WORST FEAR

A List of Recent Titles by Matt Hilton

Tess Grey Series

BLOOD TRACKS *
PAINTED SKINS *
RAW WOUNDS *
WORST FEAR *

Recent titles in the Joe Hunter Series

RULES OF HONOUR
RED STRIPES
THE LAWLESS KIND
THE DEVIL'S ANVIL
NO SAFE PLACE
MARKED FOR DEATH

* *available from Severn House*

WORST FEAR

Matt Hilton

This first world edition published 2017
in Great Britain and the USA by
SEVERN HOUSE PUBLISHERS LTD of
Eardley House, 4 Uxbridge Street, London W8 7SY.
Trade paperback edition first published
in Great Britain and the USA 2019 by
SEVERN HOUSE PUBLISHERS LTD.

British Library Cataloguing in Publication Data
A CIP catalogue record for this title is available from the British Library.

ISBN-13: 978-0-7278-8746-7 (cased)
ISBN-13: 978-1-84751-860-6 (trade paper)
ISBN-13: 978-1-78010-922-0 (e-book)

All Severn House titles are printed on acid-free paper.

Severn House Publishers support the Forest Stewardship Council™ [FSC™],
the leading international forest certification organisation.
All our titles that are printed on FSC certified paper carry the FSC logo.

MIX
Paper from
responsible sources
FSC   FSC® C013056
www.fsc.org

Typeset by Palimpsest Book Production Ltd.,
Falkirk, Stirlingshire, Scotland.
Printed and bound in Great Britain by
TJ International, Padstow, Cornwall.

ONE

The new day broke as a thread of pearlescent light on the eastern horizon, vivid delineation between the surging Atlantic and the waning night sky. It grew to a nimbus that flared and struck myriad colours from the belly of the heavens, and sent roseate fingers across the ocean. It was beautiful.

But Chelsea Grace didn't bear witness to the dawning of her last morning on Earth. Resolutely she faced west, where all remained in darkness but for a few distant pinpoints of light on the Maine coastline. Even those faint gleams were wasted on her because her eyelids were pinched as tightly as her mouth, and the skin between her shoulder blades.

She took another shuffling step forward.

The ground crumbled underfoot, and dirt and pebbles rained. She heard their clattering fall and the distant splashes as they struck water. She stood at a precipice and the only way to go was down. She rested her weight on her back foot.

Something nudged her in the spine and she flinched.

Yet she resisted that final step.

She didn't want to die. And yet behind her death was assured, before her it was only probable. She had no idea how steep the cliff was, or how high, but perhaps it was the lesser of two evils. She could hear surf lapping, and the pebbles she'd scuffed loose had found the sea below. Maybe stepping off the edge of her free will was preferable to being forced. If she jumped, arcing away from the cliff's edge, she'd plummet to open water – there was a possibility of survival. No. She couldn't bring herself to take such a leap of faith. Heights had always terrified her, and she couldn't force herself to look. Without checking she couldn't be positive what she was jumping into; perhaps there were jagged rocks at the foot of the cliff.

She should turn and fight.

Except the fear of falling had her in its grip . . . and it would be worse if she was pushed and went backwards over the edge.

Worse again if she was shot in the stomach and punched from the cliff wall by the bullet's impact.

She sobbed. Her features pinched tighter.

'Go on,' said a voice from behind her.

The barrel of the gun again nudged her.

'I . . . I don't want to die.'

'It's easy,' said the voice.

'Please don't make me . . .' Chelsea opened her eyes. Tears washed her vision and the pinprick lights of distant Portland danced wildly. Instantly, vertigo assailed her. She clenched the material at the front of her jacket, as if she could hold herself upright. 'Not like *this*.'

'I'm making you do nothing,' said the voice. 'The choice is yours.'

'Some choice,' Chelsea sobbed, and her eyelids screwed once more.

'Need some motivation?' a second voice chimed in behind her, this one higher-pitched. 'A little nudge in the right direction?'

'Please . . . please don't touch me. Just let me prepare myself.'

'I'll count to ten.' Behind her, the hammer on her first tormentor's revolver clicked back.

'No . . . no . . .' Chelsea covered her face with both hands.

'One,' said the deeper voice.

'Stop. I'm . . . I'm not ready yet.'

'Two.'

Chelsea leaned back further, and the gun barrel nestled directly between her shoulders.

'Three.'

Maybe if she threw her weight backwards, it would be enough to catch her captor off guard. She could run, find somewhere to hide until the sun was up and other people around. She would have a chance at least; better than taking either choice she was now faced with. But if she tried to run away she could still easily be shot. Shot then thrown from the cliffs weakened and bleeding, perhaps even shot dead.

'Four.'

Chelsea didn't want to be shot. No less did she fear falling to her death from a great height, but the promise of a bullet sounded more agonizing. If only she could get across to her tormentors how wrong this was . . .

'Please. You don't have to make me do this. There are other ways to—'

'Five.'

'—make things better again.'

'Six.'

'For God's sake! This is insane!'

'Jesus Christ!' the higher voice snapped, impatient now. 'You're going to keep this up, aren't you? Oh, to hell with it then.' The gun withdrew from Chelsea's spine.

The briefest spark of hope flared in Chelsea. But it was short-lived. The gun hadn't been removed as a threat, but to clear space.

The flat of a foot shoved Chelsea in the backside.

A scream rose to her lips, but was never voiced. Her feet skidded out from under her and she went down on the lip of the cliff, her tailbone smacking painfully on rock. The shock transferred from her coccyx all the way up her spine to her brain in a bright flash of agony. Her fledgling scream became a groan, and then a wild moan of dismay as she felt herself teeter, then pitch forward. In desperation, she slapped at the edge of the cliff, grasping for handholds, but her fingers found only crumbling stone and then empty air.

She prayed that the cliff was sheer, the water below deep.

Evidently her god wasn't listening.

TWO

'It's a lonely place to die.'

Nicolas 'Po' Villere's whisper barely reached Tess Grey, snatched away on the wind the instant he vocalized his thoughts. If she hadn't been standing so close to him she wouldn't have heard. He was behind her, one hand on her shoulder, as if fearful she would stumble off the cliffs, but he was taller and his view uninhibited. She glimpsed back up at him, but his gaze had settled on the narrow strip of sand below. A high tide hissed and popped on the beach, foam the colour and consistency of spilled beer littered with detritus marking its furthest reach, and obscuring the place where Chelsea Grace's body had washed ashore. Directly beneath their feet shattering waves boomed with metronomic regularity against the cliffs.

Tess pushed down the hood of her parka. The wind tugged at her pale hair. It wasn't raining hard, but the wind had a sting to it, and threw grit and sea salt against her face. She ignored the discomfort as she peered down at the place where her friend's corpse had recently been discovered. In summer holidaymakers would overrun the beach, but it was winter, the beach was deserted and Bald Head Cove *was* a lonely place to die.

'The cops are certain she jumped from these cliffs?' Po went on.

'They found blood on a rock part of the way down, where they surmise she struck the cliff as she fell. She hadn't been in the water long, and they believe her corpse washed up only minutes after she died.' Tess again glanced back at her companion. He'd donned a baseball cap against the inclement weather, and its peak shadowed his face, his usually vibrant turquoise eyes now reflective of the steel-coloured sea. 'But they're still unsure if she jumped or was pushed.'

'Her message didn't read like a suicide note to me,' Po said.

Tess exhaled slowly.

She didn't think so either.

When people planned to take their own lives they didn't tend to pen their suicide note weeks in advance, and if they did she thought they'd be less enigmatic in its wording.

If I'm dead, contact Sergeant Teresa Grey at Cumberland County Sheriff's Office. Tell her

Even the way Chelsea's final note had been delivered made no sense. Who scheduled a Facebook post to a specific time and date, when announcing their self-inflicted death? OK, there was some validity to using the scheduled post function, because until the specified time and date her status update would have been invisible to all but Chelsea, thus ensuring her privacy until after the deed was completed. But if Chelsea had used the function for that purpose, she had gone through with her suicide a full two days ahead of plan. Then again, perhaps her timing was deliberate, so her message wouldn't appear on her timeline prior to her taking her own life, ensuring no one could stop her. They were questions Tess had mulled over since receiving a telephone call from a Sagadahoc County Sheriff's deputy, asking similar questions of her. Other mysteries plagued Tess, prime among them why Chelsea, who she'd had no contact with in years, had specifically requested that Tess be informed about her untimely death. The investigating detectives wanted to know the same thing. But Tess had no idea, because she hadn't spoken with Chelsea since they were roommates at Husson University. With little in common besides their interest in history and cultural anthropology they'd parted ways after graduation, and the wording of Chelsea's message proved they hadn't been in touch for some time. Last she recalled Chelsea had taken a teaching position at a high school in Chicopee, Massachusetts, while Tess had followed the family tradition and enrolled with her local Sheriff's Office. Chelsea would have known that, but not that Tess had retired from the CCSD on medical grounds almost three years ago.

She stared again at the flooded beach, clucking her tongue against the roof of her mouth, and distractedly rubbing at the raised skin that almost entirely circled her right wrist.

'You seen enough, Tess?'

'I guess.'

'Then please come away from the edge,' Po said, exerting

gentle pressure on her shoulder. 'You're making me nervous. We don't want any more blood on those rocks, 'specially not yours.'

Po wasn't keen on heights.

Tess didn't move. Bald Head Cove was at the southern tip of a rocky promontory known locally as Cape Small, and was part of Sagadahoc County, situated to one side near the mouth of the Kennebec River. On the other side the sea stretched almost twenty miles across Casco Bay to her hometown of Portland. On a clear day she would be able to see the lights of the city, or at least those of Chebeague, Peaks, or Long Islands, but today the elements had closed in. There was no view beyond a few hundred yards of churning waves before everything grew misty and formless.

'C'mon, Tess, you've seen where Chelsea died. It's best we get back before the storm blows in.'

'Give me a few more minutes,' she said, and again peered down at the high-tide line. The police had already gone over the beach, and the cliffs on both sides of the cove, with a fine-toothed comb, but she couldn't help feeling they might have missed something important. But without climbing down to the beach and conducting a fingertip search there was little hope of turning up anything evidential in the flotsam and jetsam. For certain she would spot nothing from the edge of the cliffs. She looked for a footpath down, but knew they'd approached the wrong way from Navy Road to the beachhead. They'd have to backtrack and come in following a circular route via one of the hiking trails.

Thunder rumbled in the north. It was barely discernible over the constant booming of waves, but she could sense the shift in the atmosphere, the air growing denser and charged with electricity. Standing exposed on the cliffs wasn't sensible in a lightning storm.

She allowed Po to gently tug her away from the edge, and fell in step behind him as he loped through trampled grass to the trail leading to Navy Road. It was days since the police conducted their investigation on the cliffs, but the grass was still flattened by their feet and equipment. She almost expected to find remnants of crime-scene tape fluttering on the wind, but not a scrap had been left behind. As she followed Po the rain spattered around them and she tugged up her hood, tucking her chin into the fur lining. Undoubtedly a beauty spot during the more clement months, the promontory was exposed to the elements come winter, and not a place Tess would choose for her final resting place. Why had Chelsea come to this remote place to die?

Po's Mustang was beaded with rain, glistening darkly beneath the baleful sky. The windows had misted. Po got in and started the engine, and turned on the blowers to clear the condensation. Tess climbed in and sighed, grateful for the warmth. Doffing her hood, she could taste salt on her lips and her features felt gritty.

'You want to come back to my place?' Po offered. 'We could grab some take-out food on the way back, talk this over . . .'

She shook her head. They'd been partners for more than a year now – in every sense – and Po had hinted about her making a permanent move to his house, but as yet she hadn't given him a decision. These days Tess spent as much time living at his ranch-style property near Presumpscot Falls as she did in town, but more and more she had been thinking of her own apartment as her sanctuary, where she could go when she wanted to think. Not that it made a difference if Po accompanied her or not: it wasn't a privacy issue, just that her own little house, where all her familiar things surrounded her, helped her relax and clarify her thoughts.

'Back to Cumberland Avenue then,' said Po, as he turned the muscle car on a circle of beaten dirt at the terminus of Navy Road. It was an hour's drive back to Portland, under good conditions. The heavens opened and the rain deluged. Ribbons of lightning danced on the northern horizon and a few seconds later the thunder rumbled so loud it obscured the growling of the Mustang's super-charged engine. 'Gonna be a hell of a night.'

'I don't expect to get much sleep anyway,' Tess said.

He glanced over, and she caught his lazy smile.

'Sorry, Po,' she said, 'that wasn't an invitation.'

He laughed. 'You don't say? Tess, I know what you're like. You're not gonna let this rest until you know what the hell really happened to Chelsea.'

Her cheeks flushed, and she eyed him with moist eyes. 'It's not as if Chelsea and I were good friends. We weren't even that close when we shared a room, and we lost contact after graduation. But I can't help feeling that she reached out to me for help and I wasn't there to give it.'

'She made sure of that,' he reminded her.

'I know. But still . . .'

'I get you. You don't have to explain. You want to do some digging, and I'll be too much of a distraction. Hey, I can understand that.' He stuck his tongue in his cheek, inviting a friendly gibe. Tess purposefully glanced away, just as lightning flashed, engulfing the windshield with white light. Black dots danced in her vision. When Po came back into view, he was studiously watching the road – he'd gotten that she wasn't in a teasing mood, and respected her wishes.

The going was slow, the rain coming down in curtains. The foliage on both sides of Navy Road was thrashed by the storm, throwing litter on the windshield. But once they reached Bath and found a highway, things got easier and Po picked up speed, following the adjacent Androscoggin River to Brunswick and then on towards Portland, finally drawing the Mustang to a halt outside Tess's house more than an hour and a quarter after leaving Bald Head Cove.

During the drive their conversation had been limited to comments about the harshness of the storm. Before getting out of the car, Tess leaned toward him and they kissed briefly, before she flicked up her hood. It was only a short jog to the steps that led up to her upper-storey apartment above an antiques shop, but the rain was solid and would soak her the instant she was out of the car.

'Anything you want me to do?' Po asked.

'There's nothing immediately to mind. But I'll call you if anything comes up. Are you going home?'

'I might drive by the bar; Chris has a problem he wants to talk over with me.'

Po was the owner of a retro bar-diner, and as with Charley's Autoshop, it was in a silent capacity. Chris Mitchell managed the bar on Po's behalf, while Jasmine Reed was in charge of hospitality.

'Tell Chris "hi" from me,' said Tess, 'and Jazz too, if she's still there.'

She got out of the Mustang and stood at kerbside as Po

drove away. Raindrops as thick as her fingers battered her. She turned and went up the stairs and indoors. The wooden house creaked and groaned, the storm beating tympani on the roof, but the compact home felt safe, a haven. She hung her dripping parka over her bath, and prepped her coffee maker. It was going to be a long night, and the caffeine would help sharpen her mind. She hoped. Because at that moment she had no idea where to begin.

'Start with what you know, Tess,' she said aloud.

But that was the problem.

If I'm dead, Chelsea's Facebook post had read, *contact Sergeant Teresa Grey.*

'Why contact me?' Tess had posed the same question dozens of times. Each time there had been only one answer. 'Because I know something important about *why* she died.'

Except she didn't have a clue what it was she knew about Chelsea Grace's death.

THREE

The storm didn't let up for hours, but Tess was so caught up in her thoughts that she was barely aware of the racket overhead. Rain drummed down, ran like flumes from the guttering, and the thunder rattled the windows in their frames, but Tess had drawn up her bare feet beneath her backside and settled her laptop on her knees and was lost in the digital world. The laptop was hot from prolonged use, causing the skin on her thighs to prickle. On an occasional table alongside her she'd set the jug of coffee, most of which she'd drained. Dressed in pyjamas and dressing gown, comfortable and warm, she found she did her best work; and yet tonight the mystery surrounding Chelsea Grace's untimely death thwarted her.

She had collated a document, cutting and pasting details she had gleaned concerning her old roommate from various online sources, and had built a fair picture of Chelsea's life since Husson, but it was unremarkable and gave no clue as to why she'd died. From her social network updates Chelsea came across as the wholesome, unexcitable individual she'd known at university. Up until the end of last fall's semester she'd taught history at a school in Chicopee – having never transferred from the high school Tess originally knew about – before suddenly, and without explanation, serving her notice and dropping out of educating. Tess wondered if she'd left her job because of what she planned to do in the near future . . . ending her life. Or if leaving her career behind had set her on a downward spiral of depression that had ultimately led to her death. But there was nothing in any of her status updates that hinted at any disillusionment at life: her posts were upbeat in the whole, and featured the usual gamut of shared jokes, viral videos and pictures of cute kittens and puppies. Unlike some social network users who ranted and raved, or sought a sympathetic digital pat on the shoulder from strangers, Chelsea wasn't one to air her dirty laundry in the public realm. In fact she mentioned very little about her private life, and certainly didn't hint at any relationship, or lack of. The Sagadahoc County detectives would be pursuing any leads in that respect. As sad as it was, the first suspect in any murder inquiry was always the partner of the deceased. Next up, family members or close acquaintances – sometimes even distant friends like old roomies who hadn't been around for years.

It came as no surprise that her mind had swiftly jumped to murder, because there was no way Chelsea took her own life. Not by jumping from a cliff: if there was one thing that she recalled about Chelsea it was her intense fear of heights. When they worked at a summer camp even sleeping in the top bunk was out of the question.

Tess abruptly walked to her bedroom. She dug through drawers, and then stepped inside the walk-in closet where she kept her grandfather's service revolver in a lock-box. The Service-6 was of no interest; she reached onto the shelf again, feeling around, and dragged forward a battered loose-leaf folder bulging with packets of photographs. These days most pictures snapped were on smartphones and tablets, but back when Tess and Chelsea were at university, people still took photographs on traditional cameras. She'd almost forgotten the pictures were buried at the back of her closet until she recalled Chelsea shaking and sweating at the prospect of having to sleep five feet above the floor.

She laid the folder on her bed, and began pulling out individual packets. The first few held old family snaps of Tess and her two older brothers, Alex and Michael Jnr, as well as those of her parents and grandparents and other relatives: birthdays, vacations, Thanksgiving, Christmas. The temptation to indulge in nostalgia was strong, so she set them aside. She dug for more recent packets and found a couple of possibilities. She carried them to her sitting room, and began sorting through the pics. Most of those recording her time at Husson University featured a fresh-faced Tess Grey, usually in a slight state of inebriation. Friends or acquaintances who'd snapped her in moments of high jinks or celebration had given her the photos: most weekends were cause for celebration back then. In the pics other young women often accompanied her, occasionally she was with guys who had come and gone. Very few included Chelsea, but it was unsurprising. They hadn't been close, and Chelsea hadn't attended many of the weekend parties Tess did. But she found the snaps she was looking for, those taken at the summer camp. She set all the others aside and teased out the small handful of photographs onto her knees.

'God! Look at my hair! What was I thinking?' Tess wheezed as she eyed an unflattering image where her hair had been cut pageboy-style, dyed black with midnight-blue highlights – all the rage at the time but ugly as all hell to her current tastes. Shaking her head in bemusement she set the photo aside. Picking up the next, she studied it with more interest. It was a group shot taken in the summer of 2003, during the third year of four at Husson. Student fees were very high, and in return for her parents funding her education, Tess worked during vacations, taking a position at the summer camp with a bunch of her fellow undergraduates. She stared at the smiling faces of girls and boys she'd rarely seen or even thought of in fourteen years. The names of some came immediately to mind – Chelsea Grace's already in the forefront – but other faces took a little dredging from her memory.

She began jotting names, matching them to the faces. There were thirteen individuals in the scene, dressed in matching T-shirts, shorts, and hiking boots, ten of them female. The names of the boys came to mind, but usually it was their nicknames she recalled first and had to think harder for their full names. Some of the girls had been friends, the others simply workmates, but she found she could recall most. Two of the girls had been on the fringe of their social circle and it shamed Tess now that she had been as aloof to them as the other popular girls in their group. Typically clichéd, one girl was fifty pounds overweight, with frizzy black hair, a prominent nose, and large spectacles. The other was tall, skinny, almost to a point of waif-like emaci-ation, with straight hair hanging to her shoulders, dyed as black as a raven's wing, to match the thick eyeshadow and lipstick she wore to show her affiliation to the Goth culture she'd embraced.

'Thing One and Thing Two,' Tess intoned, and was embar-rassed that she had joined in with the group in naming the two outsiders, who were also collectively derided as the Geek Squad – ironic when they were all studious geeks in varying degrees – or worse, the Beaver Munchers. Back then Tess had believed herself a nice person, tolerant and understanding of other people's race, religion, and sexuality . . . and yet she had been as quick to sneer at those two girls as their other supposed friends. Tolerance, it seemed, had only mattered back then as long as it meant fitting in with the consensus.

She told herself she was still young then, and eager to please, and had sought to fit in, even though she knew it was wrong to target those two girls in what amounted to psychological bullying. These days she wasn't as easily manipulated, and in fact embraced people's differences: hell, she was an ex-cop in a relationship with an ex-con, and one of her greatest friends was a gay man: the irrepressible Pinky, whom she'd met through Po. But being so open now didn't excuse her behaviour back then, and if she could turn back the clock she would greet those two girls with kinder words, and their actual names.

Except the shame continued to burn her when she realized she couldn't recollect their full names. She'd an inkling the larger girl was called Gina, but the Goth girl . . . she racked her memory. Couldn't think.

But she was digressing. She looked again at the picture, focusing instead on Chelsea Grace. It was the Chelsea that Tess remembered, and almost unrecognizable as the woman she'd more recently viewed on her social media pages. Similarly to Tess's, she'd worn her hair cut in a short bob, with reddish highlights added to the tips of her brown locks. She still carried a little baby fat, giving her a toothsome smile topped off with chubby cheeks. But there was something in her gaze as she peered back at the camera that spoke of a less than happy-go-lucky individual; there was a hint of sadness, as if she had seen a foreshadow of her fate and knew her days on Earth were numbered and the clock was ticking faster than for others.

No. Tess was seeing things that weren't evident, fitting Chelsea's expression to what had recently happened. How could that young girl be aware of what would become of her fourteen years hence? She couldn't. Still, with nothing else to work with, Tess thought that perhaps something had happened back then which had prompted Chelsea to leave her death message personally for her old roomie.

'What the hell were you up to, Chelsea?' she asked the girl in the photo. 'Why didn't you leave a clearer message? I don't know what you want from me.'

Except, she did. It was apparent that despite her ambiguous message, she wanted Tess to show the world *why* she died, be that by her own hand or another, and bring resolution or – if she was a victim – justice to her killer.

And yet there was something else Tess couldn't ignore: what if Chelsea's words were meant as a warning?

FOUR

'What the hell is that?'

Rick Conklin rubbed his calloused hands over his features. His cheeks were rubbery with fatigue, and his eyeballs gritty, as if the Sandman had dumped a sack full of sleeping-dust under each eyelid. Not that it had helped him sleep, he'd only achieved a few minutes of shut-eye since midnight and didn't expect much more before dawn. The medication he took for chronic pain dulled his agony, but also made him jittery and restless.

He was still seated in his chair in front of his TV in the lounge, the players on screen over-exaggerating their mannerisms and voices in some ancient black-and-white gangster flick on the TCM channel. He blinked again, trying to focus, and James Cagney swam into view, tilting his hat at a rakish angle and snarling at the camera. The sounds of Tommy guns rattled, startlingly loud. But that wasn't what had roused Rick.

He heard the clicking noise repeat from somewhere back in his ground-floor apartment. Someone was trying the catch on his back door.

'Sons of bitches!'

His wasn't the best of neighbourhoods in Bangor, Maine, and it wasn't unknown for a sneak thief to try to liberate their neighbours' belongings. Rick had been burglarized twice before, but this was the first time anyone had tried when he was home. He had his disabilities, but he wasn't totally useless, and those who knew him well would say he wasn't to be fucked with.

Rick muted the TV. Earlier a storm had raged overhead, but it must have swept south, because now there was a lull, the only sound the steady drip of rain from the gutters. He listened, wondering if he'd mistaken the sounds of rain droplets for the clicking of his door latch.

A creak was followed by a soft *snap!*

Rick slapped his palms down, grabbed the wheels – only one

in a firm grasp – and spun his wheelchair to face the kitchen door.

'Who's there?'

All was silent again. The home invader holding their breath in anticipation of being caught red-handed.

'Yeah! I hear you,' Rick hollered. 'You'd better get the fuck out now!'

Something scraped on the linoleum flooring in his kitchen. For a second he wondered if a cat had found its way in through the flap he hadn't gotten around to securing since his own tabby got flattened by a car last year. But he knew he was hoping for the best, because no cat had been working on the locks until they opened.

'Who is there?' he snapped again. 'I'm warning you, man, don't think you can push me around.'

Rick was in his second year at Husson University when the deadliest terrorist atrocity in modern history happened, when planes were flown into the World Trade Centre and the Pentagon or brought down in a field in Pennsylvania when the passengers fought for control with the hijackers. Up until that moment his life map had been laid out only as a fuzzy sketch and he had no real sense of what he wanted to do after graduation. But as he watched – alongside billions of others across the globe – those terrifying images relayed live on TV a switch was thrown in his mind and he had singular intent after: as soon as he graduated he left one institution and enlisted directly in another. He had the intelligence and aptitude to enrol as an officer candidate, but he was eager to serve his country, to avenge the thousands of his fellow countrymen murdered on September 11th 2001, so instead joined as a regular in the 187th Infantry Regiment, which had recently been deployed to the Middle East, so he could get his boots on the ground faster. During his first tour he was soon conducting combat operations in Husaybah, Iraq alongside the 3rd Armored Cavalry Regiment, and after redeployment to Iraq again in the fall of 2005 was involved in 'Operation Swarmer', defeating insurgents and terrorist cells throughout Salah ad Din province. There his war against terror ended when he was caught in the blast from a roadside IED that took the lives of two Iraqi Army soldiers, and both Rick's legs from mid-thighs down.

That was the end of one fight for him, but the beginning of another. The going had been slow and torturous, but he'd adapted well to a life on wheels, and these days even played competitive wheelchair basketball. He'd been fitted with prosthetics, and had mastered them, but preferred his chair. His legs still required the assistance of crutches to walk any distance, and he preferred to have his hands free: it was better for him that at least one set of limbs remained liberated. He had the upper body of an athlete, and if anything, beating his wounds had toughened him both mentally and physically in ways even two tours of combat duty hadn't. Tethered to the chair, his appearance made some people under-estimate him, and that was to his advantage, and usually their peril.

He'd discarded his prosthetic legs after arriving home earlier. They were lying on the rarely used recliner sofa on the opposite side of his lounge. He ignored them, calling out to the trespasser: 'Y'hear me? I don't need my fuckin' legs to kick no cowardly thief's ass.'

In a show of fearless challenge he wheeled his chair forward, and slapped both palms flat on the doorframe to the kitchen. It was habitual to leave the doors open, to aid in his movement through the apartment. The kitchen was in darkness, the only lights the soft glow of LEDs on his low-line cooker and micro-wave ovens. Behind him the muted TV cast flickering blue shadows over his shoulder, but they barely reached a foot or so within the deeper darkness of the kitchen before being swallowed up. Rick craned forward, staring, watching for movement.

Nothing.

He thought about hitting the light switch, catching his home invader in the full glare of the overhead striplights, but that might be advantageous to the burglar. Perhaps he was unaware that Rick was in a chair; showing him might invite a response that could yet be avoided.

'Get out of here,' he snarled. 'Last warning, 'cause I'm calling the cops.'

There was still no hint of movement.

Had he imagined the sounds? Maybe as he wakened from his fitful sleep he was still clinging to the end of a dream, and the noises had been nothing but figments dragged into the real world with him. That *had* to be it.

'Anyone there?' This time his voice was less challenging, holding a hint of embarrassment at his foolishness. There was no response, and he was relieved, despite feeling like an idiot.

But then he felt the wash of cold wind over his face and bare forearms, and a colder chill danced down his spine.

He knew for certain that there were no open windows: he'd earlier battened down the hatches against the storm, and his air-con was switched off until spring. That damn cat flap could have allowed in an errant breeze, but he doubted it.

He slapped the switch and the lights stuttered to life.

His back door stood wide open.

Raindrops dripped from the lintel, striking the concrete ramp installed to allow him access to the small back yard. The patter matched the racing beat of his pulse. He told himself he wasn't afraid, but the reaction of his body said otherwise. When scared, Rick's response was anger.

He glanced all around his kitchen. It had been adapted to suit a person constrained to a wheelchair, sparse and uncluttered, offering little in the way of hiding places. He was confident that nobody was in the room, but there had been somebody there. On the linoleum just inside the open door he spotted small wet patches. They weren't distinct footprints, but neither were they stray raindrops blown through the open door. It looked as if somebody had stood there a few seconds, listening perhaps, while the water sluiced from their clothing and shoes. One of the tracks was scuffed in a tight arc, and he recalled the scraping sound he'd heard after first shouting a warning. Apparently the home invader had taken heed. The scrape had been them turning abruptly and fleeing, albeit leaving open the door they'd escaped through.

Rick pushed forward, neck straining as he peered at the small puddles, then up at the open portal. 'Yeah! You'd better run!'

He should call the cops. He'd deterred a burglar, but they were still out there and would probably prey on another of his neighbour's homes. There were a few elderly and vulnerable residents in his street alone. And yet . . . not one of his neighbours ever gave him as much as a howdy if he passed them in the street, so why the hell should he give a damn about them now? Let the burglars steal from them; at least they'd leave him alone. He wheeled forward, going around the dining table and chairs reserved for when he had guests – it hadn't been used in years. He tracked through a faint line of rain droplets unaware. Reaching the open door, he pushed far enough out so that he could see into his back yard.

A gardener kept his lawn in decent order, and had pruned the shrubs back at the end of fall, but he wouldn't return now until spring, so his yard was looking a bit worse for wear. The recent storm had left the grass battered and sodden with puddles. Unused garden furniture had been spilled by the wind. Of much else he couldn't make out any detail in the darkness, so he wheeled out onto the ramp, glancing first along the path that led around the side of the house to the carport. He suspected that after he'd disturbed the burglar, they would have made their escape in that direction. The view was blocked any further by the dim bulwark that was his nearest neighbour's home, all lights extinguished due to the late hour. Outside, though the storm had blown over, the wind still dirged mournfully and rattled the skeletal branches of the trees surrounding his property. He had no hope of hearing the flight of his would-be burglar.

Still angry, but a tad braver, he shook his head, and again muttered that they should keep on running. He placed his hands on the rims of his wheels, about to back inside the kitchen.

The wheels abruptly jerked in his grip. Rick made a wordless gasp of surprise, and his instinct was to look back over his shoulder. In that instant he got a fleeting look at a burly figure looming over him, hair spiked up on a broad skull. The damn burglar hadn't fled; he must have hidden in the doorway to Rick's basement. Having no use for a basement, he sometimes forgot it was there. The son of a bitch had snuck out behind him and grabbed the push handles at the rear of his chair.

'Hey!' Rick tried to snatch back control by pushing down on one wheel rim. 'Get your goddamn hands off me!'

The big guy said nothing, only yanked the chair from side to side, laughing at the way Rick was jerked around.

Rick threw an elbow back at his tormentor. He missed and received another taunting laugh.

'Get off me!'

His demand was complied with this time. But the hands were

snatched away only after a sharp thrust forward. Unbalanced, Rick was thrown from his chair, and went chest down on the ramp. His wheelchair added injury as it tumbled over him and crashed down in the mud at the edge of his lawn. He'd taken plenty of spills when trying to get used to his prosthetic legs, and on the basketball court, but on most occasions they hadn't troubled him, and he'd bounced back from the falls. But this was different. He felt the impact with the concrete ramp go through his body as if he'd been caught in another explosion, and the tumbling chair struck the back of his head solidly, laying open his scalp. He lay there, his skull ringing, arms outstretched before him, fingers spasming uselessly as he tried to make sense of what just happened. Before he could claw himself around and grab for his chair, his assailant came down the ramp behind him and planted a solid kick in his butt.

The pain almost engulfed the insult.

More laughter, but purely sadistic.

This wasn't simply about hurting him: his treatment was meant to debase him.

Cringing in pain, Rick managed to flop ungainly on his right side, an elbow holding him off the concrete, but at an awkward angle to look back up. The light flooding from the kitchen door limned his attacker. Rick couldn't make out any details; his abuser was a backlit silhouette.

'What the hell, man?' Rick pulled away, folding at the waist to pull his backside out of range of a second kick. But that only invited a boot to his gut. He wheezed out, and tasted bile in the back of his throat. Rick shouted again, this time in fury.

He was no weakling. As a third kick was swung into his body, he folded around the leg, wrapping it with both arms and squeezing with boa-constrictor intensity. He reared up, jamming a shoulder under the knee, locking the leg into immobility as the big guy hopped for stability on the ramp. Rick wrestled the leg, twisting it one way then the other, and the big guy responded by grabbing at Rick's hair. He kept his hair high and tight, so it made for poor handholds. His attacker windmilled his arms, then pitched down on top of Rick, grunting in pain as the knee was wrenched unnaturally. In a tangle they rolled sideways down the ramp and into the mud. Instinct kicked in and Rick began pummelling his attacker with both fists. His attacker responded in kind. There was no clarity in Rick's mind, he simply endured the chaos, landing blow for blow, and with each punch landed felt he still had a fighting chance. On the ground like this, he'd taken away his opponent's mobility, evened things up. He finally managed to wrench around and began climbing atop his foe: Fingers clawed at his face, and at his windpipe, but Rick gave as good as he got, punching down solidly into the other's broad face. He got only the briefest of glimpses of his attacker's features, and was only glad that they were screwed in effort, and spattered with blood from both nostrils and a split lip.

Emboldened by the injuries he was doling out, Rick swore down at his larger opponent. 'Think you could fuck with the cripple, did you?' He smacked his knuckles into the face again. He felt the strength go out of the guy beneath him, but he wasn't finished. 'Who's fucking laughing now, huh?'

He was on fire, and winning, and not about to give up. He punched down again, and felt the skin over his knuckles split. He cringed, as he reared back and shook droplets of blood in the air. His other hand was clamped firmly on his opponent's neck, his stumps locked astride the solid body.

He had no defence against the second figure that rushed from the shadows and swiped a baton into his face. He experienced the impact as a popping in his skull, a scarlet explosion behind his eyes. Then darkness.

FIVE

'A warning?' Po pursed his lips as he again considered Tess's hypothesis concerning Chelsea Grace's final words.

'It's what it sounds like to me,' Tess said as she settled down at a workstation and began logging in. He'd collected her from home earlier, and they'd driven to the offices of their employer, Emma Clancy, situated in a civic building further up Cumberland Avenue. Clancy's company set up temporary quarters there after arsonists targeted the firm's original building at Baxter Boulevard, as they primarily served the Attorney's Office in a specialist inquiry capacity. Tess worked for Clancy on a self-employed basis, while Po's name was kept off the books. Though he wasn't an official employee, he was no stranger to the building, and had become a familiar face in its corridors. Unlike Tess, he wasn't allowed to use any of the encrypted systems available to Clancy's team, but that suited him fine. Po's allowance to the digital age was carrying a cellphone, and occasionally adding figures to an archaic spreadsheet on an even more archaic PC at Charley's Autoshop. He was literate, intelligent, but in an old-fashioned manner, and knew to keep out of the way when Tess was at work. He'd planted his backside on a desk behind her, arms folded as he conversed with the back of her head.

'A warning about what though?'

'I'm guessing that she wanted me to figure that out by myself.' Tess continued to tap keys, bringing up various programs on screen.

'Why didn't she just say, "Tell Tess Grey to watch out for . . ."
I dunno: "Watch out for black cats crossing her path" or something like it.'

Tess glimpsed back at him, her mouth set sourly. 'Well that would have been helpful.'

'You know what I mean. If she was murdered and knew who she was in danger from beforehand, then why not just say?

If it was a warning, then she made a poor job of conveying its seriousness.'

'Maybe she didn't know who she was in trouble with. Or maybe she had no proof that she was in danger, only a suspicion, and that's why she left such a vague message. There's always the chance that she scheduled that message with the full intention of deleting it if her suspicions proved unfounded.'

'A lot of maybes.'

'Lots of maybes often add up to a sure thing.'

'Sometimes they just add up to a steaming pile of crap.' Behind her he smiled at his wit, but she wasn't listening. Her shoulders hunched as she tapped on the keyboard. 'Got a bit of a problem at the diner,' he said.

Tess didn't respond at first: too engaged in what she was doing.

'Tess? Y'hear me?'

She turned and looked back at him, annoyed having been stopped mid-flow. 'What is it?'

'We've got a problem at the diner. It's what Chris wanted to talk about.'

Now Tess was more concerned. She turned the office chair fully to give him the attention due.

'He's been getting trouble from some Neanderthals who miss the old days when Bar-Lesque was a strip joint.' Po shrugged his shoulders, without unfolding his arms. 'Said I'd go in for the next few nights in case they come back.'

'That's OK by me.' He was apologizing for not taking her dilemma seriously enough, having double-booked his services. 'It's like you said, Chelsea didn't give any direct warning, so maybe there's nothing in it. I'll be fine without you if that's what you're worried about.'

'You sure you can spare me? It's not as if there's anything concrete on the horizon . . .'

'We've talked about hiring bouncers before. You should consider it again.'

Po nodded. But wasn't happy. 'Was trying to make the place family friendly, attract the tourists, sometimes having gorillas on the door gives the wrong impression.'

'You don't need to hire flat-nosed thugs, get somebody who can act as a gatekeeper without making things too obvious.'

'There's that,' he agreed, 'but these idiots ain't the type to walk away when asked nicely. They've got a stick up their butts because the bar manager's a faggot.' He held up his hands. 'Their words not mine. The irony is they were too busy ogling the dancers at Bar-Lesque to notice that the guy serving their drinks then was the same one serving them now.'

'So they're a bunch of homophobes?'

'They probably don't know the meaning of the term. They're simply haters; wouldn't matter what you put in front of them, they'd still find something to complain about.'

'So maybe they've moved on and won't bother coming back.'

'Maybe.' He shrugged again. 'Then again maybe not. Don't matter which way things add up, I'd be a poor example of a caring employer if I don't look after the welfare of my staff. Think I need to show Chris some support with this.'

Tess was in agreement. Until she knew otherwise she wasn't prepared to jump to a conclusion that she was in any danger from the same person that had pushed Chelsea to her death, whether that was physically or mentally. 'You know, I've been thinking that you've missed a trick with the bar. You said you want it to be family friendly, but these days families come in all shapes and sizes. You should have Chris organize regular LGBT-friendly evenings and embrace that community too.'

'I get the lettuce, bacon and tomato, but don't know what the 'G' stands for in that acronym.'

Tess grunted in mirth. 'How long have you been saving that lame joke?'

This time his shrug was more expansive, both open hands involved, his smile wider. 'Believe it or not I was quoting Pinky.'

'If you do begin doing gay friendly nights, you should invite Pinky along. I'm sure he'd love to see Chris again.'

'He's visiting next month with Amelia,' he reminded her. 'Maybe Chris can get something organized for then. But you know what Pinky's like; he might turn his back on such a gathering. He enjoys being the centre of attraction, but I'm unsure how things'd go down with him if he's in a roomful of other camp guys.'

'Sheesh, Po. Now you sound like those other Neanderthal jerks you mentioned.'

He grunted, acknowledging his faux pas. 'I didn't mean it to sound like that. I was thinking about Pinky's attitude. He's gay – I guess – but isn't into the overexuberant shenanigans of some of his contemporaries. Y'know, all that wrist-flapping flamboyancy?'

Tess gave him the stink eye.

'Jeez. Maybe I should shut my mouth now before I say anything else offensive. And there was me thinking I was all PC these days.' He scowled back at her, matching her stare. 'You know exactly what I meant.'

She broke the staring match with a smile. Pinky Leclerc was an enigma. He was a gay man, or perhaps bisexual, because she'd also noticed him eyeing plenty shapely women with interest, and yet neither of them had heard of him being in any kind of sexual relationship with anyone. Tess had grown to wonder if he was in fact asexual, and remained celibate due to his condition. He suffered from a medical problem that affected his body shape, bloating his lower torso and legs – sometimes painfully she thought – and she had wondered if he had a psychological hang-up about getting naked in front of others, let alone being intimate with them. In her opinion he had nothing to worry about, he was who he was, and that was a lovely guy. But Po was correct: Pinky did frown at some effete guys, and literally squinted in annoyance when they camped things up for effect. When he wasn't being a nice guy, and the best friend anyone could ask for, he was a criminal. She knew that he occasionally dealt in illegal firearms, which should make him unconscionable to her, and that those weapons were undoubtedly used in the wrong hands for nefarious reasons, and yet she couldn't help but love Pinky. She guessed though that to maintain his status in his circle of customers he had to portray an image that could be only undermined if he displayed any form of perceived weakness. To the criminal fraternity, an overtly gay man would be greeted with disrespect, perhaps hatred.

'He might love it,' she said. 'He wouldn't have to maintain an image, could really let his hair down for a change.'

Po nodded in agreement. 'Guess I'd best make sure there's still a bar for him to visit. I told Chris I'd come on over for evening trade. You've got me till then . . . unless something more urgent comes up.'

'Hopefully I can get through my work before then and come on over too.'

Po didn't answer.

'What? You don't think I can handle a bunch of drunken idiots?'

'Things might get rough.'

'Is that what you mean by family friendly?'

'You've met *my* family, right?' He grinned, but it slipped as he considered what he had in mind. 'Thing is I might have to bust a coupla heads to get my point across, and it's not a side of me I like you seeing.'

'It's a little late for that, Po. Besides, you've seen my ugly side plenty of times too. Listen, you don't need to go all Steven Seagal on them; show you're above that kind of behaviour and you'll be doing everyone a favour.'

'Sometimes violence is the only language butt-heads understand. They come looking for a fight, I'll give them one they can't handle. Can assure you they won't want a return match.'

Tess exhaled. She didn't want to see her man fighting, certainly not getting hurt. But she'd learned quickly enough that Po wasn't the kind to walk away from danger. His method of handling the bestial nature of humanity was by being the most feared thing in the jungle. It was how he'd survived incarceration at Louisiana State Penitentiary: he'd fought so hard the first few times that he was rarely challenged for dominance later. His credo was that if you hit first, and hit hard, you rarely needed to keep on swinging.

'I can speak to Alex, see if he can have a patrol in the area.'

Alex was Tess's brother, and an employee of Portland Police Department. Recently he'd been promoted to patrol sergeant, and Po's bar-diner came under his patch. It was his sworn duty to protect Chris and the other employees from thuggish behaviour.

'Best he doesn't,' Po countered. 'Don't want to put your brother in an awkward position.'

'I meant he could have a patrol in the area to head off any trouble.'

'Yeah. I got that. But it won't deter the a-holes for long. They'll just come back another time when the cops are busy with something else. I'd prefer if they come looking for trouble while I'm there, and the sooner it's done the better.'

Tess took a furtive glance around them. They were talking about conducting vigilante action in the office of Emma Clancy, who worked on behalf of the DA. But worse than that, Emma was also Alex's fiancée. If Po wanted to keep his plans totally off the books, this wasn't the best place to arrange them. She held up her hands, and swung back round to the workstation. 'The least said the better then,' she announced. 'But the offer stands: if you want me there tonight, I'll be there.'

'It goes without saying.' Po rested his hands on her shoulders, kneading them gently. He bent so his mouth was close to her ear. 'But your time is best served here doing what needs doing to put Chelsea's death behind you.'

She hadn't told him much about the photographs she'd studied last night, other than that she hoped to trace contact details for some of their classmates who might have kept in touch with Chelsea after they graduated. From them she hoped to build a clearer picture of what was going on in her old roomy's mind leading up to the point when she fell from the cliff at Bald Head Cove. She had considered making enquiries directly with Chelsea's parents, but had put it off. She doubted that Chelsea would have shared any details with them, and if she had then the detectives on her case would have followed them up by now. But the police were still treating her death as a suicide, so obviously there was nothing Chelsea's mom or dad had divulged to make them think otherwise. Besides, Chelsea had reached out to Tess, and that told her that whatever led to Chelsea's death, it had its source back in the days they'd last been together.

'This is all boring stuff,' she told him, without taking her attention off the screen. 'My morning's going to be filled with phone calls, so there's no need for you to hang around here. If there's something else you want to get on with, I'm good. I'll call you and we'll meet later.'

'Ordinarily I'd jump at the offer,' Po admitted, 'but what if Chelsea was warning you about danger? I'd be a poor example of a partner if I don't look after my woman.'

Tess laughed. 'Po, you said you thought you were politically correct these days, but you're still a male-chauvinist pig. You can dress things up as old-fashioned chivalry, but sometimes you open your mouth and say something totally inappropriate. But don't worry, I knew you were a caveman the first time we met, and it's still what I love most about you . . .' She thumped him playfully with her elbow. 'Your concern is perfectly appropriate to me. But misguided. Now get out of here before I have to show you who's really boss.'

Po kissed her on the side of her neck, a wet smacker. 'Yes, ma'am,' he said, and moved rapidly for the door, grinning back at her. Tess balled a slip of paper off the desk, dabbed her neck dry with it and hurled it after him. He was still laughing as he retreated down the corridor.

Tess shook her head, smiling. But as she returned her attention to the screen, the smile faded and her brow tightened. Back to the serious stuff.

SIX

P o returned to the office in less than an hour, urgently hailed by Tess on his cellphone. When he left he'd been laughing, but now his face was rigid, the only emotions in play were through the turquoise flash of his eyes as they settled on Tess. 'You found something?'

'Are you free to drive us up to Bangor?'

It was still morning, his services at the bar not required until evening. 'F'sure. What's up?'

'Let's get going, I'll explain on the way.'

They took Po's Mustang; her Prius was still parked on the slope outside her house. These days it got little use, and Tess had noted this morning that it had gathered a new pile of leaves on its hood after the storm. The supercharged car would make shorter work of the drive to Bangor, and more importantly to Po, with more street cred.

En route she told him about collating the contact details of her small circle of classmates while she was at Husson University, and that while checking out one individual his name had been flagged in a police report taken during the early hours of that very morning. Richard Wade Conklin had been the victim of a serious and sustained assault.

'He's dead?' There was genuine concern on Po's usually austere features.

'Thankfully he survived. But he isn't in a good way.'

'You think his attack had something to do with Chelsea dying?'

'Could be purely coincidental, but what are the odds?'

'Assaults happen all the time. 'Specially to younger guys.'

'Yeah, I'm sure they do. But how often do they happen in their own homes?'

'Plenty I guess.'

When she was with the Sheriff's Office Tess had attended a number of assault and battery calls and yes, many did occur in the home environment, but usually with young guys it was in or

outside a bar, or on the way to or from some drinking establishment. Often, when attacked in the home, it was by a family
member, friend, or acquaintance, rarely by a stranger.

'Richie disturbed a burglar trying to break into his apartment
and was beaten senseless.'

'It happens. Best advice if you discover an intruder is to just
let them take what they came for, and call the police.'

Tess glanced at Po. 'Like you'd do that?'

'I'm not the kind to take good advice.'

'Richie wasn't either.' She had defaulted to using the name
she'd known Conklin as when he was a youth; in some respects
it seemed like yesterday since last she'd seen the young man.
Back then he'd been known as a tough guy, a typical jock who
drank and fought as hard as he trained. His outward nature didn't
match the keen intelligence he exhibited in class though, and as
she recalled Richie had graduated with honours a year or two
before she had. In some respects he was a contradiction in terms,
not unlike the man seated opposite her in the driving seat. 'But
he wasn't exactly in a position to give his attacker a fair fight.
Richie is a double amputee, Po.'

He frowned across at her as she unconsciously kneaded her
thighs. She caught him looking and offered a grimace. 'IED out
in Iraq,' she explained.

'Damn, the scumball beat on an injured serviceman?' The
thought that a mindless thug had targeted a veteran angered him.
He gave the Mustang extra gas and it surged forward. It was as
if Richard Conklin's attack had taken on gravitas now that his
past and his disabilities had come to light.

They arrived at the hospital in short time. Tess asked about
Conklin at a nurse's station and they were directed to a ward. She
expected to be confronted by police officers guarding his room, but
there were none: she was mildly relieved; if the police were treating
Conklin's attack as more serious he would have been under their
protection until the perpetrator was brought in. It was also helpful
that she didn't have to explain herself to any detectives, and had
simply told a part-truth to the nurse when asked about her business.
She'd said she was an old friend. In lieu of any other visitors –
there'd been none – Tess and Po had been granted permission to
speak with Richard before the doctor's rounds commenced.

She recalled a tall boy, wide-shouldered, with a firm jaw, clear green eyes, and a reddish tint to a mop of unruly curls. The man lying propped in the hospital bed bore no resemblance to the guy Tess once had a crush on. A fist encircled her heart and gave it a squeeze as she paused in the doorway. The Richie Conklin she knew had diminished, and not merely through the loss of his legs. His upper body was still strong, and yet he'd lost something: the self-assurance of youth had left him, replaced by despondency. He used to attract approving looks from girls, and was known to preen under the attention. Now he looked . . . sunken. The pride that once puffed out his chest had fled him, that roadside bomb had taken his heart as assuredly as his legs. Then again, he would hardly look his best lying in a hospital bed, with dressings inadequately covering the breadth of his recent beating. His torso was hidden beneath a sheet, but his arms bore scarlet and purple bruises and scrapes. His head had taken the brunt of the attack: His jaw was inflamed, as were one cheek and eye, as swollen and shiny as a ripe plum, and a turban of bandages compressed his skull. His reddish curls were a memory. What she could see of his hair had been shaved to the skin, and perhaps it was as a result of his injuries and their subsequent patching up. Conklin looked asleep.

But when they stepped in his room, Conklin jerked, and one eyelid darted open. He wormed his body beneath the sheet, then visibly deflated as the kicking of his phantom legs failed to assist his escape. Tess again felt that fist squash her heart as Conklin's face screwed in despair. Conklin sucked in air, and expelled it equally as noisily. His one good eye darted from Tess to Po and back again. Again he appeared to try to climb up the bed and failed.

'Richie?' she said to waylay his obvious discomfort. 'Take it easy. Nobody is going to hurt you.'

'I . . . I thought I was back home again.' His voice was whisper-thin. He appeared bewildered. He shook his head, winced at the pain it caused, and his single eye settled on them again. 'Who the hell are you?'

Before Tess could answer, Conklin rolled on his side, reaching for something at the side of his bed: a button to hail a nurse. Pain made him withdraw, and he folded his arms around his ribs. Again he exhaled loudly.

Tess hurried to his side, while Po took a position at the foot of the bed, arms crossed. He tried not to look at the empty space where Conklin's legs should have been. Tess reached for and patted Conklin gently on the shoulder. 'Richie,' she said, her voice as tender as her touch.

He rolled on his back, face screwed again. 'Leave me the hell alone.'

'Richie,' Tess assured him, 'I only want to ask you a few questions.'

'I already told the other cops what I can recall. Now please . . . let me be.' He reached to push away her fingers, but bypassed them and cupped his mouth. His fingers trembled. He studied her acutely. 'You're not the cops.'

'You might not remember me,' Tess said. 'I was at Husson University with you. You were a couple years older but . . .'

'Teresa?' His head shook as if palsied. Relief flooded through him, and the shaking stopped. 'Teresa Grey, right? Yeah . . . I remember you . . . of course I do.'

She smiled. 'Yeah, it's me. But call me Tess, OK?'

He touched his chest. 'It's Rick these days. Wondered why you kept calling me Richie. I haven't been called Richie since I don't know when.' He glanced up at Po.

'We haven't met, buddy,' said Po. 'Nicolas Villere.'

Conklin nodded, after further scrutiny of Po. He returned his attention to Tess. 'It's been a while, right?'

'It has.'

'You look good,' he said, and his mouth quirked in a rakish smile. It would have worked better if his lips weren't swollen. 'I guess life's been a bit kinder to you than it has me.'

It was all a matter of perspective. She had come very close to being a fellow amputee, and only a half-inch of flesh and a team of skilled surgeons had managed to save her severed hand. By comparison to the major trauma he'd suffered in the bomb blast, she had gotten off lightly. But he was unaware of her past injury, and wasn't referring to his either, but his recent scrape with death.

'Is it as bad as it looks?' Po was forthright.

'Does it look bad?' Conklin responded, then gave a sour laugh. 'Got a couple of cracked ribs. My head feels like a drum line has been at it. And I've an itch on my right foot that's sending me nuts 'cause I can't scratch it. Otherwise, I guess I'll pull through.'

'I see your sense of humour is still intact,' said Tess, and immediately wished she'd kept her mouth shut.

Conklin snorted at her faux pas, but made an exaggerated sweep of his hand over his lower body, then grinned. 'Hey! It saves me a few bucks when it comes to buying new shoes and socks, I guess.'

Tess chuckled politely, but felt uncomfortable. Conklin had obviously taken to managing his disability through self-deprecating remarks. Often when people made jokes at their own expense it was a way of armouring themselves: get in first and you take away the opportunity for hurtful comments.

'You heard what happened to me?' he asked.

'You mean in Iraq?'

He opened both hands in emphasis, as if he hadn't been obvious.

'I only heard this morning,' Tess said. 'I was looking into something else and your name came up.'

'You joined the cops after graduation. You still with Portland PD?'

'No. Never was. I was with the Sheriff's Office. But, well,' she glanced at Po for the right words. He offered no hint. 'These days I work privately.'

Conklin's one open eye sparkled with interest. The swollen one stayed resolutely closed. 'Like a private detective?'

'Like that, yeah.'

'And my name came up?'

Tess warded off any concern. 'Only through association. Do you remember another girl from back at Husson? Chelsea Grace. She was the same age as me, was my roommate in fact.'

He glanced surreptitiously at Po before answering. 'When we were together I was never in your room.'

Tess's cheeks flushed. She too batted the briefest of glances at Po, but he was untroubled by the subtext in Conklin's proclamation. She quickly changed tack. 'She was part of the gang that time we worked at that summer camp.'

Conklin nodded. 'The girl that got stuck up the tree and screamed blue murder?'

Tess smiled. She'd forgotten that incident. They were supposed to be building a jungle gym for the kids, fixing rope swings and wooden platforms in the trees, when Chelsea had to be rescued from a ladder after holding so tightly to a tree trunk that she'd practically left her fingernails buried in the bark.

'She never was good with heights.' This time when she looked over at Po it was to ensure he'd caught her point. Someone as terrified of heights as Chelsea was didn't choose to jump off a cliff. 'She used to get a nosebleed in thick socks.'

'Quiet girl, as I recall. Didn't join in with the fun much.'

'That was Chelsea.'

His gaze settled on her. There was a subtext to her comment too.

'Chelsea died,' Tess announced sombrely.

'When? What happened?'

'About a week ago. You didn't see anything in the news?'

He shook his head.

Chelsea's death had been reported in the press, and on TV bulletins in Portland. Perhaps her death hadn't been newsworthy in Bangor though. Or it had simply bypassed Conklin's notice. She had to prompt his memory to recall her, so it would have been easy to take no notice of the reports.

'The police say it was suicide. She jumped from a cliff at Bald Head Cove.'

'Suicide? I doubt it. Not like that anyway.'

'My thoughts entirely,' said Tess.

Conklin paused. 'You said my name came up in connection to her?'

'Only in a roundabout fashion.' She told him about Chelsea's final message on Facebook, and how it had led Tess to looking into her death, and finding the old photographs from their time at the summer camp. 'I was going to call around our old gang and ask if any of them had recently been in contact with her. That's when I came across the news about your attack. Hope you don't mind us dropping in like this?'

'You're my first visitors. Apart from medics and cops, oh, and some guy preaching the Good book. Guess you could be my last visitors too. I kinda lost track of all my old pals.' He didn't mention family members, and Tess wasn't prepared to press him on it. 'Not sure I can tell you anything about Chelsea. I haven't seen or heard from her since I graduated.'

Tess nodded at him, but in a way that indicated his recent injuries.

'Do you know who did this to you?'

He shrugged. 'They jumped me in the dark.'

'At home?'

'It was as if they wanted to lure me outside. Funny behaviour for burglars.'

Po finally interjected from the foot of the bed. 'Maybe they wanted you out so's they could ransack your place without you getting in the way.'

'That's what the cops think. Thing is, once I was knocked unconscious they left. They didn't take a thing with them.'

'They were disturbed in the act?'

'A neighbour heard the ruckus, called the cops, but they weren't to know that. No, it was more like they broke into my house with the intention of taking me, not my DVD player.' His face pinched momentarily, quite a feat considering the extensive swelling. 'They wanted to hurt *me*.'

'You upset anyone lately?' Po asked.

'No more than usual,' he grunted. 'They didn't say a damn thing. Just set on me. Dumped me out of my chair, and laughed. I said they wanted to hurt me, by that I mean *punish* me. And they took enjoyment in doing so.'

'Punk ass cowards,' said Po.

'I got the better of one of them,' Conklin said, as if he needed to save some face. He didn't want to admit to being beaten by any number of punk ass cowards. 'Then the girl snuck in and hit me with a bat or something.'

'What?' Tess said. 'One of your attackers was female?'

'I only got a glimpse of her. Didn't recognize her before you ask, just that she was a skinny chick. I was too busy wailing on her fella. After she hit me with the bat, he must have kicked me around my backyard like a football.'

Tess thought back to his reaction when she'd entered his room with Po. For the briefest of seconds he thought his attackers had returned for round two. 'I'm not the skinniest of chicks,' she said, 'but was your other attacker similar in build to Nicolas?'

Conklin shook his head. 'Not as tall, but – no offence, man – he made you look like a weakling.'

Po was nonplussed.

'Muscular?' Tess asked.

'A goddamn steroid freak! Neck like a propane tank. Fat head, spiky hair. But that's about all that I can remember. Was too busy punching his face to note any detail other than if it hurt.'

'Least you got your licks in,' Po said, impressed.

'Might not have if he hadn't slipped. I ain't gonna lie to you, buddy, for a minute or two I didn't expect to wake up again.' Conklin touched his bandaged skull. 'And that was before that sneaky bitch treated my head like a piñata.'

SEVEN

The trip back to Portland was spent mulling over what they'd learned from Richard Conklin, and the strange circumstances surrounding his assault. The police were pursuing leads, and Po suggested that Tess should coordinate with them. But from what Conklin said, the cops were treating his assault as a consequence of disturbing burglars in the act, not as a personal attack. During the same night, another two dwellings had been burglarized in and around Bangor, so his case wasn't unique. Neither of them believed that was true; it was assumed that petty criminals had conducted all the other home invasions, seeking easily transportable goods that could quickly be sold on for drugs, alcohol, or whichever vice drove the criminals to steal. There had been no violence involved. No hint that more than one perpetrator had been responsible.

'So Conklin's assault is unrelated to the other cases, and therefore unique,' Po said.

'But is it related to Chelsea's death?'

'Does it need to be for you to get involved?'

'As much as I'd like to see justice for Rick, I can't let him distract me.'

'Really?'

She glanced across at him. 'Yes, really.'

'I just got the impression you had a soft spot for the guy; not like you to turn away when someone you know is in trouble.'

'Soft spot? I felt sorry for Rick because of his injuries . . . if that's what you mean?'

'It's exactly what I mean.'

Tess snorted. 'Are you asking if we were once an item?'

Po didn't reply, just concentrated harder on the road.

'We fooled around a little back then, sure.'

He glanced sharply at her, but instantly returned his attention to driving.

'Some drunken fumbling took place, but that was all.'

'Hey, I ain't judging.'

'You've been with other women, right?' She clenched her teeth, speaking through a clamped jaw. 'Plenty I bet.'

'A gentleman doesn't brag about his conquests.'

'But he doesn't mind hearing the gory details of mine?'

'I'd rather not.' He snorted in forced humour. 'Tess, I ain't challenged by your past relationships. I'm certainly not jealous of Rick Conklin.'

'Why? Because there's no competition from a crippled man?'

'Jeez, Tess, where'd that come from? I only met him and I respect the guy. He's a damn war hero, for Christ's sake. But I'm not jealous of any guy, because I trust your feelings for me are as strong as mine are for you.'

'On any other occasion that might sound romantic,' she snapped.

'Man.' Po's southern drawl drew the word out. 'All I was saying was that I sensed you still had feelings for the guy. And that's OK by me. There's nothing wrong with holding affection for old friends, even if only in a nostalgic way. I'm surprised you ain't interested in taking on his case, is all.'

'If Rick's case was connected to Chelsea's death then I'd be all over it,' she said, still angered, 'but as far as we know it's unrelated. Finding out what really happened to Chelsea is what's important to me right now, not chasing after some mindless thugs out for their kicks at a disabled man's expense.'

'You think that's all there was to it? Some drunk dude out to impress his girlfriend by beating on a handicapped guy?'

She shrugged. It sounded unlikely, but not unknown. From experience she knew that society's most undesirable occasionally targeted people with disabilities. Hell, sometimes even everyday folks could be guilty of bullying those they perceived as lesser individuals. It was a sad reflection of modern civilization.

Po grunted. 'Well, if anything, Conklin got the last laugh. The idiot's girlfriend had to rescue him when Conklin turned the tables. Things coulda turned out very different if she hadn't been there to save that punk's ass.'

Tess shared a sly grin with him. She wasn't as miffed with him now that the subject had changed. But she couldn't hold the smile. 'The fact that the girl had a bat troubles me.'

'Yeah,' Po agreed. 'Sounds as if she went expecting trouble, otherwise how was it she was already armed?'

'Rick's positive they lured him outside with the intention of beating him up, so maybe she was always going to join in whether her friend got the best of Rick or not.'

'Punish him,' Po stated. 'That's what Conklin felt they wanted to do. Punish.' He looked across at her for emphasis. 'What if Chelsea's death was also a form of punishment?'

She had to admit, she was thinking along the same lines. Forcing Chelsea to jump from a cliff was possibly her worst nightmare. But punishment for what reason? Nothing she'd learned yet gave any clue, so maybe Po's suggestion of cooperating with the Bangor police investigation into Conklin's attack made sense. If and when they identified a suspect in Conklin's attack she'd like to be informed: if only to rule them out of any involvement in Chelsea's death. She made a mental note to contact Bangor PD via Clancy's office, make things official and above board.

Their drive took them down I-95 south of Augusta, where Po took the exit onto I-295 to cut around Brunswick and follow the rugged shoreline along Casco Bay. Tess considered asking her driver to divert to Bald Head Cove, but what purpose would staring out over the cliffs again serve? While Po concentrated on the road, she fished out her tablet and powered it up, looking at the list of names she'd collated. Conklin, for all he was woolly-headed from medication, proved to have a more astute memory than she. He'd offered the full name of one of the girls that had continued to foil Tess. Not Gina, as she'd thought, the girl she'd horribly recalled as Thing One was named Mina. Mina Stoll. She set about tracing a current location and contact details for her, but was almost instantly thwarted by a lack of signal.

'How soon can we be back in Portland?' she asked.

'Forty minutes, give or take.'

'Drop me at my place?'

'Sure.'

'Po?'

He glanced over.

'I'm sorry,' she said.

'For what?'

'You know what. For giving you a hard time.'

He frowned as if he'd no idea what she was talking about. But she wasn't fooled. His silence had told her that she'd stung him earlier. If he were envious of her feelings for Rick Conklin she should accept it for all the best reasons. Po had been pushing her to make their partnership more permanent by moving in with him, and maybe he'd taken her reticence wrong. Maybe he was experiencing insecurity about just how strongly she'd bought into their relationship. Seeing her showing affection to another man, one she'd undeniably dated before, had perhaps given him a twinge or two of jealousy, despite his denial, but that only meant he felt so strongly for her. She should have been flattered instead of biting his head off.

'I don't recall being given a hard time,' he said. 'Fact of the matter, it was kinda mild coming from you, Tess.'

Her eyebrows gave an involuntary jump. But he was correct. She could be snappy. But Po could also be infuriatingly laconic at times, where the only way of prompting a response from him was to go for him like an angry terrier. But their bickering was rarely heartfelt, and simply their way. She knew that Po was amused when he earned a rise from her, and often pushed her into snarky mode for effect. Making up was part of the process, and unashamedly for her, it made for better sex.

'I'm just . . . I don't know. My head's all over the place.' Her tablet was on her lap, her web browser still refusing to log on. In the top-left corner alongside the 'No Service' message, and a dead Wi-Fi signal, a wheel icon continuously whirred around. Tess's thoughts were like that turning wheel, ever seeking, but never finding connectivity. Visiting Conklin's sickbed had been akin to following a single spoke of that revolving wheel, and it had gotten her no closer to finding out why Chelsea died. She had to find other spokes, and hopefully one of them would snag something meaningful.

'I guess that you and Chris are going to have to handle those troublemakers yourselves. I need to concentrate, try to find something worthwhile. I can't do that if I'm waiting for trouble to brew.'

'Sure thing,' Po said, and she could tell he was happier that she wouldn't be in the line of fire at the bar. She knew he'd been trying to find a way to dissuade her from joining him, and she'd just given him an out. It wouldn't surprise her if he'd manipulated her into getting angry with him so she'd be happier with her own company, the devious swine!

She gave him the stink eye again.

'What?'

'If we weren't driving so fast I'd give you a slap around the head.'

Po grinned. 'Now there's the Tess Grey I know and love!'

'Just be careful tonight, OK? I've had enough with hospitals for one day.'

'Don't worry. Ain't no girl gonna sneak up and knock me on my butt, Tess.'

'Oh, yeah?' She backhanded him playfully on his shoulder. 'You'd better watch yourself when you get home: I still owe you a smack.'

EIGHT

Rayne frowned at the abrasion on Cable's head, teasing aside clumps of spiky hair now as rigid with dried blood as with styling gel for a better look at the injury. 'You need to shower,' she said.

'I already washed my hair.'

'You've bled again. You need to get that clean or you might get infected.'

'It won't get infected. It's just a scratch.'

'It's raw and bleeding, Cable. Go and wash and I'll put something on it.'

'Stop fussing, Rayne. I'll get to it, just not right now.'

Cable was hunched over a laptop set on a counter in their RV. Coincidentally, on screen was a list of names comprising a similar group of students from Husson University that Tess Grey was studying many miles away. Cable had highlighted in red those that had already been dealt with, but was unsure about Richard Conklin's name. Conklin had been beaten, but not to Cable's satisfaction.

'We have to go back and finish the job on that fucking crip.'

Rayne shook her head. 'Not now, Cable. We wait. If we go after him now we'll be caught, and that will be the end of it. Is that what you want? Before you're done with the others?'

'He's already hurt, will be easier to deal with next time,' Cable said.

'Or maybe he'll be ready for us next time. Even taken by surprise he put up quite a fight.'

'I slipped,' Cable grumbled. The bulging muscles of Cable's left shoulder twitched violently, and Rayne stepped closer and laid a gentling hand on it. 'Otherwise there's no way he'd have gotten a chance,' Cable assured her.

Rayne patted Cable's neck, then hooked her palm more securely round it and pulled Cable back for a lingering kiss. As they parted, Rayne was breathing heavily, her lips glistening. It took a moment before she could speak. 'I don't think any less of you, Cable. You're more of a man than that piece of shit, even before he had his balls blown off in Iraq.'

Cable looked back at the screen. 'How'd you know his balls got blown off?'

'I took a peek up his shorts after he was knocked out.'

Cable squinted back at her, mouth working in revulsion . . . maybe jealousy.

'Chill, Cable, you know I've no interest in anyone's bits but yours.' Rayne ran the tips of her sharpened nails through the spiky hair again, making Cable wince.

'You would have handled Conklin, whether I'd helped or not.' Rayne moved alongside Cable so that she could see the laptop's screen. 'Don't dwell on it, or him. Like I said, we'll go back once he's returned to his miserable life. Next time he won't get away so lightly. Next time you can use the bat on him.'

'No, that'd be too easy,' Cable grunted. 'I want to kick him to death, treat him like a mangy dog.'

'You'll get your opportunity. I promise you. We'll make it happen, the way we did with the other two.' Again Rayne moved in, this time wrapping both arms around Cable's neck and forcing her butt in to sit. She was half her lover's size, willowy and sparse where Cable hulked. She snuggled on Cable's lap as she again roamed her wet mouth from chin to eyelids and back to Cable's lips again. This time when they parted Cable was breathing equally deeply. Rayne gently stroked the discoloured bump on her partner's nose. 'Does it hurt?'

Conklin had pounded his fist into Cable's face half a dozen times before Rayne turned the tables by smashing him unconscious with the baseball bat. Cable's nose had streamed blood, but it hadn't been broken. The swelling and the deep bruising under both eyes only added to his brooding good looks in Rayne's opinion. Again she probed at the slight malformation of Cable's nose. Cable sat stoically, resisting the urge to draw away.

'It does hurt,' Rayne teased. She pouted her glistening mouth. 'Let me kiss it all better.'

Cable stood abruptly, but Rayne's arms were still looped around his neck, tightening so she wouldn't slip as his hands grasped her backside. Her toes wiggled clear of the floor. She peered up at Cable, whose face was more brooding than ever.

'I asked you not to fuss,' Cable growled.

Rayne mashed their groins together. To her delight Cable clutched her butt tighter. 'You love it when I fuss over you,' she said.

'I've stuff to do.' Cable glanced down at the laptop.

'*We've* stuff to do,' Rayne corrected.

The motorhome was old, shabby, but it was roomy. At the back there was a separate bedroom complete with a double bed. Between it and the sitting area were a tiny kitchenette and two stalls, one of which contained a chemical toilet. The other stall held a shower, but the cubicle was tiny. 'I'm not showering in there,' Cable stated bluntly.

'Then let's go to the shower block.' Rayne's features lit up. 'We can get naked together.'

They had parked on the RV site in the early hours, after fleeing Bangor fearful that the police were hot in pursuit. Before they'd gotten to beat Richard Conklin to death – always Cable's intention – some nosey neighbour had hollered that they'd called the police, and neither of them was fool enough to ignore the warning. Rayne had driven the huge Winnebago while Cable sat dejected in the back, mopping blood with a damp towel and trying ineffectively to keep the swelling to a minimum by rolling an icy cold Coke can across the aching flesh. Before they'd entered the RV site, Cable had joined Rayne up front, so both had taken note of the communal bathroom facilities as Rayne drove them to a vacant space: it was an ugly cinderblock structure, separate entrance doors for men and women situated at either end. Rayne hadn't joined Cable in the men's washroom, because there were already other campers up and about, but she'd been dying to lather up her lover and was no less eager now, hours later. By now she could give a damn if anyone spotted them entering a shower stall together, in fact, if the truth be told, the very thought of raising an eyebrow or two made her hotter.

Cable hadn't yet set her down, and didn't as he lurched towards the bedroom with her. 'Fuck the shower,' Cable grunted. 'I bathed already, and intend getting much dirtier before I do again.'

The bed was already an untidy bundle of sheets and a rucked-up duvet. Cable almost threw Rayne down, and she lay there as

Cable loomed over her. She bit her bottom lip, supposedly coy but Cable knew she was anything but. Cable filled the entire doorway, but managed to yank open the front of his shirt, displaying thick wedges of pectoral muscle, and abdominals that bulged as if there was a rack of snooker balls beneath the pimpled flesh. Rayne's eyes widened, as they always did when Cable displayed like this, and latched onto the vivid red scars on her lover's heaving chest. The recent scars should have been repulsive, but she found them fascinating, and so unlike the silken silver mutilations – barely noticeable now as she'd entered her early thirties – she'd inflicted to her forearms in her teens.

NINE

It took only a brief, though admittedly uncomfortable, telephone call to Husson University for Tess to complete the list she'd been collating. She should have thought about ringing the administrator responsible for student intakes before, but her head had proved a mess of whirling and conflicting thoughts since receiving the sad news of Chelsea's demise. Too many why's and how's had been vying for answers, and she'd given them undue attention rather than concentrating on facts. Tess was supposed to be all about the details, but she was also prone to allowing her wondering mind to take over at times, and had to reign in her tendency to extrapolate. Sometimes thinking outside the box helped, but mostly it hindered her, the case in point how she'd wasted hours trawling through pages of online data when a polite request on the telephone had gotten her the exact details she was after.

When calling the university, she'd first thought about spinning the administrator a line about how she was hoping to organize a class reunion and was missing the names of some of her fellow students, but had taken the snap decision to go with the truth: though she did make her request sound official by mentioning she was a specialist inquiry agent attached to the DA's office – not a lie but a slight bending of the actual nature of her call. And it was a good job too, because the administrator, a woman who identified herself as Jenny Elam, immediately broached the subject of Chelsea's untimely death.

'Hi there! Are you following up on the request for information by the Sagadahoc Sheriff's Office? I already emailed over the information to their office in Bath and to the chief at Phippsburg PD.' Jenny was breezy, used more to speaking to prospective students than investigators. It took her a moment to recall the circumstances that had prompted Tess's call. 'Gee . . . it's really sad about Miss Grace. Such a waste of life; she was a fine young lady.'

'You knew Chelsea?' Tess asked.

'No, not personally. But as an alumna of our fine institute I can imagine she was held in high regard by all that knew her. It's so sad to think how badly her students must feel about losing such a fine teacher.'

They probably felt anything but *fine*, Tess thought, echoing what sounded like Jenny's favourite word. Unfortunately, if her suspicion was correct, then it might very well have been another alumnus of their class that had pushed Chelsea to take such drastic action, and they were anything but *fine* in her estimation. But she kept her opinion to herself.

'It's incredibly sad,' Tess said. 'And why her case should be given the amount of attention it's due. I could get the information from the investigation team up in Sagadahoc county, but it would sure speed up the process if you'd send it across.'

Jenny was apparently seated at her computer, because she hummed an agreement, and said, 'I've the email I sent them up in front of me now. I could forward it to you?'

'Please.' Tess gave Jenny her email address.

'It should be with you now,' Jenny said.

From behind her Tess heard the musical chime announcing the incoming message.

'Thank you,' she said, 'you've been a great help.'

'My genuine pleasure,' Jenny said, but Tess caught the hint of an unvoiced question. Jenny had made a connection. 'Umm, can I just say . . .'

'You noticed my name was on the list of students?'

'So it is you? Teresa Grey? You're also an alumna of Husson?'

Tess sensed that Jenny now regretted emailing the list of names prior to taking steps to confirm that Tess's request had come through official channels. But her fears were allayed by the address to which she'd sent the email: Tess had purposefully given the one she used as an employee of Emma Clancy, as opposed to a personal one. But that was not it; Jenny had another reason to question her identity. 'You're rather famous around here,' Jenny announced.

'Really?'

'The Albert Sower case?' There was a buzz of excitement in Jenny's voice. 'The more recent one where you saved all those imprisoned girls? You've become quite the celebrity among our students, Tess.'

Tess was too stunned to respond. The cases that Jenny referred to had indeed been high profile, and had received a lot of airtime through local media channels, but Tess preferred to play down her role in what had occurred and had never dreamed that she had achieved any level of fame through her involvement. She doubted that she was celebrated to the length that Jenny suggested, but it was reasonable to assume that, yes, her name had probably come up as a notable graduate of the university. Then again, she equally wondered if she'd been afforded a similar level of notoriety when she'd accidentally but fatally shot a victim and almost lost a hand while foiling a robbery. Those linked events had caused an outcry and brought her law-enforcement career to a halt. Tess certainly wasn't about to bring it up now.

Something important struck her though: she had to consider the possibility that Chelsea's last message was addressed to her because she'd come to prominence through solving those cases. You're reaching again, she warned, because if that were the case then Chelsea would be aware Tess was no longer a Sheriff's deputy.

'Can I ask you something, Tess?' Jenny's voice had dropped to a conspiratorial whisper. Tess imagined her hunching over the phone, taking occasional backward glances to ensure she wasn't being observed, and certainly not overheard. 'If you've an interest in her case, is there more to Miss Grace's death than we're being told?'

'I'm surprised that Chelsea's death has even been brought to the university's notice,' Tess replied. Best she remain noncommittal.

'It hasn't been announced beyond faculty members,' Jenny assured her. 'But it strikes us as being unusual that a suicide is being treated with so much suspicion. I mean, first the sheriffs, the police, and now a private investigator?'

Reading between the lines, Jenny had probably been the first point of call on all requests for information from the law-enforcement agencies taking an interest in Chelsea's past, so when she said 'us' she really meant 'me'. Jenny's interest had been piqued, so now would be a good time to put her off spreading any unfounded rumours. 'There's nothing else I can tell you, and not because of the confidentiality rules law-enforcement officers work under, but simply that there's nothing else to tell. Sadly, a young woman has died under dreadful circumstances, and it would be remiss of us all if we didn't investigate and rule out other possibilities other than what might very well prove to be an awful accident.' Tess was purposefully verbose, the more she threw at Jenny the more the woman would believe she'd been given a forthright answer. A blunt 'no comment' would have guaranteed gossip and speculation.

'So she wasn't a victim of foul play?'

'I'm not in the habit of speculating,' said Tess, her tongue metaphorically wedged firmly in her cheek. 'Thanks for your assistance, Jenny, but I'm very busy and . . .'

'Oh,' Jenny replied. 'That's *fine.*'

Jenny ended the call.

Tess caught sight of her face reflected in her phone's screen. She guessed that when Jenny had snapped that final word, she'd worn a similar sneer. The admin assistant hadn't been pleased at being brushed off, but Tess could care less. She was bending the truth when stating she wasn't one for speculation, but not that she was busy. Immediately she hurried to her computer and opened the email. Jenny had attached the list as a document. Tess printed it for later.

After Po had dropped her off at home she'd gotten another jug of coffee brewing, and had brought some cookies from the kitchen. Her diet wasn't the healthiest, but the caffeine and sugar rush would help concentrate her attention. Jenny had sent over the entire student enrolment for the years whilst Chelsea was at university. There were a few names missing that Tess required – Richard Conklin was two years ahead of them, for instance – but Tess had already identified the other older students who'd worked with them at the summer camp, so it was no problem. She saw that Mina Stoll's name was listed and also that of the Goth girl who'd continued to thwart her recollection: Gabriella Kablinski.

She'd kept the photographs of their time at summer camp to hand. She fished out the group photo, and laid it alongside her keyboard, glancing from photo to screen, matching names to faces. Ten girls, three boys: she was confident she'd identified all. Next she concentrated on the photo, staring into the faces of each individual, including her own younger self. 'One of you guys knows something,' she said aloud. 'But which one?'

Already she'd identified contact details for most, but with the addition of the names she'd needed to complete her list she still had some final digging to do. Or she could get on and make a start and get to the others later if she drew a blank from her inquiries.

She picked up her phone, but paused with her finger over it.

What made her think that Chelsea's death had anything to do with working together at summer camp?

They'd been in close company for the best part of four years, so why had Tess singled out that one spell in their lives? A hunch. Gut instinct. An elusive memory that she simply couldn't grasp; something mundane, everyday normal, but maybe seen differently from another's perspective. The truth was, even though they'd shared a room, working at the camp was the first and probably only time that Tess and Chelsea had considered themselves friends.

Her gaze fell on the photo once more. This time she singled out the faces of the males in their group. Richard Conklin, Kent Bachman, and Manuel Cabello. The jock, the joker, and the rebel, as she'd collectively thought of them. Clichéd, yes, but true. She tapped a fingernail on Cabello, taking in again his brooding dark looks. Chelsea – terrified to openly admit her infatuation – could barely keep her attention off Manny that summer, but Manny had not noticed. In turn he was too fixated on Tess to notice her dowdy roommate. Tess hadn't reciprocated his advances – but for one time. The gang had partied late one Saturday evening, and Tess and Manny had ended up in a drunken clinch. When Manny tried to kiss her, Tess had allowed it, but only until she'd glanced over his shoulder and spotted Chelsea's stricken face. She'd turned the kiss into a joke, and sent Manny on his way with a shove, but Chelsea hadn't taken the hint, hadn't swooped in when he was ready and willing: she'd stormed off weeping. As she recalled, later on, Manny had ended up sleeping with Mina Stoll of all people. It had surprised everyone, because up until that point the group had agreed that Things One and Two were an item, and it had come as much of a surprise to Gabriella when she'd caught Manny and Mina at it. The incident had led to a hysterical spat, and Manny wearing a sheepish grin and heavy embarrassment to what depths he'd plunged. Corny euphemisms aside, Manny and some of the other guys had gone to great lengths to put Manny's dalliance with Mina behind them, at the expense of the girl of course. Mina was broken-hearted, but then so was Chelsea. Never had Tess witnessed Chelsea angry before, but she was vindictive towards Mina after that, as if it were Mina's fault that Manny had been pulled astray by the wicked lesbian. Tess recalled her launching a juvenile smear campaign against Mina, and by virtue of their friendship, Gabriella was included in the name-calling and insults. Jeez, Tess even remembered being party to some of the bullying, and was ashamed to admit that she'd taken a certain amount of perverse delight in hurting those misunderstood girls, simply because she wanted to right the wrong she felt she'd done to Chelsea when smooching Manny. Ironically, Chelsea never got her man. Manny and Mina didn't run off into the sunset either. He met a recently divorced woman, three years his senior, with two kids, but fell instantly in love and moved away with her before completing the end of his third year at university. With Manny's sudden departure, even Chelsea understood that maligning Mina and Gabriella wouldn't bring her Prince Charming back, so had cooled things down. In their final year she had fully gotten over Manny, and any ire she aimed at either girl after that was the impersonal bullshit that youths occasionally engaged in. But what if Chelsea had never gotten over the way he spurned her: could that have been the nucleus of her depression that caused her to step off a cliff all these years later.

'Manuel Cabello,' Tess said, and again tapped the photo for emphasis. 'Have you something to answer for, buddy?'

TEN

R aised voices brought up Po's head, and he stared balefully at the group entering the diner. It took him all of three seconds to study them, weigh them, and judge them as welcome guests to his establishment. Their voices were loud, but jovial, the small group of four men and two women sharing a joke that had them all laughing as they approached Jasmine Reed, the acting maître d' that evening. Since Po took over the premises, the old Bar-Lesque had undergone transformation from a sleazy gilded cage, and was now nostalgically decked out in a style reminiscent of the Hard Rock chain. Most of the main floor where the booths reserved for private dances had been located was now dedicated to the dining experience, while the bar area was situated opposite, where drinkers seated themselves on tall stools. Most patrons visited for the food and ambience of old-school rock and roll and doo-wop tunes on the jukebox. Jasmine – better known as Jazz – led the group to their requested table for six, a stack of menus in hand. Jazz was a striking girl, her image more so for her sleeves of tattoos, vibrantly dyed crimson hair, and figure-hugging red dress – Jessica Rabbit for the twenty-first century – so was apt to attract the kind of looks she got from those following as she sashayed to the dining area. The men's eyes were on stalks, and even the women seemed less envious than fascinated. Po's mouth curled up at one side, and he allowed his gaze to slip back to the pages of the book he was reading. He enjoyed the classics, but he equally enjoyed a thumping good thriller, and tonight was following the exploits of an ex-soldier righting wrongs in America. Interestingly, a British author wrote the book, but you wouldn't know it. Po was enjoying the slightly over-the-top heroics, and had pegged the entire series as future reads.

The door opened again, and Po marked his position with one oil-stained thumbnail as he checked out the man entering the diner. Guy in his forties, shirt and tie, slacks and loafers.

He made for the bar, literally licking his lips. Po didn't yet go back to reading.

Chris Mitchell, the bar manager, was as equally eye-catching as Jazz was in looks. If she was reminiscent of a 1950s movie starlet, then Chris was the brooding rock star. He had the ebony ducktail, the sensual eyes and lips of a young Elvis Presley, but with the addition of chiselled muscles, tats, and the occasional piercing. Men and women viewed him not dissimilarly to the way their gazes alighted on Jazz, taking their own good time before slipping away again. It wasn't about sexuality, not always. Some men felt challenged by women's attraction to Chris, especially when they knew he had no interest in the opposite sex, and wondered why the hell girls grew all giggly around him. Some men's insecurities sometimes manifested in brusque aggression when ordering their drinks. This latest punter was no exception.

'Beer,' he snapped in an order that carried to Po as a sharp whip crack. By the time Po glanced across at him again, the man had turned his back on Chris, as if the bartender was beneath him. Po sought Chris's eye, but he only shook his head, his coiffed pompadour wobbling but still defying gravity, as he warded off any concern. The guy wasn't one of those who'd previously caused Chris trouble. He took his beer and moved away to the far end of the bar, propped himself on a stool, and studiously ignored all around him. Po ignored the surly customer, making another visual sweep of the diner instead.

The dining area was relatively quiet, but it was still early. Business usually built between eight and ten o'clock, and Po was reasonably sure that his services wouldn't be needed until later than that. He was happy to read in the meantime, and to sip from the glass of Sprite that Jazz periodically replenished. No booze for him. He required a clear head, and was never one who relied on alcohol to bolster his courage. He returned to his book.

Time passed. Po thumbed his way through the book page by page, chapter by chapter. Those entering the bar earned a cursory glance from him, but nobody raised his hackles. He noticed that after a couple of beers the surly customer at the end of the bar had softened enough and had even engaged Chris in small talk. Jazz and her serving staff were working at full speed now, the dinner crowd having come out in force. Po sat largely unnoticed in his chair adjacent to the hostess stand at the front of house. He'd settled there for the purpose of anonymity, but also so he could reach the door quickly if the need arose. Drinkers, diners, partygoers: all made an indistinct ripple of movement beyond the tinted windows, their voices a constant babble – some now raised to higher tones as their inhibitions loosened. The sound of traffic had now become a periodic, muted grumble, with only the infrequent keening of distant sirens breaking the mould. All aided in lulling Po, as did the high-octane antics of the hero in his book.

The solid *crack!* on the window to Po's left startled him out of his seat. He stood so abruptly that he dropped the paperback and it knocked over his glass of lemonade. He grabbed for neither. His first instinct was to look at the window, to figure out the cause of the noise. The plate glass still vibrated from the impact, and he could make out cracks radiating from a central point. If somebody had struck the window in passing, they'd have done more damage to their hand. Po took a quick check of those in the bar and dining area. Most faces had turned towards the sharp sound, and now peered at him, as if somehow he was its cause. Jazz took a few steps towards him, clutching a menu to her chest, mouth open in silent question. Po gestured, warning her to stay back.

The window imploded behind him, struck a second time. Glass rained, crashing and tinkling, and Po rounded his shoulders as it avalanched over him. The sound was momentary, but to him it seemed to stretch out the length of his silent string of curses. Chunks of glass peppered him, shards jabbed and stung. Something jagged drilled his shoulder, and another burning impact caused his left leg to buckle. Before the tinkling shards settled on the floor, a third solid object struck the next window, and it shattered first time. Glass flew inside the bar area, and Po was only distantly aware of customers scattering from the curtain of flying shards. Stools were knocked over in their haste. Diners also scattered from their tables, adding to the cacophony of shouts and yelps.

Seconds had passed at most since the first missile struck, but it was all it took for those in the restaurant to panic. Po swung

around, shedding a coat of tinkling splinters, and some larger
chunks of glass that had caught in his clothing. The window was
now framed with jagged teeth, and his view outside through the
gaping hole was uninhibited. Shocked passers-by gawped back
at him, but from the safety of about twenty feet to each side of
the entrance. Po ignored their incredulous looks as he knocked
loose some small slivers of glass from his hair. His gaze zoned
in on a pickup truck across the street. There were two figures on
the back, another two inside the cab. All wore hooded tops and
gloves; the two standing on the rear of the truck had scarves
wrapped around their faces. One of them held half a building
brick aloft. Po's mouth opened in warning, but before the shout
left him the brick sailed across the street and crashed through
the glass of the entrance door, and rebounded off Jazz's hostess
podium.

Po raced for the door, his hasty passage slowed by the glistening carpet of broken glass underfoot. He yanked open what
remained of the door, and lurched outside, volcanic in his anger.
But already the men on the rear of the pickup were slapping
urgently on the cab. The driver gave it gas and it squealed away
from the kerb, smoke billowing from its overheated tyres. All
four occupants hooted and hollered, and one of the men on the
back risked letting go of the cab to flip the bird at Po. 'Fucking
faggot!' the man screamed, his words barely muffled by the thick
scarf. Then the pickup rocketed away and he had to grasp at a
handhold to avoid pitching off into the street.

Po charged after the truck, but it was a race he couldn't win.
It roared away, those on the back hollering and challenging Po
to follow. But then they didn't seem overly keen on allowing
him to catch up. The pickup skidded around a corner at the end
of the block, and was gone.

Po came to a halt, staring at the empty spot where the pickup
had disappeared. He turned, heading for where he'd left his
Mustang, but was caught in indecision. Witnesses milled around
outside his bar, some now bending to peer inside through the
broken windows. There was some glass on the sidewalks, and
he could spot one of the bricks used in the attack. He loped back,
calling at people to stand aside. Jazz, then Chris appeared in the
doorway.

'Po? What the hell?' Jazz knew about the troublesome customers, but none of them had expected an attack of this magnitude.

'Is anyone hurt?' Po countered.

Chris stood with the fingers of one hand interlaced in his sculptured hair. His mouth hung open in disbelief. One of the first time's Po had met the barman Chris had worn a similar shocked expression, but on that occasion his arms had been glistening with the blood of a stabbed man. Thankfully this time he wasn't gore-spattered. But then his gaze fell on Po, and his eyes widened even more.

'Are you hurt?' Chris wheezed.

Po glanced down. He had spots of blood leaking through his shirt and jeans. He could feel the sting of cuts on his face and on the back of his neck and his forearms. Thankfully, no major arteries had been cut, though he did take a second check of his leg where he'd been hit particularly hard by flying glass. His jeans were torn, the skin beneath abraded, but at least there wasn't a chunk of toughened glass protruding from his femoral artery or anywhere else.

Po shook like a hound shedding water from its pelt, and more shards tinkled around him.

Jazz touched him, carefully avoiding the slivers adhering to him, so that she could manoeuvre him around. She checked his back. 'You look like you've gone through a mincing machine,' she announced.

'I'm fine,' Po reassured her. 'Everyone inside OK?'

His question was directed at Chris.

'Nobody got hurt, but I'd best go check that none of them end up cutting themselves: all we need is to be sued and it'll just make this the perfect evening.'

'I'll help,' said Jazz, and turned to follow Chris inside. But she halted, turned back to Po. 'How do you want to deal with this, boss?'

'Those punks got away, but I'll catch up with them.'

Jazz shook her head. 'I'm sure you will. What I meant was how are you going to handle our customers?'

'Give 'em all their tabs and tell them I'll pick them up.' He thought about it. 'Tell 'em they can also eat free next time they visit.'

'You think anyone's going to come back if they're afraid their side orders might be delivered on a flying brick?'

Underneath he was seething, but Jazz's words pulled a brief smile from him. 'Might take some recovery time, but I'm confident our customers will be back.' He scanned the gathered bystanders. Some of them were already talking on cellphones, some of them videoing the destruction of his premises. Within minutes he supposed those videos would be plastered all over the social networks. He'd rather have kept the police out of his business, but their involvement was inevitable. Best he beat anyone else to the punch before the police suspected he had something to hide. He took out his cell.

Once that was done, he called Tess.

ELEVEN

'Teresa Grey,' said Kent Bachman, affecting a reasonable impression of Obi-Wan Kenobi. 'Now that's a name I've not heard in a loooong time.'

For good measure he listened again to the voicemail message, this time straining to associate the officious voice with the younger Tess he once knew. He couldn't, and neither could he easily dredge a face from his memory. To be fair, back when he knew her, his attention had been fuelled by the raging hormones of youth so he was more apt to linger on her butt and boobs than on her face. Hell, all these years on and he hadn't changed much; his wife was forever digging an elbow into his ribs whenever a good-looking girl was nearby. Lois, wife and mother to their three children, was used to his wandering eye, and took it as part of the package that was Kent: she knew he would never get to stray, or if he did he'd have to pay for the services of some hooker because he wasn't the kind of guy to attract any attention from the pretty girls he so openly ogled. He had let himself go. She'd an excuse for not being as sylph-like as she'd been when they married – bearing three kids could do that to a woman – but Kent's only excuse for piling on the pounds was that he could rarely keep his mouth shut, and stuffing fast food into it didn't help. Kent was positive his wife was happiest when he was eating, because she'd grown weary of his jokes and impressions to a point where if she heard another Sean Connery or Clint Eastwood skit she'd beat him to death with her bare hands. These days, he tried to express his impressions when she was out of earshot, the way he made sure that she wasn't around when checking out any pretty young things.

He'd missed his vocation in life. He should have been on stage, or even better, on TV. In his opinion he was as good as any other current impressionist playing it for laughs. He'd considered auditioning for *America's Got Talent* but the suggestion had earned him only a scornful laugh from Lois who reminded him that his impressions were about three decades out of date. Kent disagreed; 'Fred Flintstone is timeless, right?'

'No,' Lois had replied, 'he's from the Stone Age, just like your act.'

'Jeez, Lois,' he'd said, 'maybe you should be the comedian instead.'

But Lois was too much of a pragmatist than to aspire to something she wasn't, and she made sure that Kent knew his place too. He couldn't feed and clothe his kids with the non-existent earnings from a pipedream; he had to get a *real* job. So there he was, tending a counter at a Walmart Supercenter a stone's throw from I-95 in Augusta. Customers had been few and far between in the last hour, but there was still plenty of work to be getting on with. As a supervisor, Kent got to boss his assistants around, so didn't do much of the manual lifting himself. But he still had to keep a close eye on his staff, so he patrolled the aisles, periodically tucking in his shirt as the rise and fall of his expansive gut rucked it up. It was during his overseeing duties that he'd pulled out his personal cell and checked for any last-minute instructions from Lois. She'd left a message telling him she'd left dinner in the oven, that she'd be asleep when he got back, so he'd better not cheat on her at Wendy's on the way home. He had no intention of it; he was planning a detour to the nearby Denny's when he got off shift at midnight, his grumbling belly fixated on one of their all-day breakfasts. Then, somewhat surprised, he'd picked up Tess Grey's message, eliciting the impromptu – again decades old – impersonation of Sir Alec Guinness.

Tess's message wasn't long. Simply an introduction and reminder of where they knew each other from, and requesting that he call her back as a matter of urgency. She left her number for him. Hearing that Tess Grey was now a private investigator surprised him. He had assumed that she had followed some line of work more appropriate to the qualifications she'd earned at Husson. Then again, who was he to speak? He hadn't put his own education to much use, unless majoring in history was the reason most of his jokes were historical.

The notion elicited a grunt of sour mirth.

The shop was closing up, and behind the scenes the security guard would be making his rounds, locking doors, turning off lights. A manager had to stay behind to set the alarms and finalize the lock-down procedure, but being a lowly supervisor, Kent got to leave with the other few members of staff on the back shift. He thought about returning Tess's call, but it was midnight, and that she'd have probably retired for the night. He put away his phone, then went and fetched his jacket and rucksack from his locker. On his way out the staff exit, he waved and said goodnight to the manager and guard who were now stationed near the alarm panel. They ignored him, too keen on getting off home to spare any time in small talk or pleasantries. He ducked outside, one hand over his head to ward off a spatter of chilly rain. His car was parked to the side of the building: the lot had been almost filled when he'd arrived for his shift. His shoes slapped the wet asphalt in his haste to reach his car, and his belly bounced as he broke into a graceless jog. He was out of breath by the time he reached it. He dug for his keys in his trouser pocket, recalled they were in his bag with his wallet and lunch pail. Scowling against the rain, he placed his bag on the hood and began digging for his keys, struggling in the dimness. Ordinarily it would have been light enough to see by, but a quick glance at the side of the building told him the external light had blown its bulb. By touch alone he found his keys and pulled them out, moving for the door as he hit the fob to disengage the locks.

'Excuse me, sir.'

The voice was so unexpected that Kent jumped a foot in the air and his fingers flexed, his keys and rucksack flying out of his hands. His first instinct was to go after them, but his mind was in flux, and instead he rounded quickly on the young woman who'd appeared from the gloom behind him. He held the flat of his right hand to his chest. His mouth hung open as he gasped noisily.

'I'm sorry, sir,' the young woman said, 'I didn't mean to surprise you.'

'You nearly gave me a heart attack,' he said, patting his chest rhythmically.

'I shouldn't have snuck up on you like that.' She opened her mouth in a wide smile of apology.

It was after midnight, dark, the rain pattering down around them. Kent's suspicions were rightly on high alert, and yet he couldn't help himself. He glanced down from her unremarkable face to check out her breasts and then her legs where they poked from beneath a short leather skirt. Her breasts were hidden beneath a padded jacket, but her pins were bare and though slim were shapely enough. Nicer than her face he had to admit, which as he glimpsed back up at her unwavering smile was a touch on the hard side for his taste, and that scar on her lip didn't help. Her hair was straight to the shoulder, and lank, but that could have been because it was damp. He got a waft of her perfume, stale with what was almost an undercurrent of ammonia. Distractedly he wondered if she was homeless, and perhaps about to offer favours in return for cash. He checked her teeth: too white to be those of a drug addict, he decided. He wondered how her malformed mouth would feel on his Johnson, and experienced a tingle of excitement.

'What are you doing out here?' he asked, but then waved off any answer by leaning and searching for where he'd dropped his keys. His rucksack was partly under his car. He grabbed a strap and picked it up. As he did, the young woman turned side-on and gestured deeper into the dimness towards the rear of the store. Kent followed her gesture but could make out little of what she indicated.

'I've a flat battery,' she explained. 'I can't get my darn car started. Was wondering if . . .'

'You don't have Green Flag?'

She shrugged slim shoulders.

Kent scowled a moment. Then offered a reciprocate shrug. 'I don't have any starter leads. Sorry.'

'What about a push start?' The woman looked him up and down, appraising his size with interest. 'There's still a little juice in the battery, just not enough to turn the engine. I bet a big strong guy like you could get me going.'

Kent experienced another tickle of baby fingers in his stomach. Those words were suggestive if ever he'd heard a lascivious invitation: maybe he should give her a jump.

'I'd love to, but, uh . . .' He rubbed a palm over his damp features. 'Well, uh, I'm married.'

The woman shoved her hands in her jacket pockets. One foot was slightly in front of the other. Her shoulders gave a little wiggle as she peered up at him. Her smile had barely slipped. 'I'm pretty sure your wife wouldn't mind you helping out a girl in distress, sir,' she said. 'If it were your wife who was stuck, wouldn't you hope someone would come to her rescue?'

'Well . . . yes, of course.' He glanced back the way he'd come from. The last he wanted was for any of his colleagues spotting him with the woman: despite agreeing to help her, he didn't want anyone telling Lois about it. She wouldn't approve. It was all clear. The manager and guard must have left by a different route. 'Just let me find my keys.'

The woman crouched and picked up his keys. She hung them over a finger, but as he reached for them she backed up a step, smiling coyly.

Kent's fingers fell short.

'Promise me you aren't going to drive off and leave me all alone,' she said, her eyes flashing.

'I promishh,' Kent said, slipping into his best Sean Connery. 'And my promishh is my bond.'

The woman blinked at him, emitting a tiny guffaw, but her laughter sounded more like confusion than humour.

'Shorry,' said Kent, still unable to let it drop. 'That was shupposed to be James Bond. Y'know . . .'

'You're funny,' she said. 'I like guys who make me laugh.' She tossed him the keys and turned away, began walking into the darkness. 'You coming, then?'

Giving back his keys was a sign of trust between them. Kent was tempted to climb into his car, head on home – without making his planned all-day-breakfast stop – and snuggle in bed alongside Lois. But those baby fingers continued to tickle his stomach lining: his promise was made and if he'd correctly read the girl's tone then he was also on a promise of sorts from her. Still on a James Bond trip, he whispered under his breath, 'I musht be dreaming.'

After locking his car again, he followed. He was surprised to find that she wasn't leading him to the back corner but across the deliveries yard. Here the night-lights still glowed, but there was no sign of her car. She crossed a narrow service road and entered a turning circle used during the day by trucks after offloading their freight. Parked at the end was a huge recreational vehicle reminiscent of a cowshed on wheels.

'Hey!' Kent called. 'Is that your motorhome?'

Without stopping the woman said, 'Sure is.'

Kent was torn. Motorhomes came equipped with beds. But they were also huge and heavy monstrosities – at least this vintage model was.

'You expect me to push that thing?'

'No,' said another voice from behind Kent. 'I expect you to get inside.'

For the second time in as many minutes Kent jumped, and spun around. This time he managed to keep hold of his rucksack and keys, but neither would do him any good.

A figure had snuck up on him while he'd followed the flashes of the young woman's slim ankles across the asphalt. Backlit, Kent couldn't make out any detail of the newcomer. But the figure was large. Maybe even as big as Kent, though stocky and solid where he was all flab. He did a double take, first at the young woman who'd led him into a trap, then at her companion who was about to spring it.

'G-get inside?' Kent wondered. 'What do you want from me?'

'What do we want?' asked the big guy. 'Now I can't speak for Rayne, but I want a piece of your lard ass.'

Kent threw down his rucksack. 'My billfold's in there. Just take it.'

'I'll take it. But you're still getting in the van.'

Kent shook his head, searching for a quick escape route from his predicament.

The figure brought out a gun and moved towards him. Kent didn't need to see it to know he'd nowhere to run: any gun would bring him down before he ran a few yards. A shaft of light from the distant lamps cut across features vaguely familiar to Kent.

'Hey!' he croaked. 'Don't I know you?'

'You might,' replied Cable. 'Now get in the fucking van before I shoot you in the gut.'

'What do you mean? Why?' Kent's spine straightened up a notch or two. 'You can't make me,' he said, his voice reed thin.

'We can.'

Rayne clubbed him over the head with the bat she'd retrieved from near the motorhome.

Kent sprawled on his belly in a puddle.

Cable frowned at Rayne.

'I could have walked him over, now we're going to have to carry that fat ass.'

'Kill him here and have done,' Rayne said dispassionately.

'I want to punish him first,' Cable reminded her.

'Fine. So do I. Just let's not fuck up this time like we did with that dumb cripple.'

TWELVE

'This isn't going to be good for business,' Tess said as she watched the emergency glaziers at work. They had sawhorses and power tools strewn across the sidewalk in front of the diner, and their vehicles parked at the kerb. At that late hour they weren't replacing the broken windows, just fixing boards in the frames to secure the building until they could return for the repairs. Chris, Jazz, and their staff had tried tidying up earlier, but Po had sent them home, arranging for a specialist cleaning company to attend the following day to conduct a full – and safe – deep clean of the glass-strewn premises.

Po stood with his thumbs hooked in his waistband.

'Wasn't expecting things to get this far outta hand,' he finally admitted. 'I've got the glaziers coming back in a few days, but we're gonna have to shut up shop till then.'

'You could stay open; put out some "business as usual" signs,' Tess suggested.

He shook his head. 'I'll wait till the place is back to lookin' its best.'

'And what's to stop those idiots coming back and smashing the place up again?'

He didn't reply, only gave her a steady look. Oh, right. He was going to stop them.

'Have you any idea who was responsible?'

'One thing I know, this wasn't down to a bunch of drunks pissed that they missed out on a lap dance.'

'Smashing the windows was a bit extreme,' she admitted.

'They planned the attack. Wasn't a kneejerk reaction to being kicked out.'

'What did the police have to say about it?'

Po's mouth quirked briefly.

'You didn't tell them much, did you?' Tess shook her head at him.

'Told them what I was prepared to say,' he replied.

In other words he told them only what he could without jeopardizing his own attempt at revenge.

'Have you angered anyone lately?' If Po had attracted any personal trouble he would have mentioned it to her, but he wasn't the most ebullient when it came to sharing his thoughts. If he'd felt that it wouldn't have any impact on her then he would keep her out of the shadier side of his business dealings.

Again he didn't answer her.

He handed her a slip of paper.

She glanced at it. Written in Po's neat hand was the make and model of the pickup truck used by the attackers, plus a licence number.

'You didn't give this to the cops?'

'Told them about the truck, didn't admit to catching sight of the plates. Thought you could check 'em out, give me a head's-up first.'

'Po, maybe you should just let the cops handle this. I'll get Alex on to it and . . .' She stopped. He'd turned to watch the workmen drilling boards into place: he'd made up his mind. She knew what he was thinking: what could the cops do? Even if they traced the truck, the owner would claim it had been stolen – there was the possibility it was already burned out someplace – and his pals had been wearing hoods and scarves, no way of identifying them that would satisfy the legal process. On the other hand, Po would feel confident he'd be able to recognize them again to dole out some of his own brand of private justice.

Vigilantism wasn't tolerated by any law-enforcement agency. If Tess used her connections to identify the owner of the truck and Po took action, she'd be complicit in his criminal activity. She wasn't comfortable with the idea, but neither would it stop her assisting her man. The attack on Po's premises was an attack on him, ergo it was an attack on her too.

'I'll see what I can do.' She put away the slip of paper for now.

The workmen were finishing up and putting away their tools.

'How long do you expect to be stuck here?'

Po glanced over at her Prius.

'You may as well get off home now,' he offered. 'I only need lock up and I'll follow you back.'

'Changed my mind. How's about I come on up to your place?'

'F'sure.'

He turned and studied her with interest.

She fought to keep any hint of trepidation off her features. She wasn't about to admit that she'd grown nervous about being home alone. Perhaps her warning antennae were malfunctioning, but after identifying the remaining individuals in her circle of old friends she'd grown more nervous with each message she sent. If her gut were to be trusted, then one of those people she'd reached out to was responsible for Chelsea Grace leaping off a cliff, and by contacting them she'd given them reason to recognize her as a possible threat to their liberty. Yes, part of her motive for calling them individually was to try to draw out a negative response, but she didn't want to be in a position where she was paid a home visit, not while alone and vulnerable. She wasn't afraid of confrontation, but neither was she stupid. Not long ago she'd suffered an attack at her apartment when a violent rapist had fixated on her, and she had no desire to attract similar attention again. Her home was her place of safety, and the last she wanted was for it to be violated. She hadn't told Po, but she'd loaded her grandfather's Service-6 and kept it alongside her while finishing those calls and typing up messages. When Po had rung, telling her about the vandalism at the bar, she'd felt immediate anger, but also a little relief. It gave her an excuse to drive over, and she'd done so with the revolver nestled in her purse.

'I've been so busy with the police and everything else that I didn't ask how you'd gotten on,' Po said.

'I could be reaching,' she said, 'but a name came up that got me thinking about some stuff. It's too early to say, and I need to speak with him first, but there was one guy who caused a little trouble for the gang back then. It seems an inconsequential lead now, but I've got this feeling gnawing at me, and I need to follow it up.' She took a look around. It was a weekday night, and most of the party crowd wouldn't come out until the weekend, so the streets and nearby bars had quietened dramatically. 'But it's either too late or too early to do anything right now. I think the best idea is to sleep on it, and that may as well be back at your place as mine.'

'You won't hear me disagreeing.' Po caught the attention of

one of the glaziers, the foreman Tess assumed. 'Be with you in a minute, buddy.'

He turned back to Tess. 'Who knew that having a few windows bust would cause so much fuss? The cops were all over the place earlier, trying to round up witnesses, taking statements. Checking for CCTV footage at some of the other establishments. Didn't sound like they picked up on anything promising. Could do with an early start to make my own enquiries. If you head on back to my place now, do you think you'll be able to run those tags before I get back?'

'Depends on how long you're going to be.'

Po observed the glaziers taking their own good time putting away their tools in their vans. 'Shouldn't be too long I hope.'

'If I get you those details, you aren't going to go out again, are you?'

There must have been a 'tell' in her face, if not her tone.

'You OK, Tess?'

'I'm fine,' she said, too quickly to be sincere.

'This entire thing has you rattled,' he said. 'It's not like you.'

'Fear of the unknown,' she admitted. 'I must admit, having no idea who is behind Chelsea's death is worrying.'

'If anybody *was* involved,' he reminded her. 'You feel strongly that your friend didn't take her own life. Are you worried you might be a target?'

'I've no reason to think that way,' Tess said, but a visible shudder ran through her body. 'It's not as if any of the others have been hurt, right?'

'What about your buddy Conklin?'

'Coincidence.'

'And none of the others have had any trouble come their ways yet?'

'That still remains to be seen. I haven't spoken to any of them yet.'

'I'm sure if anything bad had happened, you'd have found out. All those programs you have running, I just bet you've set 'em to alert you if any of their names pop up in any news or police reports.'

'Believe it or not, I'm not that far along with the investigation yet. I'm still waiting to make personal contact before I do anything else.'

'That's probably for the best. Speak to them, Tess; you'll hear they're all fine and well, and that you've nothing to worry about.'

'I'm not worried.'

'And I ain't cabbage coloured,' Po retorted. 'You ain't actin' like yourself, Tess. I can tell. But you're probably frettin' over nothin', you'll see once you've talked to your old friends.'

THIRTEEN

He was seated in a chair and his feet were wet. Not just damp, they sloshed as he moved them the few inches of freedom he'd been allowed. His shoes had been removed, but his socks were still in place. Sodden. The cuffs of his trouser legs had adhered to his shins: equally wet. The sharp odour that rose to engulf him in a heady miasma each time he shifted his feet had Kent Bachman fearful of wetting his drawers. At first he thought he'd awoken seated in a puddle of gasoline, but the smell was sharper, the fumes less choking. Not that he was any less terrified, because paraffin would burn him no less painfully than gas.

His hands were tied behind his back, strapped to the back of the chair with duct tape, and more tape had been wound around his upper face as an impromptu blindfold. Until recently a wadded cloth had gagged him, but it had been removed, his retching as he attempted to purge his gut partly responsible for wakening him. There was a strange numbness at the back of his skull, as if the flesh had swollen to twice its normal size, but he felt little pain from where he'd been struck unconscious. He didn't know if a lack of pain was a good sign or not: probably the latter. Had he suffered brain damage from the hefty clout he'd taken? The duct tape blinded him, but otherwise his other senses were working at a higher intensity than usual, so probably not. But he did think that his skull had probably been fractured, and the swelling was a sign of debilitating complications in the future if he didn't seek immediate medical assistance. For all he knew he was bleeding to death, but with no way of knowing, the pool in which his feet squirmed could be crimson with his blood. When he thought about it, he could feel moisture between his shoulder blades, which went all the way down to the cleft of his butt. It was probably blood, but it could be sweat, or even rain water. There were puddles where he'd been knocked down.

He was terrified, confused, but he remembered how his

assailants tricked him. Two of them working in tandem to walk him directly into a trap. The first playing the damsel in distress, only to lead him back to the second, the ogre lying in wait for the unwary. That wasn't entirely true, the young woman had turned out to be the main aggressor, having no compunction about beating him senseless with a Louisville Slugger. He'd known instantly that it was no ordinary mugging, first the couple showed no interest in taking his wallet, secondly he'd vaguely recognized his ambusher. A face from way back when, from around about the time he was at university with . . . shit! Was that call from Tess Grey to warn him that he was in danger?

'Hey! Hey? You there?' His head swung to and fro as he tried to pinpoint his abductors' locations. They ignored him.

They were in the room with him though. He could hear them, scuffing boards with their feet as they moved, conversing in whispers – about him – making random bumps and knocks as they arranged objects to their satisfaction.

'What do you want?' Kent tried again. 'Whatever it is you're holding against me, I apologize. But I swear to you, I don't know why you'd want to hurt me. Jesus . . . I'm a married man. I've three small children.'

'Shut your mouth.' The voice was the young woman's, a sharp hiss that held promise of further violence. 'You sound like a snivelling bitch!'

'For God's sake! Why are you doing this to me?'

The staccato clip of shoes on hardwood predicted what was coming. An open hand slashed across Kent's face. The slap wasn't delivered with power, but the shock of it was enough to set his ears ringing, and his exposed cheeks to burn.

'What did I just tell you?' the young woman demanded. Kent tried to recall what it was the other called her. Appealing to someone by their given name could sometimes defuse a situation. His brain still rang from the slap, but her name came to him accompanied by a dull flash behind his veiled eyes.

'Please, Rayne? I only wanted to help you. Why treat me like this?'

'You wanted to get in my pants,' Rayne snapped back. 'You're a dirty pervert who thought he was going to get his wicked way with a vulnerable girl. Pig!' She slapped him again, this time harder, and across his jaw. He tasted blood in the back of his throat.

His other tormentor had moved in, silent for one so big. Cable's fingertips dug into Kent's shoulders from behind, and bore down. 'Is that what you planned, Kent? You thought you would get Rayne all alone and then rape her?'

'No! No, for Christ's sake! She asked me for help, and I was only being—'

'What, a fucking gentleman? Don't make me laugh, you piece of shit! You were never a gentleman.'

'Kind!' Kent yelped. 'I was going to say I was only being *kind*.'

'You expect *me* to believe that you've changed?' Cable's voice dripped with scorn.

'I was never cruel to you—'

Before the sentence was out of his mouth, Cable's thick fingers were around Kent's throat. They squeezed savagely, and Kent bucked and wrenched where he sat, the oxygen instantly sealed off from his lungs. In his ear, Cable raged, though the tirade was pointless: all Kent was aware of was the pounding of his heart. If it beat any harder it would shatter his brittle cranium. Absurdly he was grateful of the tape wound round his skull as he felt it was the only thing holding it together. Rayne saved his head from exploding. She pulled Cable away. Kent's head fell forward, mouth gaping, before he threw it backwards and sucked air into his lungs. As he expelled the first grateful lungful it was with a deep sob. He dragged in air again, and once more flopped forward. Distantly he heard Cable and Rayne arguing: Cable's voice was higher-pitched than normal with emotion. According to Cable, Kent thought he was the class joker, but his humour had been spiteful, hurtful, barbed so sharply it had cut deeply.

'Well he's no joker now,' Rayne assured her friend. 'He's just a big ol' joke. Look at him, Cable. Sitting there wetting his pants like a fucking baby.' Scornful laughter punctuated Rayne's point. But that was not the extent of her cruelty. She marched forward and slashed her palm across Kent's face a third time.

A blub left Kent, coppery saliva dripped from his bottom lip.

'Look at him, Cable. Just look at him. He's pathetic! How did you ever let this coward bully you?'

'It was different back then,' Cable muttered, sounding ashamed that Kent Bachman had ever held the upper hand. 'I was different back then.'

'If you'd been with me things would have been very different,' Rayne crowed.

'You weren't there. You have no idea . . .'

'Well,' Rayne said, and Kent sensed that she was offering Cable a tender embrace, 'I'm here now. Nobody . . . *nobody* will ever hurt you again. Not while there's a breath left in my body!'

And Kent knew.

This wasn't about some imagined slight that had psychologically scarred Cable. Rayne, for all she was a sparrow by comparison to Cable's hulking form, was the dominant force in their relationship. She was a manipulative monster. To listen to them, this was supposed to be some kind of revenge trip for Cable, but there was no denying who was pushing all the buttons. Cable was as much a victim now as when a vulnerable youth. Rayne was using his insecurities to appease her own sadistic kicks. It was pointless trying to appeal to him for mercy, but if he could get the idiot to see sense . . .

'This is wrong!' Kent yelled.

His shout startled his tormentors, momentarily throwing them into silence.

'Do you hear me? This is wrong! You have to stop right now!'

He heard the clip of Rayne's shoes again and steeled himself for another slap. But it didn't come. Instead Rayne leaned so close that he felt the short jabbing of her breath on his face as she snapped, 'You are not calling the shots here, Kent.'

'No, I'm not,' Kent replied sharply. 'It's obvious who is though. You're insane, you fucking twisted freak!'

'What did you call me?'

'You heard me! Fucking freak! Cable? Cable! Do you hear me? This crazy woman is making you do this. Don't you see?'

There followed a deep rumble, originating not from Rayne but from her lover. Cable charged in and slammed a fist into Kent's gut, swearing savagely to silence him. Every atom of Kent's being wanted to shrivel in response, and if he could he would have buckled over in his seat too. But his bindings held him in place. He shuddered out what little breath was left in him, fighting against the painful contractions in his abdomen. Cable's hand slapped down on his face, ramming his head backwards, bending it tortuously over the chair's back. Kent took a second clubbing thump, this time to his ribs.

'That's it, make him shut the fuck up!' Rayne urged.

Kent yelled in frustration. There was no hope of getting through to Cable, not while Rayne tugged all the strings. Kent's wordless shout became a plea for help. He had no idea where he'd been brought, and assumed it wasn't in earshot of any help, but it didn't matter. He yelled again and again, before Cable's palm slipped lower and forced his mouth shut.

'Should I gag him again?' Cable asked.

'On second thoughts you want to hear him scream, right? So let him. Nobody will hear but us.'

Cable's hand withdrew, and Kent tried to shout for help, except his mouth was full of bile and all that came out was a splutter. As he sucked in air, his throat burned. And it reminded him of where he was, what he was seated in, and sudden panic sent him crazy. He threw himself around in the chair, and felt it buckle beneath him.

'Shit,' he distantly heard Rayne say. 'If we're going to do this, we'd better do it now.'

'He's going to kick loose.'

'So do it *now*!'

'Oh God noooo . . .'

It took Kent a few seconds to realize the plea was his. And when he did so, he repeated it, this time as a high-pitched squeal. He'd heard the scratch of a wheel on flint.

Feet on floorboards rumbled, as Cable and Rayne sought a safe distance. But the sound was engulfed by the *wumph* of igniting fuel. Flames sucked all the oxygen from around Kent's open mouth as he screamed in terror. His throat constricted, and his entire body clenched in anticipation as crawling fingers of flame writhed up his fuel-soaked trousers. It took a moment before he experienced the first searing bite in his flesh, but then that moment stretched into endless agony as the rest of his clothing was set aflame, and Kent within them.

FOURTEEN

'Aaron Noble? I'm sure I've heard that name before.' Po was fresh from the shower, a towel around his waist, his greying hair darkened with moisture. Immediately above the towel a scar was vivid against his swarthy skin, pink, and puckered like a mouth in a tight grimace. When Tess glanced up it matched the expression on his face.

'Any reason why he should want to ruin your business?'

'None that I can think of. But you're forgetting something: not a lot of people know I own Bar-Lesque. Far as they're concerned Chris is the owner.'

'So the trouble isn't directed at you but at Chris?'

'Makes sense.'

Tess was seated at the breakfast table, already showered and dressed. She'd woken at dawn and had gone back to work, first checking on any replies to the mass of calls she'd put out the night before. Already she'd spoken directly with Alicia Thomson and Callie Burke, but neither of her old classmates could offer anything except sad platitudes on hearing about Chelsea's death. Tess had ruled them out as suspects because one resided in Fairbanks, Alaska, the other in London, England. In this modern era where bullying had grown easier through the digital medium, either woman could have pushed Chelsea to suicide from a distance, but Tess was more inclined to think a physical hand was in her friend's back when she'd plunged from the cliff. Besides, she didn't get as much as a whiff of suspicion off either Alicia or Callie, and hadn't expected to. They'd only ever been at the outer edge of their circle of friends.

Po was waiting for her to respond. His words had been loaded.

'You're suggesting that I'm reading too much into Chelsea's death?'

He shrugged. 'All I'm saying is you might be inviting trouble that wasn't originally marked on your card.'

'Yeah,' she agreed. 'But it doesn't make it any less troublesome.'

'F'sure. Lookit what I've got to attend to now.' He meant dealing with those responsible for smashing up his bar. Whether the attack was directed at Chris or at him, it made no difference. The same was true for Tess: if she was a target or not it wouldn't stop her from investigating, and hopefully bringing Chelsea's killer to justice.

'If you're going to do anything you'd better get dressed first,' she said.

'There are some things I can do naked,' he said, and dug a finger in the top of his towel. He was a beat from whipping it off when Tess's cellphone rang. She held up a warning finger.

'Damn! Saved by the bell, huh?' Po grinned, but took the hint, retreating to the bathroom.

'Hey, Alex,' Tess said.

'Hey, sis.' Alex paused. She imagined she could hear the wrinkling of his forehead. 'Man, how do I say this? Have you seen the news this morning?'

She hadn't. She'd done most of her work while seated at the kitchen table.

'What's wrong?'

'What the hell have you gotten yourself involved in this time?'

'What do you mean? Come on, Alex, just tell me what's up.'

'We just got a call through from Augusta PD. Seems someone up there was burned alive last night. The thing is, when they dug through his personal belongings, they found his cellphone. Tess, I don't know how to take the sting out of this so I'm just going to say it: the last message the victim received was a voicemail from you.'

'What?'

'Yep. You know the vic, Tess.'

She tried to make the connection, but the announcement had set off an explosion in her mind. It flared briefly, pushing aside all cognitive process. For a second that intense flash morphed into a scene of horror. She pictured a form engulfed in immolating flames, a figure on whom she couldn't place a face. But there was only one person it could be. As the initial shock subsided, his name inserted itself at the front of her mind as a second detonation.

'Kent Bachman,' she croaked. He was the only one of her old friends who lived in Augusta.

Alex's silence confirmed her fear.

'You said he was burned alive?' Tess said. 'You mean murdered, right?'

'He wasn't able to have done that to himself. His bindings had been burned through but there was evidence he'd been duct-taped to a chair. Get this, Tess. The poor sap was made to sit with his feet in a trough filled with accelerant. First guess is whoever set him on fire used barbecue lighter fuel, gallons of the fucking stuff.'

'Oh God . . .' Tess rested an elbow on the table, her face in her cupped palm.

'He was also one of your buddies from Husson?' he asked. Alex was aware she was interested in Chelsea's death, and making follow-up inquiries with all their old friends.

'Do you remember when I took a summer job to help pay my way?'

'At that adventure camp out in the boonies? Yeah, I remember. Mom wasn't impressed.' The thing was, their mother was rarely impressed by any of Tess's career choices.

'Kent Bachman was one of the counsellors. He was a big dope, Alex. Thought he was funny, but was more annoying really. Shit . . . listen to me speaking ill of the dead.' Tess couldn't equate the younger Kent – full of fun, bad jokes, and cheesy impersonations – with a scorched corpse. 'He never took life seriously; I can't imagine him doing anything to deserve being burnt to death.'

'Sometimes murderers don't need a reason, not a logical one at any rate. Their motive for killing him might be based on something as trivial as an imagined slight. You know as well as I do, sis, murderers aren't suave psychopaths like you see in the movies, they're usually pathetic little fuckers with an inferiority complex.'

His description was a broad whitewash of many murderers, but it far from covered all. During his law-enforcement career he'd come across a murderer called Hector Suarez, who broke the mould, but in general the killers he'd dealt with were of the common or garden variety: drunks, drug addicts, and enraged spouses, all doing harm to each other for what amounted to ridiculous trivialities.

'What's the consensus of Augusta PD?' Tess asked.

'Bachman's death is being treated as a homicide; there's no way around it. It's the reason I'm giving you a head's-up. Expect a call from one of the detectives on the case, Jolie Carson. She'll want to know why yours was the last call on his cellphone.'

'He was burned to death, but his phone survived?'

'It wasn't on him when he was set on fire. The killer had placed it and his wallet with some other personal items in a rucksack safely out of reach of the flames. Detective Carson reckons it was so there was no issue when it came to identifying him. Otherwise it would have been down to dental records or DNA. I don't want to put any pictures in your head, Tess . . .'

'It's too late for that,' she said. 'You said he was seated with his feet in a trough?'

'Uh-hu. Whether it was intentional or not, his killer ensured Bachman suffered before he died. The flames would have ignited his legs first, then crept up his body. He would've lasted longer than if he'd poured petrol over him and torched him.' Alex stalled; sickened by the horrifying images he was conjuring. Cops – Tess included – grew toughened to sights that would turn the stomach of most members of the public, they learned to compartmentalize and shove horrific images aside while they concentrated on the facts and brought to justice the perpetrators of such inhumanity. But it was difficult to inure oneself when it came to personal friendships. Years had passed since Tess had last laid eyes on Kent Bachman, but it still hurt and upset her to imagine his horrible fate.

'His torment was deliberate.' Tess immediately thought of her recent visit with Rick Conklin, and how he'd believed his attackers wanted to hurt him. *By that I mean* punish *me,* he'd iterated. *And they took enjoyment in doing so.* Kent was being punished too, and what better way to terrorize a woman with a profound fear of heights than to make her jump off a cliff? Prior to Kent's murder there had been nothing to connect Chelsea's death with Rick's beating, but it was different now: there was a definite pattern, and Tess was more convinced it had something to do with their time together at the summer camp.

Po appeared in the doorway. He'd dressed in a T-shirt, denims, and high-topped boots. His hair was still damp, but combed neatly. He clutched a jacket down by his side. He was ready to go out, but not too impatient to wait until Tess finished speaking with Alex. Tess nodded, grim, importing the gravity of the call to him. His mouth formed a tight line, but he didn't speak. Instead he filled a mug with coffee and replenished her cup. She could drink something much stronger but was grateful nonetheless.

'Have you any suspects yet?' Alex asked hopefully.

Tess was tempted to mention Manuel Cabello but until she'd something more incriminating on him decided she'd stay quiet. Though Manny had caused some discord among their group, never had he done anything to suggest he was capable of murder. In fact, if anything, it was more likely he was another potential victim and should be warned. When she'd sent out her call for information she hadn't thought about warning the others that they could also be on the killer's radar: things were different now.

'Am I a suspect?' she countered.

'If you were I wouldn't have called you.' Alex grunted, realizing what he'd just said. 'I mean that Detective Carson wouldn't have given me a call, she'd have had you brought in instead.'

'But it looks suspicious, right? How Chelsea's last message was to me, and then I'm the last person to contact Kent. If I were Carson I'd be asking questions too.'

'She's had no reason to connect the two cases, being as they're in different police jurisdictions, so why would she?'

She told him about the assault on Rick Conklin.

Alex was silent for a long beat. Then he said, 'Is Po with you?'

'He's here. What? You think I need protecting?'

'That's what *you're* suggesting, Tess,' he reminded her. 'That for some reason your group of old friends are potential targets of this killer.'

'Killers. Plural. A man and woman attacked Conklin.'

'Makes sense,' he concurred. 'From what I've learned about Kent Bachman's murder, it would have taken more than one person to abduct, imprison, and then torture him.' He went on to relate how Kent's car had been found at his workplace, while his body had been discovered miles away at an abandoned warehouse after his wife had reported him missing in the early hours of the morning. At first, the disappearance of an able-bodied adult male hadn't raised much concern with Augusta PD, and little would have been done initially to find him; it was only after the fire department responded to an anonymous call reporting smoke at the disused warehouse that his corpse was found.

Tess wondered if the killers had made the call, considering they'd ensured that Kent's corpse would easily be identified. Maybe they weren't responsible, and the latter was a mistake. Announcing that they were killing their victims would send other potential targets into hiding or under protection. If they still had an agenda to fill they were going the wrong way about it. Tess decided that leaving Kent's phone to find was an error, because to date the killers hadn't taken credit for Chelsea's death or the assault on Conklin. It was as Alex pointed out earlier: most murderers weren't the psychopathic masterminds promoted by Hollywood and mystery novels.

'Did Detective Carson leave a number?' she asked.

'You want to beat her to the punch and call her first? No need, Tess. I assure you, you aren't a suspect. I already attested to the fact you were in Portland last night, tied up with the vandalism at the diner.'

'I think the sooner I pass on to her my suspicions that the three victims are all connected the better. The sooner some cross-jurisdiction investigation gets underway the sooner the killers will be identified and stopped.'

'The connection's still sketchy,' Alex cautioned her. 'There's nothing in the MOs that connects the murders. In fact, up to now the only homicide we have is that of Kent Bachman.' Tess was about to argue the point, but Alex sensed it coming. 'I'm not saying you're wrong, Tess, just that Chelsea's death has already been written off as suicide, and we don't know enough about this other guy's assault – whaddaya call him: Conklin? – to think it was anything other than a burglary gone wrong. All I'm saying is don't be offended if Carson laughs you off as a paranoid crank.'

'All the more reason somebody should be at the helm of a

concerted investigation into all the attacks. There's somebody travelling around New England punishing people for some perceived grievance, and they need stopping before anyone else gets hurt.'

'Just make sure that isn't you, sis.' On that note, Alex made his goodbyes and ended the call.

'Well?' Tess eyed Po.

'We'll deal with it.'

'So you don't think I'm reading too much into Chelsea's death now?'

He hadn't heard the news about Kent Bachman, but had absorbed the gravity of the call simply by observing Tess's body language. His outward appearance grew equally grim. 'Like I just said, Tess, we'll deal with it.'

FIFTEEN

I t was one thing shaking the images of a burning corpse from the mind, quite another the stench. Cable's history was a comic strip illustrated with violent and depraved imagery, so the terrible pictures didn't trouble him – a blink or two and they were banished. But, even so many hours later, shifting the god-awful stink was proving more difficult. Some people said that the smell of burning human flesh was akin to that of a hog roast: if that was the case then Cable would never eat barbecue again. Admittedly there had been an undertone of sizzling pork fat as Bachman writhed within the flames, but the toxic smoke rising from his cheap clothing had obliterated any mouth-watering odours beneath a sharper, sinus-stinging noxious cloud.

Cable had retreated from the bilious stink more than the intense heat, watching from a distance as Bachman at first struggled to free his feet from the inferno ignited under him. He'd drummed his soles, spattering flaming fuel yards all around him, only adding to the conflagration. His trousers were already sodden with lighter fuel, but his exertions added to the pyre, sped up the spread of flames up his body. Briefly the flames had gathered in his lap, roiling like a ball of copulating serpents, before writhing up his shirt, the flames bluish-white and intense. His mouth opened in a wordless scream, and it was as if the fire was sentient, and seeking entry to his deepest core. He began swallowing flames. As his exposed skin blistered then curled, and the impromptu blindfold crinkled and shrank, his eyes sank back into their sockets – liquefied – and he began constricting in on himself. Victims of intense heat were often discovered curled into a foetal position, hands in a pugilistic pose, knees almost fused to the forehead, a reaction to the shrivelling of muscle and ligament tissue, but strapped to the chair, he couldn't follow the natural process. Cable heard the competing pops of his elbow and shoulder joints coming unhinged. The synthetic fibres of his work uniform melted as much as burned, adhering and becoming one with his blackened hide, and sent up dirty black smoke, the source of the acrid stench. Cable placed a hand over his mouth and nostrils, observing the demise of his enemy in silence.

Rayne displayed her fascination more vocally, hissing a sibilant '*Yesssss* . . .' as she danced from foot to foot, her fists clenched before her hipbones. Taking a glance at his lover, Cable saw the flames reflected in Rayne's wide eyes and bared teeth. She was enjoying the destruction of Cable's past more than he did. Somehow her reaction to their victim's death was both disturbing and exciting. When Rayne was excitable she manifested it as a sexual charge that took some sating. Pleasing Rayne pleased Cable. If he were to be honest, he experienced little satisfaction from the killing of the individuals on his list, but derived great pleasure from making Rayne happy. If it weren't for Rayne, or at least the desire to appease her, then Cable doubted he'd go to such twisted lengths as he had.

Seated, arms wrenched out of their sockets, Bachman began to fold at the waist. His hair was gone, and most of the scalp that once bore it, and yet his skull guttered like a torch. Cable had seen enough, and took another step backwards. The flames from the human pyre reached for the ceiling of the abandoned warehouse. The smoke was rolling in the rafters, lowering, the stench more ascorbic now that treated timber had begun to scorch. It was time they got the hell out of there before they succumbed to the poisonous fumes.

'His knapsack!' Rayne pointed at where they'd dumped Bachman's belongings. Other than the cash from his wallet, they hadn't yet had a chance to riffle through and find anything worth pillaging.

'Leave it,' Cable said.

'We should take it.'

'I'm not going back in there.' For emphasis Cable coughed, and then couldn't stop. Grabbing Rayne's wrist, he hauled her with him for the safety of the door.

'We should take it,' Rayne repeated more stridently.

But there was no way that Cable was going to risk death for the sake of a few trophy items. 'The fire will spread, burn it, there'll be nothing left behind but ashes.' He looked up and spotted embers glowing amongst the thick smoke. If the warehouse didn't burn down around Bachman, he'd be surprised.

Their motorhome was parked close to the derelict structure, intentionally so that they didn't have to move Bachman too far in the open. When they'd led him inside, he was already tied up, gagged and blindfolded, and the last they wanted was for any witness to spot them leading the shambling figure to his death. In the early hours of the morning, rain falling steadily, it was doubtful that anyone would be abroad in the abandoned industrial site, but who knew. Homeless people sometimes sought shelter in such places. Rayne was unconcerned by the prospect of being observed by some street bum, but Cable was more cautious. It had never been his intention to remove Bachman's gag, but Rayne wanted to hear him beg for his pathetic life. She'd also urged Cable to remove the condemned man's blindfold, but he'd resisted: watching him burn was horrible enough without peering into Bachman's soul as it shrivelled to nothing.

They had the motorhome peeling away in seconds, this time with Cable at the wheel. Rayne was still hanging out the open doorway, a jack-o'-lantern grin painted on her slick face as she scanned the receding warehouse for the first sign that the conflagration had it in its grip. Cable had to reach over and yank her inside before he took the sharp right turn at the end of the industrial site. The door slammed shut as he made the manoeuvre, and Rayne bounced happily in her seat. 'That was a fucking rush!' she crowed.

'Can't get the damn stink out of my nostrils,' Cable countered. 'I can even taste it.'

Hours later and he could still imagine the taste as a film of oily soot in the back of his throat. His nasal hairs had singed, he was certain, and the mucus dried to powder, impairing his scent receptors, and yet it didn't lessen the intensity of the bitter tang ingrained in his memory for ever. Throughout the morning, he'd hawked and spat, blown his nose, but there was no shifting it.

Rayne offered a tube of vapour rub.

'Put some of that on your top lip, it'll take the smell away.' Cable declined.

'So let's go do something to take your mind off things.'

'Like what?'

'I dunno. What do you want to do?'

'Take stock,' Cable replied.

Rayne only stared at him.

Cable held up the list of names they'd been working their way down.

'If you don't put that damn list down you're going to wear holes in it with your fingers.' Rayne had dressed in jeans and sneakers, a padded coat over a woollen sweater: the weather had turned decidedly colder these past few days. She pulled a woolly hat down to her ears. To Cable she resembled a waif-like boy. Not an image he was attracted to. So much different from when they'd writhed naked on the bed together once they'd driven a safe distance away from the burning warehouse, and found an overnight camping place deep at the end of a farm track. Then, Rayne had been all woman.

'Where are you going?'

'Out. You're not the only one who can't shift the stench. It's those clothes we took off last night, stinking up the place. Smells like a campfire in here. You coming?'

'Where?'

'We'll gather up the clothes and burn them.'

'I think I've had enough of bonfires for a while,' Cable said.

'We have to get rid of the evidence, Cable. If the cops stop us and find those stinking clothes they'll easily put us at the scene.' She shoved an errant lock of hair under the edge of her woolly hat. 'And that list of yours, you should burn it too. You have all those names in your head, and know who still needs punishing. Burn the note before it incriminates us both.'

'Should I burn the gun too?' Cable said sarcastically. 'And the knife? That baseball bat you're so fond of? Hell, why don't we just set fire to the Winnebago with everything in it and have done?'

Rayne scolded him silently with a cold gaze.

Cable sniffed, rubbed his tender nose with the back of a tattooed wrist.

'Are you done?' Rayne demanded.

Cable shrugged. 'Sorry. Over-reaction.'

'And then some.' Rayne approached him, ruffled his spiky hair, and then dragged her fingernails round to the nape of his neck: Cable liked the feel of her nails on his skin. He was easily appeased, easily manipulated by Rayne, but wasn't so stupid not to recognize he was being played. Not that it made a difference. 'Now come on. Shake off this sullen mood, why don't you? We'll get rid of the clothes, and then walk into town, yeah? I don't know about you but I'm famished.'

'I'm hungry,' Cable admitted, 'but let's stay far away from anywhere with pulled pork on the menu.'

Rayne nodded at the piece of dog-eared paper Cable still clutched in his hand. 'Really, you should burn it too.'

Cable shook his head. 'Not until I've marked every last name off it.'

'You know that won't be possible, right?' Rayne tossed her head dismissively. 'Some of those bastards are out of our reach: you can't change the inevitable.'

Cable stood abruptly, gesturing down his burly form, demanding that she look.

'Nothing's impossible,' he reminded her. 'I'm living proof of that.'

SIXTEEN

He had more faith in Tess's ability to look after herself than in his own to keep out of trouble. The fact was, Po was actively looking. Tess was no barroom brawler, no kung fu-kicking hard ass, but she could still get stuck in when the chips were down. Actually, when he thought about it, Tess had proven that in most dangerous situations they'd fallen into, her employment of strategy, force of will, and a level of bravery becoming a wildcat protecting her cubs had seen them safely through. She had a gun, and a cop – her brother Alex – and Po on speed dial, so she should come to no harm. Nevertheless, he still wasn't comfortable about leaving her behind. The recent events had set a worm of unease wriggling in his stomach, because he now believed that there was more to the death of Chelsea Grace and the attack on Richard Conklin than he'd initially credited. After the burning of Kent Bachman, he was as certain as Tess was that there was a crazy man somewhere out there who'd go to any end to hurt her along with others associated with her college days. He trusted that whoever was responsible for the other attacks could have no way of tracing her to his home near Presumpscot Falls, and that she'd be fine until he returned, and yet he couldn't shake the twinge of guilt he felt at abandoning her like that. Hell, he hadn't actually abandoned her; it was at her urging that he'd left to take care of business. She knew as well as he did that he had only one way of facing danger and it was head on. When incarcerated in Angola he'd learned that when you got pushed you pushed back harder. Give way to an abuser and you were perceived as weak, and you continued to get pushed until you were little more than a crimson smudge on the prison floor. It got to a stage with Po when he pushed back not only on his behalf, but for others too. He'd made a lifelong friend of Pinky Leclerc by standing up for the young black kid about to be gang-raped by a bunch of twisted white supremacists who took umbrage against gays, and black gays more than any. He could have walked away, abandoned Pinky to his

fate – after all he wasn't any man's keeper – but it simply wasn't
in his nature. It was why he felt so bad about leaving Tess to fend
for herself while he went off on his own errant mission.

In a skewed manner, he'd concluded that the sooner he put to
bed any further trouble directed at either Chris or his diner, the
sooner he could devote all his time to supporting Tess. At the
moment, Tess was safe, buried under the workload she'd taken
on, fielding telephone calls between cops in Augusta, Bangor,
and Sagadahoc County, encouraging some cross-jurisdictional
cooperation, so he had a window of opportunity. He'd driven to
the address Tess supplied to him for Aaron Noble, owner of the
pickup used during the attack last night, but wasn't of a mind to
rush in before he knew for certain that Noble was responsible.
He parked his Mustang within sight of Noble's home, an unremarkable structure on a shabby street in Westbrook, a suburb to
the west of Portland. Discarded kids' toys and a sunken trampoline
on the patchy lawn to the side of the house hinted that Noble
was a family man. Not the greatest role model when it came to
fatherhood, not if he was the destructive homophobe his actions
had made out. The pickup was parked out on the road, two wheels
on the raised kerb. So it hadn't been gotten rid of after all: perhaps
Noble had been confident that it had been driven off while
onlookers were still reeling from the bricks hurled at the diner,
too stunned to take note of the licence plate. To be fair, the
suggestion would have held water if not for Po noting the details,
because none of the other witnesses had been able to offer
anything to the police but a sketchy and often contradictory
description of either the truck or the group of vandals in it. Even
as he'd run outside, Po had been noting specifics, and was certain
that if he saw any of the thugs again he'd know them simply
from their silhouettes, and their individual mannerisms. Such
evidence wouldn't stand up in a court of law, but Po didn't care:
he had street justice in mind. But not here and not now.

Aaron Noble might not be the ideal family man, but there
could be innocent kids at the house, and Po wasn't about to take
trouble to their door. It irked him to have to wait things out, but
Noble would have to leave the house at some point, and could
be fronted once out of sight and hearing of his children. Po was
good at waiting. He'd had twelve years' practice when locked

in the pen, and in less comfortable surroundings than the plush leather interior of his muscle car. He had his latest novel on the passenger seat, but wouldn't allow it to distract his attention this time. He sat, smoking out of the open window as he watched Noble's house for movement.

Three cigarettes later, and he flicked the latest smouldering stump onto the kerb. Noble hadn't shown, but another vehicle had pulled up outside the house. The driver announced his arrival with a double tap on the horn. Po spotted the dancing of shadows behind the living-room window, but couldn't tell if it was Noble or someone else. The newcomer got out of his car and settled his butt on the hood, crossing his arms on his chest while he waited. The guy was in his late twenties, clean-shaven, fair-haired, built like a manual labourer. Po pictured the man holding aloft a half-brick, moments before he'd hurled it through the diner's front door. His mind stripped away the hat and scarf the man had worn the evening before. Yes, he was one and the same. Po's mouth tweaked.

Noble came out of the house, appearing harried. A toddler pursued him, a roly-poly boy whose thick mop of dark curls resembled his father's. Noble grabbed the kid by his sweater and force-marched him back to the door. Biting words were hollered at the woman of the house, and she showed up a few seconds later to take charge of the squirming toddler. No kisses of goodbye were shared by those in the Noble household, only a few more choice words from Noble, echoed as loudly by his overweight wife, who slammed the door as much on his retort as to stop the child escaping once more. Noble strode down the path to the sidewalk, showing his open palms in a shrug of apology to his pal. The blond guy punched Noble on the shoulder, and more curses were exchanged, though this time in good-natured banter. Noble reciprocated with a punch to his pal's shoulder, and then went around the car and got in the passenger seat. Moments later, the car peeled out from the kerb with a squeal of rubber and a waft of blue smoke. The car was facing Po, and passed on his left. Neither occupant looked his way as the driver took off at a dangerous speed. Po waited a few seconds more, fired up the engine, and pulled a tight turn and followed.

Those in the car had no idea they'd picked up a tail. As Po

settled in behind them he could make out their shapes as they talked animatedly. The driver barely had his eyes on the road for more than a second at a time, and drove one-handed. His other arm was propped out the open window, periodically flicking ash from a cigarette. He manoeuvred his car with a disregard for other road users and pedestrians; they would get out of his way or get driven over. His attitude to road safety told Po a lot. He was a dick of the highest order.

The pursuit led Po back into Portland via Brighton Avenue, before the driver took Stevens Avenue through Bradleys Corner to Congress Street and onward. Before they reached the Fore River Parkway, Po had a good idea where they were heading: back to the scene of the men's recent crime. He was right. Most of Portland's busy nightlife was centred in the downtown area, between Fore Street and the river from which the street took its name, but Po's diner was situated at the edge of the old downtown port district, within stumbling distance of Mercy Hospital and Western Cemetery. As questionable as his moral decision was concerned, Po thought the hospital and burial ground couldn't be better placed, because he was prepared to send his enemies to either if it came to it. Aaron Noble and his pals had only smashed a few windows, so taking their lives was supreme overkill, but should things go further . . . then Po was prepared to take things to extremes too. He was no psychopath, he wasn't going to kill anyone except in the direst of circumstances, but he was a realist. If he was pushed, he pushed back harder; hopefully a warning would be enough to make Noble and his friends back off. If they took a telling, so be it, but if they chose another route then Po would meet them head on and with no regrets.

If Tess knew the way his mind was working, she'd have a hissy fit. She was under no illusion that he intended stopping any further attacks on his property and employees, but hopefully not to the extent he was ready to go. In fact, she knew full well what he was capable of. He'd killed before, and would do so again if necessary to protect his friends and family. For Tess he'd gladly go back to prison, though not for a few smashed windows.

In full view of Bar-Lesque, the car pulled to the sidewalk. Po's Mustang settled in a few spaces back, and he watched Noble climb out and stand alongside the open door, while his pal leaned across the seats for a good view of their handiwork. All the windows were boarded up, the diner deserted. The men shared a joke, with Noble looking particularly pleased with the way things had turned out. He even took out his cellphone and snapped a few pictures of the beaten-up building for posterity: or perhaps proof. The temptation to go over and slap the phone out of Noble's hand was strong, but Po knew he wouldn't end things at that, and out in the open in broad daylight wasn't the best place to teach the thug a lesson.

Grinning in satisfaction, Noble got back in the car and the driver took off again at speed. Po's Mustang fell in behind them.

The next stop was a gas station on Commercial Street opposite the Peaks Island ferry terminal, where the blond pumped gas and Noble went inside the convenience store, returning moments later with cans of cola and a bag of Cheesy Cheetos. The breakfast of champions, Po thought sarcastically, brain food for dipshits. Then again he had no right to criticize, his nutritional intake that morning had been three mugs of coffee and ten Marlboro. With that in mind he lit up his eleventh smoke and then followed as his quarry struck across town on Franklin Street but cut a right before hitting the interstate alongside Back Cove. Near Franklin Park the car came to a screeching halt and the two men got out, Noble still lugging the huge packet of cheesy snacks, and ramming the contents in his mouth without once stopping talking. There were plenty of businesses situated in the neighbourhood, plus coffee shops and restaurants that serviced the community. Po was familiar with the area and even attended one of the nearby gyms when he felt the need to burn a few extra calories. He rarely visited any of the healthy eateries, so didn't know how long the establishment the two thugs entered had been trading, but was confident it wasn't long. The sign above the door read HappyDayz, and when he noted the decor and ambience of the diner it was apparent why the idiots had attacked Po's place – it had little or nothing to do with Chris's sexuality and everything to do with competition.

He swore at the idiocy of those behind the venture.

This place was a burger and milkshake joint. They didn't serve the dinner crowd but tourists and supposed fitness freaks bingeing out between treadmill and CrossFit sessions, and they were at opposite ends of town, so shutting down Po's place would not attract custom. Po couldn't help thinking that whoever Noble and his crew worked for was suffering the effects of the green-eyed monster rather than using good business sense.

He got out his Mustang, stood watching while he finished his cigarette. He had a view inside the burger joint. It wasn't open yet but he could make out the two men he'd followed plus two others. He wondered if they formed the quartet of punks who'd smashed up his diner, or if the two newcomers had ordered the attack. Po watched as Noble fished out his cellphone and the screen glowed brightly as he angled it towards his pals. He was displaying the evidence of his handiwork. Emerging from behind clouds, the weak sunlight struck the window, making it a blind canvas. As it brightened, all Po could see was a reflection of his own spare frame staring back at him.

He flicked his cigarette stump into the kerb, strode forward.

He pushed through the door, and stepped onto a checkerboard floor of black and white tiles. The door swung to behind him, alerting the quartet. Noble and his pal looked at him without recognition and he was a stranger to the two other guys. Po returned their surprised perusal calmly.

One of the men, a heavyweight with long arms thick with dark hair but a sparseness of it on his head, jerked his chin towards the door. 'Sorry, buddy, we aren't open for business yet.'

Po sniffed, as if taking stock of the man's words.

He walked further inside.

Now he had all four men's attention. They shared glances.

The big guy with the balding head again repeated his warning. 'We aren't open yet. You'll have to come back later.'

Po slid into a horseshoe booth and rested his elbows on the table. He looked back at the balding guy, determining that he was the owner.

The fat man approached, his huge belly leading the way.

'Buddy, we aren't open for business.'

'You're not the only ones,' Po replied enigmatically.

The guy swept a hairy arm towards the service counter, taking in the trio standing before it. 'We are having a business meeting, buddy. We'd like some privacy, if you don't mind.'

Po folded his hands on the table. 'Carry on. Pretend I'm not here.'

The fat man glanced back at his friends, unsure how he should continue. Noble had slid away his cellphone. One hand was now massaging the back of his head as he stared back at Po. Was there an inkling of comprehension in his gaze? The blond shared a glance with him, and then came forward. He stood alongside the fat proprietor, looking down his nose at Po.

'Pal, you ain't listening. You have to leave.'

'I'm fine right here, thanks.' Po glanced away, checking out a small-scale replica of a jukebox at the end of the table. Instead of songs, dishes from the menu were listed on revolving cards. 'I like this,' he said, flicking a hand at the jukebox, 'it's an authentic touch.'

The fat man nodded in thanks, but caught himself.

Po abruptly grabbed the jukebox and swept it from the table. It crashed down, making the two crowding him stumble back in surprise.

'Son of a bitch!' the fat man croaked. 'What the hell d'you think you're doing?'

Po looked down at the jukebox, as if he too was surprised by his actions.

Noble bustled forward to form a united front with the fat man and the blond. The fourth man kept his distance, watching with what appeared to be faint amusement at the turn of events.

Noble was first to make a move. He leaned toward Po, one hand reaching for his jacket. 'OK, pal, you've had your fun. Time to go.'

Po backhanded Noble's hand aside. Not hard, but with meaning.

Getting penned in the booth was never his intention. He stood abruptly, and Noble stepped back, cocking a fist.

'Strike me,' Po warned, 'and you'll be sorry.'

For a second the thug looked ready to punch him, but the first inkling of fear crept into his features. When presented by Po's cold certainty, it had the desired effect.

'You'd better leave, or we'll call the cops.' It was the fat man who'd interjected. He stabbed a finger at the faux jukebox. 'Think yourself lucky you're not going to be made to pay for breaking that.'

'Call the cops,' Po offered. 'I think they'll be interested in hearing about how your boys here broke something too.'

It was only minutes ago that they'd all been admiring the results of a few well-flung bricks.

'Hey!' said the blond. 'He's that freakin' dude that chased after—' A sharp look from Noble silenced his admission.

Noble pushed in. 'I don't know what you're talking about, pal. Now you heard Bernie, get out or else.'

'You're going to throw me out?' Po faced the man directly, settling his feet. 'You're welcome to try, but I'm warning you: I'm heavier than half a brick.'

Noble sneered.

'So who the fuck are you? King Dick? You're forgetting something, pal, you're only one man and there's four of us.'

Po's hand flashed up, his knuckles jabbing into Noble's throat. Bright orange flecks erupted from his mouth as Noble gasped and dropped to his knees, clutching at his windpipe.

'Only three of you now,' Po stated to the choking man. He'd barely struck Noble's Adam's apple, but it was enough to set off his gag reflex. He stepped aside in case the thug vacated his stomach full of cola and cheesy snacks.

The sudden unexpected downfall of Noble held the other three men in stunned immobility. But it wouldn't last. Po shoved the fat man backwards, and in the next instant had his finger aimed at the blond guy. The man reared back as if it were a loaded pistol. 'I'll be with you in a minute,' Po promised him. The guy retreated, his attention shared between his downed friend, his two bosses, and the door to Po's left.

Po eyed the fat man from his heaving belly to the top of his balding head. 'HappyDayz, huh? Isn't that copyright infringement right there? I guess not. But you're no Fonzarelli, you're more like Arnold, right?' Po ignored the fat guy, and looked past him to the fourth man. 'I guess you're the one I should be speaking with.'

The fourth man reeked of arrogance. He was around Po's age, not as tall, but solidly built. His smile was smug as he glanced down at Noble, who was still gagging for breath. He didn't approach Po, only swept a hand to indicate the diner. 'If you're asking if I'm the boss, then you've got me, pal.' His accent

showed a Boston upbringing. 'But that leaves me at a disadvan-
tage. Who the fuck are you?'

Po wasn't ready to exchange names.

'Someone you don't want to get to know,' Po told him.

The man snorted. 'You're a real tough guy.'

'When necessary.'

The man aimed another sneer at Noble. By now, Noble had
caught his breath, but was still in a crouch, peering up at his
boss with teary eyes as he manipulated his throat. 'You took a
liberty with poor Aaron just now,' said the man.

'He got less than he deserves.'

'Mind telling me what's got you so pissed?'

'You know. You just checked out the evidence on *poor Aaron*'s
phone.'

'What if he was showing me pics of his lovely family?'

'He wasn't.' Po had seen the wife and one of Noble's children
and neither was anything to brag about. 'He was showing you
photographs of last night's handiwork.'

'You're Chris Mitchell's man?'

The blond interjected. 'He was there last night. He—'

The Bostonian's hand came up silencing him.

'Let's not pretend,' Po said. 'You sent those assholes to
vandalize my bar. I'd like to know why.'

'*Your* bar? It's Mitchell's joint, isn't it?'

Po didn't correct him. It didn't really matter if his ownership
of the diner came out: he was doing nothing illegal just keeping
his business matters close to his chest. Instead he asked: 'What's
got you so pissed at Chris?'

'Not your concern,' said the man.

'I assure you it is. When you attack my friends, you attack
me. I'm not one for turning the other cheek.'

The man merely looked back at Po; his dark gaze steady and
unperturbed by the warning. Noble had made it to his feet, his
oily curls hanging low over his forehead as he glared at Po. He
was still trying to straighten out the kink in his windpipe. The
fat man had edged away, placing the blond between him and Po.
One person should not intimidate four men prepared to do criminal acts. But Po stood firm before them, allowing his silence to
convey his message. If they rushed him he'd be hard put to stop

them throwing him out – without responding in the extreme – but none of them appeared ready to make the first move.

'Whatever your cockeyed reason for smashing up my diner, it doesn't match what'll happen next if you try again. You get me?' Po eyed the Bostonian: he was the one calling the shots.

The man looked purposefully at the jukebox Po had swept to the floor. 'Likewise.'

'I didn't start this,' Po reminded him.

'But you'll be the one to finish it?' The man's laughter was cynical.

'Don't try me.'

'Likewise.'

Knowing nothing about the man other than what their short interaction had told him – he was an arrogant piece of work – Po wasn't about to immediately take things to the next level. Knowledge is power: a truism he bought into. But neither would he walk away with the asshole's counter-threat ringing in his ears. Turning the other cheek could be the morally correct course of action, but not if it was taken as a sign of weakness.

'I told you I'd get to you in a minute. Time's up.'

Po smashed a fist into the blond's face.

He fell, unconscious before his skull cracked off the checkerboard flooring.

Noble had more guts than Po would have credited after the cowardly missile attack he'd launched last night. He came at Po, shouting in anger at the mistreatment of his pal, his fists swinging. Po caught one fist on an uplifted elbow, the other he allowed to skim past his shoulder. His forehead met the bridge of Noble's nose. Noble flopped down beside his blond friend, equally unconscious.

Po looked down at the two dispassionately. Then he raised his gaze to meet the Bostonian's.

'Try me again, you should send better men than those two punks.'

Done for now, Po turned and pulled open the door.

Behind him he heard the man laugh once, a short, bitter sound, and knew that things would not end there.

SEVENTEEN

Her Prius rumbled to a halt on Cumberland Avenue, and Tess made a note to have Po check the tyre pressures, the annoying squeak from one of its brakes, and a constant rumble emanating from the front, manifesting as annoying vibration in the steering wheel as soon as they could get it over to Charley's Autoshop: the car had sat largely unused for weeks and she should've ensured its mechanical integrity before using it again. With that in mind she wondered where Po had gotten.

She was aware that he'd gone to check out Aaron Noble as a possible suspect in the vandalism of his diner, but he hadn't reported back to her yet. No news was hopefully good news. Po was calm to the point of sanguinity most of the time, but she knew his outward manifestation was barely more than a shell – a grenade shell. When his fuse was lit he was apt to explode. If she'd accompanied him she would have influenced the way he dealt with Noble, but Po was off his leash. She could only hope that he'd managed to restrain his violent urges through reason and logic. But she didn't have much faith in that outcome.

Having spent the morning cooped up at Po's place, she was ready to get moving again. Her Prius was parked outside, but she decided it would stay off the road until it had been through the shop. Before going inside, she composed a text, asking Po to meet her at the office. Her apartment was only a few blocks down Cumberland Avenue, but she preferred to keep a closer eye on Po since he'd set himself his righteous mission.

Distracted as she typed, she barely gave a passing vehicle more than a brief lift of her head. She only noticed it at all because it sounded less roadworthy than her Prius, the exhaust growling and sputtering, the large, ramshackle body creaking on its springs. In the passenger seat was a woman with sharp features, in direct contrast to the doughy face of the hulking driver next to her. Motorhomes weren't uncommon around Maine, and neither were tourists: Tess gave it no more thought.

Her cellphone chimed.

ON MY WAY.

She pushed her cell into a pocket, fed a parking meter, and jogged up the steps of the civic building currently housing Clancy's specialist inquiry firm. When first they'd met, Clancy had been an Assistant Inquiry Agent to the District Attorney's Office, and had presented herself as a cool-headed professional, brisk, brusque, and ballsy, but since then had become Alex Grey's lover and Tess's friend. Tess was still Clancy's employee, but the dynamic had changed somewhat from back when Tess felt mildly intimidated by her surety. She'd seen Clancy at her most vulnerable, and at her most ferocious, and both women admittedly owed the other their lives. These days they met as equals and without formality.

They embraced briefly, before Clancy shooed her towards her private office. Not resting on her laurels, or her superior position in the firm, Clancy fetched coffees for them. Tess had sat in front of Clancy's desk, but her boss took a less formal approach. She settled her butt on the desk and crossed her ankles while sipping her hot coffee. She waited for Tess to begin.

'I won't allow any of this to get in the way of my other work,' Tess said.

Shrugging carefully, the coffee mug cupped to her lips, Clancy said: 'It's not as if there's much going on here.' She sipped. 'Most of our ongoing inquiries don't need your expertise and can be handled by my office team. Take all the time you need, Tess. From what Alex says, it sounds as if you might've been right about that girl's death being suspicious.'

The attack on Richard Conklin and the burning of Kent Bachman could be horrible coincidence, but they had come too soon after Chelsea's death to ignore. 'Somebody is definitely after us,' Tess said. She meant the others in her old circle of friends, indeed anyone close to her now, including Clancy. Fair warning should be given and preparations made.

'How was your discussion with the cops up state?'

'Those in Bangor and Sagadahoc were rightfully sceptical, but Detective Jolie Carson in Augusta was more open to the idea we are probably all investigating the same suspects.'

'Anyone in the frame?'

'I've no reason to point a finger at anyone yet.'

'But?'

Tess exhaled. 'There was a guy in our group who caused some trouble one time. Manuel Cabello. I dropped his name to Detective Carson and she intended speaking to him.' Again Tess exhaled, but this time it was a short note of exasperation. 'Trouble is he's gone off-grid.'

'You tried to find him already?'

'You know me, Emma. I can't leave well and good alone.'

'I can tell that you weren't successful.'

'No. Manny – that's what we called him back then – has been incommunicado for the past eighteen months.'

'While he has been planning and executing a decade-old vendetta against your friends?'

'Or he's a victim too,' Tess said, 'and we just don't know it yet.'

'Not a good thought.' Clancy pushed her hair back from her forehead, leaning forward. 'It was important that you bring the connection between the victims to the police; I wouldn't like to see you get in trouble for withholding information. But you know, Tess, maybe you should take a step back from all this and stay off the killer's radar. You've set the ball rolling, now you should let the police do their jobs.'

Tess didn't reply. Her silence told Clancy her counsel had fallen on deaf ears.

'I had to say it, right?' Clancy raised her cup in salute.

'It's not that I don't trust the cops to find the killers, it's just that I have an inside track on what might be behind the madness, and could speed up the process.'

Clancy chuckled, a forced sound. 'You've decided this is your case because Chelsea Grace reached out to you.'

'It would have been far more helpful if she'd told me who the hell she was afraid of.'

'There's maybe more in her message than you took at first glance.'

'It has troubled me that it felt unfinished.' Tess pulled out her cellphone and brought up a document where she'd cut and pasted Chelsea's original Facebook update. *If I'm dead, contact Sergeant Teresa Grey at Cumberland County Sheriff's Office. Tell her*

She studied it again. 'Not only does her final two words sound like a request, they also feel like Chelsea had more to add. The investigators at Sagadahoc Sheriff's Office took the words literally. Chelsea's dead so tell me, but what if she intended adding more like "tell her to watch her ass" or "tell her she's next"?' Tess snorted. 'What would really be helpful was as if she meant to say "tell her Manny Cabello is hunting and torturing our old pals".'

Clancy reached for the cellphone and Tess handed it over. Clancy eyed the screen. 'And this is exactly as the message appeared on her status update?'

'Exactly.'

'Minus the period at the end of the sentence?'

'Exactly,' Tess reiterated. 'But then some people aren't known for obeying the rules of grammar when updating their social network feeds.'

'Chelsea was a teacher, right? Wouldn't she be more careful; she has an image to keep up with her students. I hardly think that when she was typing her suicide note – if that's what it is – she was giving much thought to how her students would react to a missing full stop. But that isn't to say that her ingrained habits would change. Has her final note been compared to her other status updates?'

'The cops have looked in depth at her profile,' Tess said, 'checking for any clues to what led her to jump, but I'm unsure if they analysed the actual wording. They thought Chelsea took her own life, so why would they look for inconsistencies like that?'

'Yeah. It's a fair point.' Clancy slid the cellphone across the desk. 'But have you?'

As she retrieved her cellphone Tess couldn't hide her smile, though she tried to by tilting her mug to her mouth.

'Missing the period isn't habitual, is it?' Clancy prompted.

'No. Chelsea was very particular about constructing grammatically correct updates, almost to a point of anal retention. You're suggesting that Chelsea might not have even typed that final message? That her killer could be the one responsible.'

'You've thought of that too.'

'I have,' Tess admitted. 'But how likely would it be for her killer to have had access to her page?'

'Are you kidding me? Online accounts get hacked all the time, Tess.'

'Yeah. But why would the killer give me a head's-up?'

'Maybe to draw you out.'

Tess shook her head doubtfully. 'With all the media attention on me lately, I've had more column inches from the local press than Kim Kardashian. Anyone looking for me would have no problem finding out where I live and work.'

Clancy sat back. 'What kind of a gap are we talking about? I mean between Chelsea's last status update and the time she jumped from that cliff?'

'A day or two.' Tess told her how Chelsea had left her career behind, without any explanation, but that she'd continued to make infrequent updates to her social network accounts. Her final one had been twenty-six hours or so before the time of her death.

'So between posting it and falling to her death, could she have been held prisoner? This scheduled-post facility, does it actually make a note of when the status was typed?'

Tess didn't know. But she would check. Perhaps a request from the police would be able to determine the time from Facebook, even give them the location. Clancy was suggesting that Chelsea could have been grabbed and forced into typing the message, to be scheduled to appear after her death. Maybe the missing full stop was a deliberate mistake on Chelsea's part, or maybe her phone had been taken off her by her abductor before she'd finished typing. It was a long shot, but no clue should be ignored.

'There's no way that Facebook will play ball with me,' Tess said.

'You don't know any hackers?' Clancy smiled to show she was joking. Or was she? 'They've refused to allow the Feds access to their system before, claiming it's against their privacy policy, so I don't know how they'll respond to a request for information. Let me ask a few contacts and I'll see if I can help usher things along.'

Tess wasn't hopeful. But she wouldn't turn down the offer of help.

'I'm still waiting for some return calls from some of the other girls in our group,' she said, 'maybe one of them knows something about Manny and where he can be found. I'm not treating him as a suspect as such, but he still needs eliminating.' She paused. Her final word could be taken in bad taste. 'From my enquiries, that is. There's always the possibility he too could be a target, worse yet that he's already been a victim. He needs to be found one way or another.'

'You said this Cabello guy caused some trouble for your friends . . .'

'Yeah. Well not for them, more *between* them. It was just a jealousy thing, girls fighting over him.'

'It doesn't sound like much of a motive to be hunting and dispatching them all now. And why attack the men in your group? An injured veteran beaten in his own home, a Walmart supervisor abducted and burned to death: those aren't the actions of a guy at the centre of a catfight.'

'I know. Too flimsy to be taken seriously, right?' Tess finished her coffee in one long gulp. 'But I can't help feeling that it's connected. For the life of me, I can't recall another time when the friendships in the group were tested as much. And it was the only time that Chelsea was involved; in fact Chelsea was one of the key players.' She briefed Clancy on how Chelsea's unrequited love for Manny was derailed by him sleeping with Mina Stoll, and how she had made it her mission to destroy Mina's reputation afterwards.

'Then why aren't you looking at Mina? By the sound of things she has more reason for pushing Chelsea off a cliff than anyone else.'

'I am. But she's another who's gone off-grid. I've been unable to find her yet. It was why I came in: I was hoping to log into the national database to see if she has surfaced during any recent police investigations.'

'And here was I thinking you wanted my valued opinion.' Clancy mock-frowned.

'No. I came in for the free coffee,' Tess countered. The truth was that she had the ability to remotely access Clancy's systems but she couldn't bear to be cooped up alone at Po's place any longer. Coming to the office was an excuse to get moving, and hearing Clancy's take on things had helped clarify the misgivings that she'd formed about who might be responsible. Whether suspects or possible victims, Manuel Cabello and Mina Stoll needed to be found.

EIGHTEEN

Stripped down to a sleeveless shirt, Cable grunted and hissed with each repetition. He was standing on a stretch of beaten grass, overlooking the Presumpscot River, a rusty dumbbell in each hand. The river flowed over boulders, churned to yellowish froth. The noise was a constant rumble, a match for the blood surging through his head at each exertion. Sweat poured from his hairline, making streamers that poured down his bruised face to drip onto his engorged pectorals. His shirt was open, exposing abdominal muscles as big as clenched fists. The scars that fascinated Rayne were flushed with blood, pink against his swarthy flesh. As he alternated each dumbbell curl, his biceps bulged and the veins on his forearms stood proud.

Rayne observed him from a deck chair settled in the shade of their motorhome, the tip of her tongue sneaking in and out and darting across her lips. While she waited for Cable to finish his set, she fixed a syringe in preparation for him. He was big and buff, but had not yet achieved her ideal. Rayne was his pharmacist – illegal androgens and anabolic steroids. Cable consumed various forms of gym candy in pursuit of perfection, but Rayne was in charge of the juice administered by the needle. She had no background in medicine, but had researched the subject enough to safely inject him and encourage him to swallow a melange of performance-enhancing agents including testosterone, oxandrolone, methyltestosterone, and danazol. The drugs promoted lean muscle growth and the results had proved impressive. They did have side effects though that Rayne could do without. Oily skin and hair often left Cable looking dirty, and if he didn't regularly bathe he stank like raw liver. Also periodic swarms of postulating acne broke out on his face, neck, and back, and Rayne found the sores a disgusting marring of the near perfect canvas of his body. And unsightly hair growth where there shouldn't be hair: it was horrible, so Rayne was also in charge of shaving him, and had made it a daily ritual where she shaved him as smooth as a baby.

There were other side effects associated with steroid abuse, some of them life-threatening, but Rayne believed that Cable's regime was under control. His voice had deepened, and sometimes his mood shifted wildly from depression to irritability, to mania and uncontrollable aggression. She didn't mind his mood swings, because she was prone to them too, but not through using questionable drugs sourced through back-street gymnasiums and the Internet. She could usually cajole him into a mood suited to her present frame of mind, and if not, then she simply took him to bed. Cable couldn't always perform, but Rayne didn't care as long as she was pleasured, and that was where their toys came in. Sometimes she preferred the sex to be aggressive and noisy. Usually Cable fell into an exhausted slumber afterwards, but it did the trick to bring his mood down to a more manageable level. It was during those moments when he had been lulled by the dump of endorphins in his system that he was most susceptible to suggestion. Not only was she building him to reflect physical perfection as she saw it, but she had also gained mastery of his mind: Rayne played with him as if he were her glove puppet.

His workouts were necessary, but they did tend to get in the way of her plans. She wanted his latest session over and done with, and then Cable could take a bath in the river. After that she'd juice him up and they could get back to having some fun. Cable didn't view his quest to punish those on his list fun, just something that must be done. Rayne however was thoroughly enjoying the adventure and excitement; the associated danger of getting caught was almost as enticing as watching another pathetic fool dying. It was odd that to avenge the loss of his first that Cable was prepared to obey the lead of his latest – but greatest – love of his life. If only he knew her affections weren't as deeply reciprocated. Rayne didn't love Cable: she didn't have the capacity for love. Only enjoyment, but that was an entirely different feeling all together. Right now Cable satisfied her lust for sex and also for blood, so was almost the perfect partner. Almost.

The dumbbells thudded on the turf. Cable reared back, hands on hips as his chest expanded like a bellows. He allowed a pained – yet euphoric – groan to announce the end of the workout. Overhead the trees were shedding leaves the colour of amber. One of them had adhered to the sweat on Cable's pimply neck. Distractedly he peeled the leaf off, rolled it between rough palms and tossed it aside. He turned and looked at Rayne. She wiggled the syringe in invitation.

Cable ignored the needle.

'C'mon, Cable, you know you want some sugar.' Rayne's voice was singsong.

'I'm not going to get chance to work out for a couple of days. We should wait till my routine's back to normal.'

'Trust me, lunkhead, you'll get plenty exercise. Different than throwing round those lumps of iron, but probably better for you. You'll need the extra energy.'

Cable joined her beside the motorhome. They'd parked it under the wide boughs of trees, a shady spot, but the branches also diverted some of the breeze. Nevertheless it was cold in the dimness and gooseflesh broke out on Cable's hide. Rayne chose a spot and slid in the needle. She plunged it slowly, and all the while watched Cable's eyes for any flicker of discomfort. Cable held her gaze stonily. With a fresh dose of anabolic steroids flooding his system he reached for the door. Rayne halted him.

'Bathe first.'

'Too damn cold for bathing out here.'

Rayne pointed at the river. 'It's refreshing,' she said.

'No way,' said Cable.

Rayne folded her arms, the depleted syringe drooping by her side. 'I won't change my mind.'

'You had a warm shower,' Cable moaned. 'You want me to get in that freakin' river?'

'You're covered in sweat and stink like a rutting dog,' Rayne said. 'And you can't fit in the shower.'

Unlike the last campsite this one didn't come with a utility block. It didn't come with any amenities other than a bit of flat earth to park on. The bonus was that it was deserted but for their vehicle. They were breaking the rules, no overnight camping was allowed at this time of year: a rule enforceable by fines. They couldn't care less for rules and regulations and any fine would go unpaid. Rayne had a collection of parking tickets and fines stuffed in a loose bundle beneath the front seat in the motorhome. The fines had been served against their original identities, not the ones they lived by now.

'I'm not moving on this,' Rayne told him.

'Goddamnit,' Cable muttered. He looked back at the river. It continued to rumble over rocks, frothing and splashing. 'Somebody might see me!'

Rayne made an exaggerated sweep of their surroundings. 'Who? There's nobody for miles around. And besides, what have you got to be bashful about? You are magnificent, Cable. You've nothing to hide and everything to celebrate. If there is some creepy peeping Tom out there, give 'em the full show.' She smiled lasciviously. 'I'll tell you something: I'll be getting an eyeful, and you can take that to the bank.'

Cable took a glance down at the pumped muscles of his chest and arms. Nodded in agreement. But he still wasn't keen on plunging in the river. The water had to be near freezing.

'You want to get back to Portland, right?' Rayne went on. 'We do that only after you've cleaned up and dressed in something that doesn't smell like a two days old corpse.'

'I smell that bad?'

'Getting there, Cable, getting there.'

Rayne smiled as Cable turned and trudged towards the river, while pulling the damp shirt off. Her smile grew even wider a few moments later when Cable made an involuntary squeal as he plunged into the river. Was there anything that idiot wouldn't do to please her?

NINETEEN

The fat chef looked forlornly at the replica jukebox. He'd retrieved it and set it on the serving counter to check if it was salvageable, but the tall dude with the southern accent had done a job on it. The box had split at the seams, cheap Chinese manufacturing coming apart with little force. While he tried to push the broken edges back together with no success, the two other guys were attempting similar reconstruction of their faces and their egos. They bullshitted each other about how Chris Mitchell's bouncer had taken a liberty, hitting them both sneakily and how they'd have kicked his butt otherwise. Of the two, Aaron Noble had come off the worse, his nose bleeding, the first signs of black eyes developing, but he was also the most vocal. The fourth man, the Bostonian, walked away to find a quiet corner, ignoring their macho BS while he spoke into his cellphone.

'It's me, Jimmy Hawkes,' he announced when the phone was picked up at the other end.

'Jimmy,' a gruff voice answered. 'Been a while. You want to speak with Chapel?'

'Is he with you, Murph?'

'Right here.'

'You should both hear this. Got a job for you if you want it?'

'Hold on.' Dylan Murphy fiddled with his cellphone. 'Got you on speaker, Jimmy.'

'How's it goin'?' a second voice chimed in. It was Bryce Chapel.

'I've had better mornings,' Hawkes said. He glanced across the retro diner at where his local heavies still massaged their egos with predictions of what would happen next time they saw that Cajun asshole. Hawkes shook his head. 'I need two good men.'

'But all you got is us?' Chapel laughed at his own joke.

'You guys free?'

'To come up to an ass-end like Portland, nuh-uh,' said Murphy. 'You gotta pay the goin' rate, Jimmy.'

'That's a given,' Hawkes assured him. 'I meant have you a day or two free to come up?'

'How soon?' Chapel had moved closer to the phone, his voice much louder now. In the background was a constant hum, and Hawkes guessed they were mobile. He pictured Chapel in the driving seat, Murphy holding the phone so they could both hear.

'Soon as.'

'Can be up there today, you want? But it'll cost ya. Extra twenty per cent on top of our daily rate, plus expenses.'

'Today would be good,' said Hawkes. Even avoiding toll roads the drive from Boston to Portland could be achieved in less than two hours. He'd happily pay the tolls. 'Soon as,' he repeated, and that was all the agreement to their terms they required.

'What's the job?' Chapel asked.

'Bit of recon,' said Hawkes, 'bit of heavy lifting. Maybe some clean up if necessary.'

Neither Murphy nor Chapel required him to translate. They spoke in deliberate couched phrases they all understood for fear their conversations were being monitored. Murphy and Chapel were on the radar of various law-enforcement agencies. Hawkes suspected he too was being periodically listened in to. 'I'll brief you with the full job when you get here.'

'Email us the directions,' said Chapel.

'I'll do better than that,' Hawkes suggested. 'Call me when you get near and I'll come meet you.'

'See you this afternoon then,' Chapel replied.

That was all the conversation needed for now. Dealing with pros like Murphy and Chapel was so much easier and more satisfying than with local assholes like Noble and his blond buddy, Lassiter. He'd thrown a few dollars their way to make life difficult for Chris Mitchell. All they'd managed to do was smash a few windows, and bring down retribution on them from some hard-ass with a damn *Death Wish* complex. Instead of them getting back what Mitchell owed, they'd cost Hawkes money. They were about to cost him more, and Chapel and Murph didn't come cheap, though it would be money well spent.

Putting away his cellphone, Hawkes joined the others in the

diner. The chef shook his head in disbelief at what had happened. 'Trouble wasn't supposed to come back here,' Hawkes told him. 'I assure you it won't happen again.'

'Good,' said the chef. 'I pay you so this sort of shit doesn't happen.'

Hawkes took out his wallet. He threw twenty bucks at the chef's feet. 'Refund,' he said. 'That should be enough to buy two of those menu boards.' He ignored the fat man's look of shame as he stooped to gather up the twenty-dollar bill. 'You two, get your lame butts over here.'

Noble and Lassiter obeyed like cowed dogs. Noble still squeezed the bridge of his nose, but was unable to halt the bleeding. In his other hand he held a wad of bloody napkins. Both eyes were puffy and shiny with moisture.

Lassiter was first to offer apologies. 'We won't let anything like that happen again, Hawkes.'

'Sadly I don't have any faith in your abilities to stop that guy.'

'He was lucky,' Noble said, his voice full of mucus and blood clots. 'He won't be next time.'

'Don't kid yourself, Noble. That guy is out of your league. The two of you would be put to sleep as quick as the last time.'

'We have the others to help us.' Noble referred to the two thugs who'd joined them on their previous visits to Mitchell's bar.

'They're good for talking shit and throwing stones,' Hawkes snapped. 'They stay out of this for now. But you two . . . I'm prepared to give the benefit of the doubt. But if you want to stay employed by me you'd better get the fuck with the programme.'

'Nobody expected that guy to follow us here,' Lassiter put in. 'But we know about him now. Things won't get outta hand again, Hawkes. I promise you.'

'You can't make that promise. You know jack shit about him.' Hawkes snapped up a hand to halt any more objections or false promises. 'But you're going to do something and I want answers quick. Find out who that asshole is, where he lives, and where he likes to play.'

'You want us to fuck him over?' Noble asked. 'I've got a couple of pickaxe handles could get acquainted with his head.'

'I have this image where I see you come back with those axe

handles rammed up your butts. Don't do a damned thing except for what I just told you. You find out who he is and where he can be found. You get me?'

Both men nodded.

'Good. Then get the fuck out of here.' He scowled at Noble, then thumbed at the fat chef for clarity. 'There's enough for Mr Addison to clean up without you dripping any more blood on the fuckin' floor.'

TWENTY

After graduating from Husson University, Wilhelmina Stoll moved west, starting a new life in Hillsboro, a suburb of the other Portland, in Oregon. Why she happened to relocate to a namesake city was anyone's guess, perhaps it was simple coincidence. As did Tess, she didn't go into a line of work expected of her university majors, but into an advertising role, employing her skills in computing with a small web-design outfit – no longer in existence – and appeared to have been successful enough. She met and quickly married another tech geek, called Daryl Gearhart, and bore him two sons. Her one-night stand with Manny Cabello had already set aside some of the rumours that Mina was a lesbian, but her matrimony and childbirth had put a lid on them. Maybe it wasn't her sexuality, or the fact that she repressed it for appearances' sake, but Mina had remained a troubled young woman who suffered from bouts of depression, the last of which took her to a seriously dark place and led her to end her own life.

It wasn't through access to Emma Clancy's national databases that she'd discovered Mina's story. Another of their old friends had told Tess about her sad fate when responding to her calls for information. Tess hadn't found the reports of Mina's death because she had been following leads connected only to her maiden name. Hell, during her recent investigation she'd been shamed on a few occasions already, not least that she hadn't even known Thing One's full name: she'd assumed it was Mina, not that it was a composite nickname that would give her a more contemporary identity. Tess was certain she'd never met another person with the name Wilhelmina. As an adult she saw nothing wrong with the old-fashioned name, but could see how as teenaged Mina might want to disassociate from it: she'd been bullied enough for other reasons ranging from bad hair to her large nose, jam-jar spectacles, and husky build, let alone juvenile aspersions concerning her friendship with Gabriella, also known as Thing Two, without also being ragged about her given name.

In a phone call with Daryl Gearhart, Tess had first expressed how sorry she was to hear of his wife's passing, but it had been years ago, and though Daryl hadn't fully gotten over Mina's suicide, he'd learned to handle his emotions, and speak contritely about it. He explained that Mina's mental health had declined over the first five years of their marriage, and he'd had to watch while she gradually became a shadow of the happy-go-lucky woman he'd fallen in love with. When she'd spiralled to the lowest depths Mina had taken a bottle of wine into the bathroom with her, using it to wash down the contents of her medicine cabinet. When Daryl had returned home from a late meeting at work he'd found their boys safely tucked up in bed asleep, and Mina still in the bathroom. By then the bathwater had grown tepid, and Mina was cold to the touch. He tried to resuscitate her, but knew she'd been gone far too long. He didn't hate Mina for leaving their children motherless, or him a widower at a very early age, but did hate that she'd taken her own life. He had been concerned about her bouts of depression, but being a man, he couldn't offer the sympathetic ear she desperately needed, and to be fair had expected her to bounce back again the way she had previously. He partly blamed his ignorance for Mina's death. As a result, he'd dedicated himself to retraining and in learning all he could about counselling individuals through their lowest times. Since then he'd worked tirelessly with a local charitable society, which offered a support network for adults suffering depression and other mental health issues. He'd even set up his own funding project, called 'The Mina Gearhart Trust' to help raise donations to the charity: before Tess had ended the call, she'd promised to pledge fifty dollars via his TMGT 'Just Giving' page. She'd kept her word, and in a fit of guilt that she might also have had something to do with Mina's descent into darkness, she upped her pledge to one hundred dollars.

As she clicked away from the page, Po walked into Clancy's office after a rap of his knuckles on the door. He cast her a wry smile before sauntering in and settling his butt on the desk alongside her. He folded his forearms, a pose she'd come to recognize when he was about to make a point.

'The gay thing was all a misdirection,' he said.

'The attack on the diner?'

'What else?'

'Seems like we were both following similar leads, both of us were wrong.'

She briefly explained about Mina Gearhart née Stoll's untimely death before adding: 'I was hoping that I'd learn that Mina and Manny Cabello had hooked up after university and they were the two on this lunatic punishment mission. A part of me is relieved that Mina had nothing to do with it, another part saddened that I'm back to square one.'

'What about Manny?'

'Off the grid.'

'You can't find him?'

'Not a trace. I was able to plot his movements until eighteen months ago, but then he just dropped off the face of the earth.'

'These days, going totally off-grid isn't as easy as it once was. I've read a few thriller novels about a big guy who walks around America with nothing but a toothbrush. That was OK fifteen years ago when they were first written, but I noticed that in the later books the author has addressed things by giving his guy a driver's licence or passport or something. You can hitchhike, catch a bus, maybe a train, but if you want to move about the country any other way you need identification. You want to put down roots, you need identification. It's too difficult to be a ghost otherwise.'

'Manny could be using a fake ID, they're still available.'

'Could be. But why? Got to be involved in some heavy shit to go to all the trouble of hiding, and paying someone for an ID that'll fool modern technology.'

'I'm guessing that if he's on a murder spree he'd want to ensure his identification remains a mystery until he's finished.'

'Or he got a hint that someone was after him and didn't want to be found.'

Tess hummed in agreement, but wasn't fully convinced.

'So you've fingered this Manny Cabello dude as your guy?' Po said.

'I can't strike him off the list until I know otherwise.'

'How long's your list?'

The sharp tug of her lips told Po all he needed to know.

She stood up, knuckling her lower spine. 'You said the attack on the diner had nothing to do with Chris's sexuality?'

'The homophobia was just another weapon of the a-holes sent to damage my business. If Chris had been black, they'd have probably called him names based on the colour of his skin. If he'd been overweight or wore glasses they'd have picked on those traits. You know how ignorant bullies work.'

A twinge of guilt knotted her stomach: Po's words almost echoed how Mina had been bullied. 'Looking at Chris you'd never guess he was gay.'

Po glanced at her as if she were nuts. 'Your gay-dar not working, Tess?'

'OK, so what I meant was he isn't your clichéd camp man. Looks more like a rock and roll star than anything. So what exactly was Noble and his friends up to?'

'They're only hired punks. You know a burger joint called HappyDayz? It's over near Franklin Park?' He waited, but Tess was clueless. 'It's themed like my place; y'know, all of that retro nineteen-fifties ambience? The guy bankrolling the joint put them up to the vandalism: at first I thought it was because he doesn't want the competition.'

'Resorting to smashing up your place is a bit extreme.'

'Yeah. I don't buy it. The a-hole wasn't clear, but I got the impression his grievance is with Chris, not with my bar. I'm not sure that Chris has been totally honest with me.'

'I've still some stuff to do here, if you want to go speak with him.'

'I'll call him,' Po offered.

'Better to speak with him face to face.'

'You're right. But are you sure you don't need me?'

'Was going to ask for a lift home to your ranch.' She thumbed in the general direction of where she'd left her Prius. 'My car's playing up a bit, maybe you can get Charley to take it down to the autoshop later? I can walk back to my own place from here, so why don't you meet me there after you've seen Chris?'

'I'll get Charley to bring over the tow truck.'

Tess eyed a single stain on Po's shirt.

'Is that blood?'

He glanced down dispassionately at the droplet that had dried almost black.

'Not mine.'

'Po?' She shook her head like the long-suffering parent of a disobedient child.

'I had to introduce Noble to my forehead,' he said.

Tess's eyelids pinched. 'Violence only begets violence.'

'Yeah, Noble got the message.'

She almost did a double take. He offered the slimmest of smiles, and turned quickly on his heel.

'Hold it,' she said, and grasped at his elbow. 'This trouble with Noble; is it finished with?'

'The ball's back in their court,' he admitted.

'Who is the person behind it? You didn't exactly make it clear.'

'Some punk outta Boston.'

'You didn't get a name?'

He shrugged.

'Want me to look into it?' she said.

'Haven't you enough to do trying to find Cabello?'

'You said this guy bankrolls HappyDayz?'

'Well, that's an assumption,' he said. 'But he has some interest in it. Maybe like me, he doesn't have his name above the door. You don't have to worry your pretty head about him; you've enough on your own plate.'

'So you're confident that there'll be no more trouble from him and his pals?' Her tone said she was doubtful.

'There are no flies on you, Tess.' He pulled her to his chest and placed a kiss on her forehead. 'But you don't have to worry. They push me and I'll push back. But if they step down I'm happy to let things be. It's a few broken windows: I'll take the hit on my insurance, pay the excess, and won't be first to escalate things further. I'm more interested in learning why Chris has bent this guy all outta shape. Be good to know what we're fighting for if that dude tries anything stupid again.'

'Then you'd best get on with it. Maybe Chris can tell you who he is, save me the trouble of doing more digging around. See you back at my place in . . .' she checked the time on the computer screen '. . . say two hours?'

'You got it.'

'Don't forget to ring Charley about my car.'

'On it.' He pulled out his cellphone. 'Now you go find Manny Cabello, so we can strike him off your list.'

'On it,' she echoed with a smile. As he turned and left the room the sentiment slipped from her lips. The truth was she'd no idea where to look for Manny next. She had a horrible feeling that she'd been as wrong about his involvement in the recent events as she'd been mistaken about Mina. Sometimes when people dropped off the face of the earth it was because there was no way of coming back. She hoped the dead end her investigation had hit wasn't a metaphor for something far more horrible.

TWENTY-ONE

When Cable drove their motorhome past the civic building on Cumberland Avenue earlier, they'd no idea how close one of their potential victims was to grabbing and pulling into the van. Rayne had even glanced once at Teresa Grey as she fed a parking meter only a few yards away, but with no previous contact with the woman hadn't a clue who she was looking at. Cable's attention had been fixed on the road, watching for a landmark that would pinpoint the address they'd traced Grey to. Even if Cable had glanced over at the opportune time it was unlikely he'd have made the connection: the youthful Tess Grey looked nothing like the woman she'd become. Gone was the fashionable black and blue bob, and heavy make-up, replaced by her original corn-coloured hair, pulled back in a utilitarian ponytail and only a liberal addition of lipstick and a hint of eyeshadow. In jeans, a crisp white blouse, and a navy blazer, this Teresa Grey was unrecognizable as the girl from school who guys – and even girls – buzzed around as if she were the Queen Shit.

As they moved further down the road away from the proliferation of commercial properties, Cable's gaze began sweeping the timber-framed dwellings and finally settled on a two-storey home set back from the sidewalk on a slight incline. It wasn't remarkable, and was similar to others on Cumberland Avenue, but it was distinguished in that the ground floor was being used as a shop.

'We're here,' Cable announced.

'Don't stop,' Rayne commanded. 'The RV's too distinctive to sit out here on the street.'

Cable only frowned across at her. He wasn't stupid. He continued along until they found the intersection with Deering Avenue and made a cumbersome turn and faced back the way they'd come from. He found a parking space at roadside adequate to accommodate the large RV, within sight of Tess's place, but distant enough that the scruffy motorhome wouldn't draw any attention if she happened to peer out of a window. The section of street on which Tess lived had speed and parking restrictions, but Cable had found the innocuous spot edging a strip of road reserved for disabled drivers, near the intersection with State Street. Other parked vehicles were decorated with fallen leaves, so it was easy to assume they'd been parked for hours or even days – they shouldn't be troubled by any nosy meter maids or cops enforcing on-street parking rules.

'I didn't see a car on the bitch's drive,' Rayne commented.

'We don't know if she has a car,' Cable reminded her.

'A hot-shit private detective? Of course she has a car. How else would she get around?'

'We'll have to wait and see.'

'She might be home,' Rayne said.

Cable nodded in agreement.

'She might not,' Rayne continued, being contrite on purpose. 'I'm tempted to take a walk up there and have a look-see.'

'You can if you want,' said Cable, 'but I'm waiting here. It's been a while, but if she lays eyes on me she might recognize me.'

Rayne's snort was full of disbelief.

'You look nothing like she remembers,' she said, 'if she even remembers you at all. From what you've told me, the bitch thought you were beneath her.'

Cable had to agree. He could count on one hand the times Teresa Grey had paid him any interest, and even then it was when he'd been the butt of a joke or target of a snarky comment. Usually she'd ignored him, an unimportant wallflower that barely shadowed her peripheral vision. He could probably walk right up to her house, say hi. He'd offer his hand, then snatch it away again – as she once had – and leave her confused as to why a random stranger had come to her door.

'C'mon,' Rayne cajoled, 'let's take a walk down. Stretch our legs. Get some fresh air . . . it stinks in here.'

'I don't think it's a good idea, Rayne.'

Her face pinched, and she nipped her bottom lip beneath her teeth, before saying: 'That's why I do all the fucking thinking. Now come on.'

She didn't wait for a reply. She threw open the door and

stepped down on the sidewalk, confident that Cable would obey. He did, though reluctantly.

'C'mon, slow coach,' she said with faux joviality. 'We'll take a peek in that antique shop, see if there's anything worth boosting while we're at it.'

'Best we keep our hands to ourselves,' Cable cautioned her. 'We don't want to go spoiling our chances at Tess Grey if we get chased by the cops for shoplifting.'

Rayne halted and turned to face Cable. The top of her head barely scraped even with his chin. He was twice her width. Yet there was no mistaking who was the dominant figure. Rayne placed a sharpened fingernail under his left eyelid, digging the tip into the parchment-thin skin. Cable endured the discomfort as Rayne held his gaze. She didn't have to say another word, but occasionally she enjoyed the sound of her own voice. 'We need cash, lunkhead. You got any stashed away in some account you haven't admitted to? No? Well, if we are going to do this, then we need a means to fund our activities. Now I'm happy to mug a guy for his wallet' – which they'd done so on a number of occasions already – 'but that will probably draw more attention than if we quietly steal something we can pawn. It's up to you, Cable. Just point me at the right Joe and I'll go bust him over the head and you can go through his pockets. If we're lucky we might make more than the nickels and dimes we did last time.'

'We've still got most of the cash we took from Bachman,' Cable reminded her.

Rayne snapped her fingernail away from his cheek, so she could aim it back at the motorhome. 'That gas-guzzler will take every last cent just to get us out of town again. Unless you want to carry the bitch off on your shoulder, you'd best come up with another way to put fuel in the RV. What cash we have left we need for *your* juice.'

'OK, Rayne. You're right.'

'I'm never wrong.' Rayne's sour mouth turned up at one corner, the scar puckering. She wasn't even joking. 'And don't you ever forget it.'

'You wouldn't allow it.' Cable offered his own sour grin, and Rayne rewarded him with a thump of her balled fist to his abdomen. Cable didn't flinch.

'You've got that right,' Rayne said and walked away, her slim hips sashaying.

Cable followed behind. He wasn't on a physical leash, but it made no difference.

They could see inside the shop before entering. It was a tiny, cluttered space, filled with curios and antiques on the less-than-valuable spectrum. A prim, elderly lady with a pair of spectacles swinging on a lanyard around her neck pottered inside, rear-ranging gewgaws on shelves. Despite the evidence of her glasses, her eyes seemed bright and alert. She glanced through the window at them, and her burgeoning smile flickered, melted away, and was replaced by a nod verging on aloofness. Cable and Rayne didn't resemble her usual clientele.

'I can't see us getting one over on that old sow,' Cable whispered. 'We should go somewhere else.'

'You forgotten why we're here, Cable? Don't forget that replenishing our coffers is secondary. If we're going to keep watch for Queen Bitch we may as well do it from inside the shop. Bet it's warmer in there than freezing our butts out here on the sidewalk.'

'Doesn't look like we'll be made welcome,' said Cable as the old woman again glimpsed back at them through the window.

'You'd let her throw you out? Scrawny little thing like her?'

'Unless we want to draw attention, best thing would be to walk away right this instant.'

'Yeah, that possibly makes sense, Cable,' said Rayne, 'but fuck it.'

Rayne pushed inside the shop, a bell tinkling an announcement above the door. Cable, wrong-footed, stayed at the window. The old woman turned towards Rayne, and despite their first misgiving, her face expanded in a grin of welcome. Bashful for no logical reason, Cable kept his head down, averted to one side as he pushed inside the shop behind his girlfriend. He was too big for the cramped space, and was fearful of knocking some of the cheap clutter off the shelves or display cabinets. Rayne wasn't as shy, she practically danced between the cluttered aisles, *oohing* and *aahing* at ornaments and trinkets. The elderly lady tracked Rayne's movements, her grin fixed in place, but even to Cable the expression wasn't genuine. There was also a hint of suspicion in the shopkeeper's pale grey gaze. Cable hooked his thumbs in the waistband of his jeans, and remained still and silent. The old woman almost forgot he was there.

'Have you visited my shop before?' the woman asked.

'We're from out of town,' Rayne answered, while picking up a small porcelain dish and holding it up as if to study its finery under the lights.

'Vacation?' the woman prompted.

'More of a pilgrimage,' Rayne said. She switched to a rack holding silver-plated necklaces. 'Or more correctly a nostalgia trip.'

'You're originally from Portland?' The woman looked doubtful. There was more of the West Coast in Rayne's accent.

'Not me. But my friend is from Maine.' Rayne indicated the large, shuffling figure of Cable, and it was enough to draw the woman's attention. Rayne pocketed the necklace she'd been fiddling with, and immediately placed her hands on a second necklace. By the time the old woman glanced back, there was no hint that Rayne's sleight of hand had gained her a few bucks' worth of cheap silver. The woman would require an exceptional memory for detail to spot her stock had been diminished. Wrinkles crinkled at the corners of the old woman's eyes, and for a brief time she clutched her lanyard as if about to put on her spectacles for a closer look. But Rayne moved away, cooing at a small collection of dolls on a shelf.

The woman again turned her attention on Cable. She appeared mildly fascinated by his appearance, but there was also a hint of unease in the way her hands dropped from her lanyard to lace together just under her sternum.

'So this is a homecoming of sorts for you?' she asked.

Cable grunted acknowledgement. But then shook his head. 'Not really. I didn't live in Portland.'

'I didn't think so. I think I might have remembered seeing you around. You're, well, rather *distinctive*.'

Cable frowned at the barely concealed insult. He was about to answer, something equally as snarky, but over the old woman's shoulder he caught Rayne's gesture to keep her talking. She was pocketing other smaller trinkets while the proprietor's back was turned.

'Wiscasset,' Cable announced, naming the first small town he could think of. Recently he and Rayne had camped overnight near the Sheepscot River, and had gone into Wiscasset for supplies.

'I have a niece lives in Wiscasset,' the woman said breezily. 'You're how old? Thirties? Perhaps you know her?'

'Uh, I haven't been home in a while,' Cable said. He didn't know what to do with his hands, began thrumming his waistband with his thumbs. Beyond the old woman Rayne was still allowing her sticky fingers to work on the appropriation of trinkets. 'Perhaps I knew her though. What's her name?'

'Jennifer Holmes.' The woman lifted a hand, made a silly me gesture. 'But of course, that's her married name. Back when you might have known her she'd have been called Jennifer Ridgeway.'

'Ridgeway? Jennifer Ridgeway?' Cable pondered, then shook his head. 'Can't recall . . .'

'Jenny,' the woman offered.

'Can't remember a Jenny Ridgeway, no,' said Cable. 'Like I said, though, it's been years since I was home.'

'So what has brought you back now?'

Cable was a beat slow in replying.

From behind the old woman Rayne announced, 'Class reunion.'

Even Cable frowned at the contrite admission; he'd been thinking of something plausible that didn't hint at their true purpose for visiting the town.

Rayne sidled up alongside the antiques seller, smiling as if she was having the most wonderful time. 'You wouldn't know it to look at him, but my friend is more intelligent than he looks. He graduated from Husson University years ago, and we're back in town to hook up with some of his old classmates.'

The woman blinked in surprise. Cable didn't look like a studious type, quite the opposite, but that wasn't what had caused her to blink. Rayne knew exactly what had caused the woman's reaction, and seethed inside. If she ever felt any guilt about stealing from the old bitch, then she could go fuck herself now.

In the next instant the woman surprised her. 'Husson, eh? Do you know my friend Tess Grey? She's an alumna of Husson, and about your age, I'd guess.' She thumbed at the ceiling. 'She shares the building with me.'

'Tess Grey?' said Cable. 'Sure, I know her. Haven't seen her in for ever. Wow, what a coincidence! She only lives upstairs?'

Rayne visibly winced at Cable's clunky mishandling of the situation. She quickly drew the woman's attention with a tug at her sleeve. 'Is Tess home now? We'd love to surprise her.'

The woman shook her head. 'If her car isn't on the drive, she's probably working uptown.'

'That's such a shame,' said Rayne, aping the woman's head-shake. 'I'm sure my friend would have loved to have said hi. But unfortunately we're only passing through on our way back west.'

'I could call her; tell her you're here,' the woman offered. 'I'm sure she'd make time to come and see you. She's lovely that way.'

'She always was lovely,' said Cable, catching a flash of envy from Rayne that for once he ignored. 'But we have to get going. Right, Shelly?'

Shelly was a fake name plucked from the air as adroitly as he'd earlier chosen to name Wiscasset as his hometown. Rayne was fast enough to know it, and respond in kind. 'Sure thing. We'd best get going. We only called in for a minute. I can't bypass a junk shop without having a root through everything. Can't pass up a bargain.'

After a brief turn up of her nose at mention of 'junk shop' the old woman found her composure. 'Anything you've seen that you like?'

'Everything,' Rayne said, making an expansive gesture of her arms. 'But unfortunately I can't take everything.' She smiled slyly at Cable, who had the manners to avert his shameful look. 'Maybe next time, eh?'

'Next time then,' agreed the old woman.

Rayne followed Cable out the door. She maintained a calm amble, although Cable was practically jogging for the haven of their motorhome. As she passed the window, Rayne glanced in, saw the old woman watching with her spectacles now in place. The old bitch wore a pinched expression, and Rayne was unsure if it was at her barely hidden sarcasm about her establishment, or if she'd guessed what Rayne had been up to. Rayne could care less. The old fart wasn't going to chase after her to retrieve a haul of cheap tat worth little more than fifty bucks. More worrying was that she might mention to Tess about her visitors. If Tess had kept in touch with any of Cable's old friends, then she might have been alerted to the fact that some of them had lately been killed or injured. They'd tracked Tess to her address after perusing old news reports about her involvement in several criminal cases, and had learned that she now worked as a private detective. What if she was already on their case? Rayne wasn't fearful, but more excited by the prospect. If she was chasing them, then more reason for catching her first. She couldn't wait to tell Cable her decision. They'd planned to take their time with Tess Grey, conducting reconnaissance, plotting her movements, and planning a scheme for grabbing her unawares. But it was now more important than ever to take the initiative. They should grab her at first opportunity, despite the fact Cable always wanted to keep her for last. She needn't die immediately, not until the other loose end was tied up, but the sooner she was in their control the better.

Rayne jogged after Cable, eager now that his slip of the tongue had ushered forward the timescale. She'd heard a lot about Teresa Grey – in Cable's opinion a snarky bitch – and learned a lot from the research they'd done on her. In Rayne's opinion – the only one that mattered – Tess Grey might prove the most formidable opponent they'd come across, and she couldn't wait to find out. Bonus: she was also incredibly hot, and Rayne wasn't averse to casting her eye, or hands, over man, woman or in Cable's case, beast. She looked forward to meeting Tess, and showing that Tess's punishment could also be her own reward. Cable had earlier described Tess as *lovely*: he was being ironic when agreeing with the old bitch in the antiques shop, but Rayne sensed there was more to his words than they sounded. Cable had admitted to having a thing for Tess back when they were younger, despite being largely ignored or even shunned, and Rayne was positive he still clutched to a flicker of hope that he'd get his chance at her. Rayne should be twisting with envy, but any jealousy over old flames was easily converted into aggressive love making, the way she enjoyed it most. Her anger ensured pleasure. And Cable would do anything to appease her.

TWENTY-TWO

'I wish you had come to me with this sooner.'

Po stood under the awning of an emergency exit door adjacent to the front of Bar-Lesque. He was smoking a Marlboro. Alongside him, Chris Mitchell smoked too. His was a different brand of cigarette: one he wasn't enjoying. Po felt a mild sense of déjà vu, as this was the very spot where he'd first made Chris's acquaintance, and they'd done so over cigarettes on that occasion too. Their reason for choosing the same spot wasn't to avoid being overheard by the police this time, but out of necessity. Carpenters and glaziers were working to repair the damage caused the evening before, and there was nowhere on the sidewalk outside the diner where they wouldn't be in the way.

'I was trying to spare you the inconvenience,' Chris said.

'As honourable as your intentions were, they kinda backfired.' Po inclined his head at the feverish activity of the workers. 'They also kinda put me on the back foot.'

'I know and I'm sorry, Po. I should've been up front from the beginning.' Chris inspected his cigarette, scowling at the glowing tip, before feeding the cigarette between his lips and trying for a more satisfying hit of nicotine. He flicked ash. 'See, I didn't know what to say, though.'

'Coulda just said what was wrong and I'd've done what I could to help you out.'

'You might not believe me, but I was trying to keep your name out of things.' Chris made a placating gesture with one palm, not that it was required because Po was as calm as ever. 'See, there ain't too many people know you have anything to do with this place, and I was trying to keep things that way.'

'I appreciate your concern. But it doesn't really matter now.'

Chris shrugged. 'I guess not. But at the start I hoped to resolve things myself, without troubling you with my problem. I genuinely didn't expect trouble to follow me back here. I certainly didn't expect *this*.' His nod took in the activity outside the diner. 'Or that it would escalate beyond here.'

'When you first mentioned the trouble with those guys, you should've just told me the truth about what was behind it. I would've handled things different.'

'Here's the truth, Po. I swear to God, when first those punks came in the diner throwing their weight around, having a go at my sexuality, I genuinely thought they were just a bunch of drunken homophobic assholes. I'd no reason to associate them with Jimmy Hawkes. They never mentioned him, or the money I owed him, so why would I?'

Po didn't fully believe him, but the point of when Chris grew aware that Jimmy Hawkes was behind the attacks was now moot. By tracking down Hawkes's associates, and beating them in front of their boss he'd most likely exacerbated the problem. 'How much do you owe him?'

Chris's face elongated with shame. 'Five thousand. Plus interest.'

'You took money from a loan shark: why didn't you come to me?'

'You'd already been good to me,' Chris admitted. 'Giving me the job, a good income, but mostly your trust. I didn't want you to think I'd become a liability to you, man. I thought I could get my debts under control, and you'd need be none the wiser.'

'Five grand? It ain't much.'

'It is when you don't have it.'

'F'sure. But if you'd come to me I coulda written you a check and had done.' It was Po's turn to nod at the workmen. 'There's about five grand's worth of expense to get the diner open again.'

'Jeez, man, as if I don't feel bad enough already.'

'Forget about it. I'm only saying. I'd rather my money was spent helping out a friend than throwing it away. The offer still stands. I can pay off your debt; let you work it off if you won't accept charity.'

Chris hung his head, his pompadour flopping over his eyes. 'I can do that.'

'Me too. But let's see if the option's still open. Tell me about Hawkes. Who is he, what's his game, and what else can we expect from him?'

His cigarette arched into the road, and Chris lit up a second before answering. Po allowed him to compose his thoughts, and took the opportunity to spark up a second smoke.

'When I first went to Hawkes for a loan, I'd no idea about him. I was put onto him by a mutual acquaintance I knew from back when this place was a strip joint. Look, I'm not an idiot. I know what kind of guys offer no-questions-asked loans, but I expected to pay him back in due time, and that would've been the end of it. Thing is, a few more unexpected expenses piled up and I didn't pay him on time. Hawkes proved he wasn't the type to wait and immediately slapped an extra thousand bucks on my bill. I contacted him, told him no way was I paying that much, and he told me that the bill was now two thousand on top for trying to take a liberty.'

'He threaten you then?'

'Yeah, but I told him to go fuck himself.'

Po's eyebrows rode close to his hairline. 'Probably why he threw a few dollars at Noble to come around here with his pals and break the place up.'

'I should've kept my mouth shut.'

'Too late for recrimination,' Po said. 'Let's see about sorting this instead. You were talking about Hawkes?'

'He's only been in town about six months, come up from Boston. I didn't expect him to have the resources to follow through with his threats.'

'It doesn't take long for like to attract like. Crap tends to stick together. So when Noble and his pals first showed up at the diner, you didn't think they'd anything to do with Hawkes?'

Chris shook his head, but it was clear from his hangdog expression that the thought had certainly gelled since. Probably before he'd drafted in Po and the missile attack on the diner. 'Sorry, man. I've been a dick. What d'you think will happen next?'

'That remains to be seen. Depends on how Hawkes wants to play this out. I'll head on back to HappyDayz and see if I can do some damage control.'

'HappyDayz? You're talking about Bernie Addison's place?'

'That's where I followed Noble and his pal, where I found Hawkes.'

'Addison has nothing to do with Hawkes. Not unless he owes him money too.'

Po flicked ash. 'It sounds I might've acted out of order with poor Mr Addison. I should go over there any way, put things right with him too.'

'How's that going to help?'

'I'm man enough to own up to my mistakes. If Addison's a victim, I didn't help alleviate his misery. I owe him an apology.'

The barman's face was glum. He knew that Po's actions were on him. His reluctance to tell the truth had led Po to jump to wrong conclusions. 'I'm the one who owes apologies.'

'And you've already given me one.' Po tossed away the stump of his cigarette. He placed a hand on Chris's shoulder and squeezed. 'You don't allow stuff like this to build up again, right, buddy? This coulda been cut in the quick.'

'Truth is: I didn't want you to know I was struggling with debt.'

'Nothing to be ashamed of.'

'Yeah, but I didn't want you thinking I couldn't be trusted around the cash register. I'd never steal from you, Po. Seriously, man, I'm full of gratitude for what you did for me.' There was a glossy sheen to Chris's eyes, and Po had no intention of seeing the man cry.

'If there was any doubt, you'd have been gone from this place the second I bought it. So let's leave it at that. I've some work to be getting on with. Watch those lazy sumbitches, will you?' He meant the workmen. 'Make sure they do a good repair job so we can get the place up and running again.'

'I can do that,' Chris said, echoing his earlier words, but this time with a metaphorical hitching of his trousers.

'Thanks, buddy.' Po turned to leave. Halted. 'Say, how did you make contact with Hawkes when you first asked him for a loan?'

'Got a phone number from my pal.'

'Give it to me.'

Chris took out his phone and scrolled through. Po took a note of Hawkes's contact details, then, while Chris set about overseeing the building work, he headed for his Mustang. He drove it across town and parked on the road opposite HappyDayz. There was no sign of the vehicle he'd followed there earlier, or of Hawkes, Noble, or his blond-haired pal. The diner was open for afternoon trade, but few customers were evident. There were three servers, all of them female, but he couldn't see Addison. Then again the chef would be out of sight in the kitchen. He pushed inside, settled his feet on the checkerboard floor.

'Be right with you, sir,' one of the young servers announced. 'Take any table you like.'

His attention slid to the one he'd earlier chosen, now conspicuously absent of its jukebox menu. Po approached the server. She was a small, slim girl who barely looked strong enough to carry the heaped plates of food she was juggling. 'Is Mr Addison in?'

'Bernie?' she replied, and her attention flicked to the serving hatch behind the counter. Following her gesture, Po caught the flash of chef's whites.

'I see him.' Po offered her a friendly smile. 'Don't let me keep you, I can see you're busy.'

Having no reason for concern, the girl bustled away, chirping a greeting to the customers eagerly awaiting their food. As she set about doling out the heaped plates, she'd already forgotten about Po.

Po didn't rest on formality. He went around the counter, and pushed through a swing door to the kitchen. The aroma of hot fat and melted cheese shrouded him. Bernie Addison, wiping sweat from his brow as he turned, was struck still as he spotted Po. His bottom lip flopped low.

Po held up a palm. 'Don't worry, buddy, there won't be a repeat performance of my last visit.'

'Wh . . . what do you want? What are you doing back here?' Addison's hand lowered, and Po thought he was actually going to grope for a nearby meat cleaver.

'I came to apologize,' Po announced. 'Thought it best I do it back here and not in front of your customers. I caused you enough of an inconvenience this morning.'

Addison's hand fell from the nearby counter, plucking instead at the front of his white jacket. Around his expansive gut he'd tied a black apron. His hair was constrained beneath a net: a gesture towards hygiene considering there was more hair on his arms than his head. He looked terrified.

'Seriously, man,' Po went on. 'I'm not looking for trouble. Not with you.'

'Didn't stop you breaking my stuff.'

'I was under a misconception.'

Addison's brow puckered at the words.

'I was mistaken,' Po clarified. 'I thought you were in league with Hawkes. I know now that I was wrong.'

'Yeah, and then some!' Addison appeared to deflate as pent-up stress melted from his body. He shivered. Again his sleeve mopped his brow, but this time of cold sweat. 'When you came in this morning, throwing your weight around like that, I admit I thought I was next. The way you slapped down Noble and Lassiter, I thought you were going to break something else. I was worried about my face.'

Po's eyebrows rose and fell.

'You couldn't be further from the truth if you thought I was working with Hawkes,' Addison said. 'I heard you mention Chris Mitchell: I know his place. Is he being extorted by Hawkes too?'

'Extorted?' Po wanted clarification.

'Protection money,' Addison stated. 'He helped me to get this spot up and running financially. At first I was thankful of the help. But then things grew sour. Soon as I began turning a profit he wanted a cut. That was never in the terms of the original loan, but he was insistent.'

Po decided he must check again with Chris, though he doubted things had gone that far with Hawkes yet. Who knew? Maybe that was Hawkes's plan: put extra pressure on Chris in regards repayment of the loan, and then demand a cut of the takings from the diner. No way was he going to put up with that kind of demand.

'When I arrived here earlier,' said Po, 'you were in a huddle with Hawkes and those other punks. Looking at the damage they'd done to Chris's place on Noble's phone. Gave me the impression that you were one of the gang.'

'Hawkes was showing me what to expect if I didn't pay up on time.'

'Yeah, I get that now.' Po exhaled slowly. 'I feel bad about breaking up your stuff. How much do I owe you for a replacement, buddy?'

Addison waved down the offer. 'Already covered.' He grunted out a scornful laugh. 'Hawkes refunded the cost of the menu board. I knew he was pissed, but what else could he do when not two minutes earlier he'd promised my place would be protected for as long as I paid up?'

Po smiled at the ironic timing of his visit.

'Where can I find the asshole?' he asked.

'I don't have an address, just his number.' Addison went to a shelf in the kitchen, dug through some papers, and found what he was looking for. He read off a number, and Po nodded along with him. It was the cellphone number given to him by Chris. Addison was man enough to let their disagreement go, but Po still offered reparation in another way. 'I'm going to put a stop to this guy before it gets further out of hand. If all goes well he won't be troubling you again either.'

Addison shrugged, doubtful. But there was also a hint of hope in his expression.

'Are we good?' Po asked.

Addison offered his hand, and Po took it.

Then he went outside to call Hawkes and arrange a meeting.

TWENTY-THREE

Bryce Chapel and Dylan Murphy looked at each other. The corner of Murphy's wide mouth curled in a facsimile of a smile.

'Fucking serendipity!' Chapel announced.

Murphy grunted. He wasn't one for big words, but he got what his friend meant. They'd only arrived in Portland a half-hour earlier, meeting with Jimmy Hawkes to be briefed on the job, and the fuckin' target only phoned and asked for a meet up. This was going to be the easiest payday they'd ever earned.

'Don't underestimate him, guys,' Hawkes said.

They were standing in the parking lot of the Maine Mall just off the intersection of I-95 and the Maine Turnpike approach. Planes flew overhead, taking off from the international airport, engines roaring as they gained altitude. Hawkes had chosen the meeting place, having business with some of the establishments in and around the mall. But he was happy to put off his scheduled meetings in order to lead Murphy and Chapel across town to another parking lot off Marginal Way. For Hawkes and his guys it was practically a straight run in once they got on Interstate-295, making getting there easy. But Nicolas Villere hadn't been thinking of their convenience: he'd selected Back Cove Park for the relative privacy it would offer should the meeting go downhill. Hawkes had learned of Villere – apparently a Cajun nicknamed Po'boy or some such shit – and he wasn't a man to be trifled with. Although mentions had been kept to a minimum in the press, Villere had proven the hard-assed hero on a couple of occasions in the past. The whispers he'd heard related to the downfall of Albert Sower's criminal network, and the capture of not one but two serial rapists. Villere was hailed as quite the White Hat: odd considering his beginnings as a convicted murderer.

'He's one man,' Murph answered, nonplussed by Villere's legend.

'And he isn't expecting us.' Chapel put in his two cents' worth.

Hawkes nodded, Murphy and Chapel were in a different league

than Noble and his pals but he'd personally witnessed Villere's handiwork that morning: Villere was in a different league too. 'He might expect me to bring Noble and Lassiter along to the meeting. He has no fear of the likes of them, but he'll still be on high alert. I don't think he'll be a pushover.'

'I don't give a shit if he's a tough guy; got me a leveller right here.' Chapel touched the bulge under his armpit. Even through the material of his padded jacket it was apparent to Hawkes that he was packing heat.

'These are my levellers,' Murphy announced, bunching his fists. His hands were the size – and Hawkes suspected the consistency – of mallets. 'Let's see him try any of that kung-fu bullshit when I'm smashing in his face.'

'Let's not get hasty,' Hawkes said, 'there might not be any need for violence.'

'You didn't bring us up here to share pleasantries with the dude,' said Chapel.

Hawkes's grin was wolfish. Then all three laughed.

Hawkes led the way across town, Murphy and Chapel following in their own car. Before reaching Back Cove Park, Hawkes pulled off the interstate and onto some waste ground alongside a building housing a credit union. He pointed out the route to the park, and asked the men to approach once he was in place: best that Villere wasn't forewarned about their attendance at the powwow.

'Are you OK meeting with him alone?' Chapel asked. 'He could get the drop on you before we arrive.'

'He mentioned making a deal. I don't think Villere's going to try anything at first. I'll keep him talking until you guys are in place.'

'You transferred our fee to the account, right?' said Murphy, offering a leer. When Hawkes nodded, he added: 'Then it don't matter if we're a bit late. It's not that important if Villere does you in first, seeing as we've been paid already.'

'Thanks,' said Hawkes. 'I'll take that comment in the spirit it was intended.'

'Take it any way you want. I give a fuck?' The more he leered the uglier Murphy's face grew. He wasn't a handsome man to begin with; his face was pitted with poorly healed scars that gave his features the texture of chipped sandstone. His hair was shaved tight to his scalp, patchy with bald spots where his hair would never regrow. His forehead sloped to thick eyebrows, and sunken piglet eyes, a huge nose, and a mouth in which Hawkes was certain he could fit a banana horizontally.

Chapel nudged his pal with an elbow. Neither man liked Hawkes, but he was a paying client, and one Chapel hoped to get more work from in the future. Insulting him would ensure that he'd bypass their services in future for more respectful help. 'Don't fuck with Jimmy, huh?' he said. While Murphy was a muscular hulk, Chapel was diminutive by comparison. He looked almost boyish, an Ivy League nerd. But there was no denying the dominant force in their partnership.

'Hey,' said Murphy. 'I'm only yanking your chain, Hawkes. We'll be there, you've nothing to fear.'

'I'm not afraid,' Hawkes countered. 'If I was I wouldn't be going in alone.'

Murphy's lips jumped again then settled into a wide-mouthed pout.

He was unconvinced, and Hawkes knew it. Truth? He was nervous about meeting Villere alone. The Cajun hadn't chosen the park so they could enjoy a pleasant walk surrounded by nature. Yet he had to be dealt with. Hawkes had worked hard to establish himself since fleeing Boston to Portland. For him to be taken seriously, and to attain the notoriety necessary to succeed in his chosen line of business, he must get over the hump in the road that was Nicolas Villere. Villere had a reputation as a man not to be messed with, then who better to take out of the picture and cement his own legend?

Despite Murphy's BS, he was confident he could rely on the two heavies to back him up and get the job done. Hawkes slid back in his driving seat and headed for the rendezvous with Villere.

Back Cove Park sat on the southern shore of the expanse of water whose name it shared. It was a popular destination for young families, and of the health-conscious who used its trails for walking and jogging routes. Had the weather been clement there would have been more people around, but as Hawkes got out his car and surveyed the area he couldn't see a living soul. The wind blowing off the cove was chilly, and rain pattered, and more storms had been forecast. He was wearing a winter coat, and he pulled up the collar around his ears, shoved his hands in his pockets, and began to walk. The grass had dulled from vibrant green to something more akin to brass dotted with verdigris. The trees and shrubs had lost their foliage, and decomposing leaves littered the paths, sometimes in stinking heaps. He walked the length of the park, approaching the point where Villere said he'd be waiting. The guy had driven a black Mustang on to the park via a connector path from Franklin Street: he wasn't above flouting rules. He stood alongside his ride, smoking a cigarette as he observed Hawkes's approach. Though he didn't appear on edge, Hawkes wasn't fooled. Villere didn't make a show of checking for an ambush, but the man's sharp turquoise eyes took in the tiniest of details with the barest glance. He was tall and lean, with wide shoulders, long arms, and the big hands of a manual labourer, and even though he had donned a jacket against the chill, it did nothing to disguise the strength in him. Secretly, Hawkes wouldn't mind pitting Murphy against him and watching who'd prevail in a fistfight: his money would be on the Cajun. Good job then that Chapel was there too, because his gun would make all the difference.

Hawkes walked directly towards him, displaying a bold front. He stopped ten feet away.

'Jimmy Hawkes,' Villere announced.

'Nicolas Villere,' Hawkes countered. 'Or do you prefer Po'boy?'

'I'm nobody's boy,' Villere told him, and flicked away the stump of his cigarette.

Hawkes shrugged. He'd expected macho bullshit.

'Hands out your pockets,' Villere went on.

'You think I'm armed?'

'Just show me your hands.'

Hawkes took out his hands, blew into them. Rubbed against the chill. 'Happy?'

'I won't be happy till we get things sorted. It's up to you whether we can come to an agreeable resolution.'

'I agreed to meet. Surely that tells you something?'

Villere snorted. He took a step forward, made a brief scan of the trail along which Hawkes had approached. 'You came alone. Maybe you're not the cowardly piece of dirt I first assumed.'

'How to win friends and influence people,' Hawkes said and offered a grin. 'Y'know somethin', despite getting off on the wrong foot, I think I like you, Villere. You're the kind of guy I could do business with.'

'Not interested.'

'I know your background. You're no saint.'

'Never claimed to be. But I still have morals. I don't work with lowlife hoodlums.'

'Is that what I am?'

'Among other things. I'm trying my hardest to keep things amicable between us.'

'Tell that to my two friends you beat to a pulp this morning.'

'An exaggeration.'

'Noble's nose is busted up; Lassiter is still seeing double.'

'Trust me, they got off lightly. I don't take too kindly to people smashing up my property.'

'Aah, poor Bernie Addison isn't too happy either.'

Villere didn't answer. Hawkes was happy keeping the tit-for-tat going, but he could tell the Cajun was growing tired of the game. 'So,' Hawkes said, changing tack, 'you said you had a proposition for me.'

'I'll clear Chris Mitchell's debt. You back off.'

'What sort of example would either of us be setting?' Hawkes surreptitiously slid his hands in his pockets once more. Villere's turquoise gaze narrowed marginally, but he didn't comment. But Hawkes sensed a shifting in the man's stance, as if a subtle change of posture would take him from a relaxed, loose state, to one where he'd blast into overdrive. Hawkes continued: 'I'm a businessman, Villere. I can't be seen as weak or my other customers might think they can refuse to pay back what they owe me.'

'You'll get back what Chris owed. I'll even foot the interest. Nobody else need know about our arrangement.'

Shaking his head, Hawkes said, 'I'll know. You'll know. Chris Mitchell will know. Pretty soon half of Portland will know. Soon as word spreads I'll lose all the respect I've worked hard to earn.'

'People don't respect you, Hawkes, they fear you.'

'Respect, fear, it's the same thing in my line of work.' Hawkes allowed his grin to build once more. 'Now . . . if you were to make a worthy offer, one that was worth the risk to my reputation, I might listen. Say fifty grand? Yeah. Make it worth my while and I might be tempted to shake your hand.'

Villere snorted.

'That isn't an acceptable resolution in your opinion?'

'I've a better one. I don't give you a goddamn dime, and you still back off. See . . . the thing is, not everyone fears you, Hawkes.'

'Hmm.' Hawkes closed his eyes, savouring the moment. 'I wish I'd laid a bet on you saying that.'

'Call me predictable. If that's the case you should know the kind of person you're trying to take on.'

'Oh, I knew that from the second you walked into the diner this morning. But here's the thing, Villere. I don't frighten easily either.' In his pocket Hawkes folded his hand around the object he'd placed there earlier; the one that made up the matching pair was in the hands of Bryce Chapel. He pressed the button on the panic alarm. It sent an electronic signal that caused the one in Chapel's hand to vibrate. 'I wonder which of us will be forced to run away today?'

The faintest of smiles lit Villere's face. Hawkes had expected nothing less. He could sense the man winding up for an attack. Hawkes didn't back off – that would be counterproductive to everything he'd set up. Instead, his hands firmly in his pockets, he nodded beyond Villere's Mustang to where another car sped down the path from Franklin Street.

Villere was either braver than Hawkes thought, or he was stupid. He didn't flee the ambush. He merely stepped out from alongside his muscle car and faced the approaching vehicle. It slewed to a halt a few yards from where he stood, and both front doors swung open.

Murphy was first out. Rearing to his full six feet of bulky muscle and foreboding face. His fists were his fortune, and he'd added to their effectiveness with the addition of brass knuckles. But Villere ignored the thug: his gaze settled on the smaller man, who appeared less intimidating than a Bible salesman. He'd good cause, because out of the two of them, Chapel was by far the more lethal. Chapel came forward first, a handgun extended at arm's length, aimed directly at Villere's chest.

Hawkes laughed scornfully. 'Run, Villere, run.'

TWENTY-FOUR

P o wasn't an idiot. He knew he was courting trouble from Jimmy Hawkes, and that there was no way that the wannabe mobster would back down from a confrontation: if he did that his future as a moneylender and extortionist would be untenable. Moneylenders thrived on intimidation, and when the customer didn't pay up on time, violence was the preferred method of negotiation. Po was happy to oblige – Hawkes deserved a good whupping – but coming at this time, when Tess needed his support, dealing with Hawkes was an inconvenience he'd prefer behind him. He'd placed the telephone call to Hawkes with the intention of getting things over with, and thus freeing up his time to help Tess deal with her problem. He'd expected Hawkes to arrive gang-handed; probably towing along Noble, Lassiter, and perhaps the other two guys from the truck who'd stoned the diner. But Hawkes had proven that he could move as quickly as Po when it came to manipulating a situation to his advantage. Whoever the two new arrivals were, they meant business, and looked the part.

Po heard Hawkes's scornful prompt to run away. He didn't, he settled his heels in the faded grass as he faced the newcomers. The threat of a gun was enough to have most men running for the hills, or throwing themselves down on their knees and begging for mercy, but Po wasn't most men. Sometimes to his detriment. On other occasions his fearlessness was enough to throw off the validity of a threat, even at the end of a gun barrel. That was all the gun was for now: even Hawkes, who was trying to establish his position in the Maine underworld, wouldn't have Po shot to death in full view of a major highway, or where there were members of the public so close by. A bunch of guys had arrived for football practice at the far end of the park, and Po had spotted at least three joggers on the path down by the shore of Back Cove.

'Didn't you hear?' The gunman stabbed his weapon at Po. 'You were told to run.'

'You going to shoot me in the back if I do?' Po asked.

'How's about I shoot you in the face?'

'Should've brought a silencer,' Po said. 'Pull that trigger, and the cops will be down on you in seconds.' He flicked his hand at the nearby highway. 'You do know there's a police station just across the interstate, right?'

The guy frowned, the question aimed beyond Po at Jimmy Hawkes. Evidently Hawkes had nothing to say about the proximity of the cops, because he understood he'd made a strategic mistake. So did the gunman. He'd happily shoot, if not for the fact they were at the wrong end of a promontory, from which there'd be little chance of escape should the cops respond. Happy to shoot, but not too happy to serve the time his actions would ensure.

Po nodded at the gun, a Dan Wesson semi-automatic pistol. It was a cannon. Overkill. Plus, if the gunman really intended putting a few rounds through him, he'd have already done it. 'Let's dispense with the dramatics, shall we?' said Po. 'We both know this isn't the time or place for a gunfight.'

'Won't be much of a fight,' said the gunman. 'I'll shoot, you'll die. Period.'

'Except we've already established that you won't shoot. Therefore you might as well put away that hawgleg before it attracts the kind of attention none of us want.'

The gun didn't waver from Po's chest.

'I hate to admit it,' said Hawkes, coming to Po's rescue, 'but I think the son of a bitch has a point. Put the gun down, Chapel.'

Po lodged the name away for later. He eyed his would-be executioner.

Chapel seethed, but he knew where this was leading. His cold anger was for show. He slid the gun in a holster under his armpit.

Cue the brute with the brass knuckles.

'There's a way we can do this without raising the alarm,' the big man suggested. 'I'll smash you so hard you won't even get out a yelp.'

Po grinned wolfishly. 'You read that line in a comic book?'

'Nah,' said the guy, and his leer was ugly. 'It was tattooed on your momma's ass when I screwed her.'

'Well, you know what that makes you, right?'

The thug's fists creaked as he tightened them. He was on a

hair trigger, ready to begin swinging, but he was waiting for Hawkes to give the word.

Po turned side-on, so he could see all three men. He wanted to speak to the main man, but not at the expense of leaving his flanks uncovered. For now the gunman had been pushed out of the picture, but that wasn't to say he wouldn't strike Po if he got the opportunity. The big guy definitely would.

'You mentioned making a bet earlier,' Po directed at Hawkes. 'You a gambling man?'

'Depends on the odds.'

'You think your man can take me?'

'I'll rip your head off and shove it up your skinny ass!' the brute growled, but Hawkes gestured sharply for silence.

Hawkes paced to one side, then swivelled to face Po. He looked him up and down, as if assessing his form. 'Wearing those brass knuckles Murphy will destroy you in seconds.'

'Fuckin'-A,' Murphy agreed.

'So the odds are in your favour,' Po said. 'Here's the deal. If I win, Mitchell's debt is clear, you leave him alone, and you don't come near my diner again.'

'And when Murphy wins?'

Po eyed the hulking man deliberately. 'If Murphy wins I won't be in a position to stand in your way, will I?'

The finality of Po's words brought a gleam of amusement to Hawkes's eyes. Those were the kind of odds that were agreeable to him.

'When?' Hawkes asked.

'Now's as good a time as any.'

'With all these witnesses?'

Po nodded towards the nearby cove. Near the shore there was a swell in the land where the grounds crew had allowed the shrubs to grow wild. 'There's a depression in that mound over there. The bushes around it will hide us from any observers.'

Hawkes shook his head. You never allowed an enemy to choose the battleground. He looked to the right, where vehicles swept by on the highway. There was an underpass to allow pedestrians access to cross safely to the park. 'In there,' he said.

Po looked doubtful. The underpass was shielded on two sides by large graffiti-daubed concrete pillars. The ground underfoot was beaten dirt, in which was sown broken glass and rusted tin cans, as well as an old armchair someone had discarded a few seasons ago, and someone else had later singed with flames, and possibly taken a dump on. It wasn't a glorious amphitheatre in which to fight, the likes of the one he'd suggested. But he accepted the challenge.

First he aimed a finger at Murphy. 'This is between us, right? Nobody else steps in or all bets are off.'

Murphy snorted. 'You think it'll take more than me to bust your ass?'

Hawkes held up both open hands. 'You have a low opinion of me already, I wouldn't like you to think I'm untrustworthy.'

'Was thinking more about him.' Po eyed Chapel steadily.

Chapel curled a lip, but his hand didn't stray to his gun.

'OK,' said Po. 'Let's do this.'

He led the way to the underpass. Confident he would win, with or without the brass knuckles, Murphy almost strutted as he shrugged his shoulders, limbering up. Hawkes and Chapel flanked him, offering encouragement.

Po angled to the left, staying near the pillars on that side. Murphy picked up pace, striding opposite Po, heading for the middle of the tunnel. Hawkes nudged Chapel forward too, to block the far end off so Po had no escape route, while he settled himself to block their way in. It was doubtful any of the joggers would run this way, but he wanted to be there to dissuade any potential witnesses if it happened. A rank stench wafted from the old armchair, pulled along by the wind tunnel effect of the underpass.

It was the moment Po had been waiting for. Chapel hadn't yet gotten in place, he was still picking his way past, trying his best to avoid the shards of glass projecting from the dirt; Murphy was engaged in a warm up, shadow-boxing his own faint image on the far wall. Hawkes had turned back to ensure they wouldn't be disturbed. Po reached down and picked up the baseball bat he'd earlier secreted behind the nearest pillar.

He didn't wait; he attacked.

Murphy wasn't his initial target; he wasn't the one to be feared. He loped directly after Chapel, the bat raised two-handed overhead, and he smashed the business end down between the gunman's

shoulders. The solid thwack of walnut on flesh coincided with
Hawkes's yell of warning. But it was too late for Chapel. He
went down like a felled ox, arms and legs splayed, the impact
powerful enough to break bone and throw him into shocked
unconsciousness: if he ever fully recovered from the blow it
would be a miracle. His gun was trapped beneath him, so Po
ignored it.

He spun to confront the next target.

Murphy bellowed in rage: either too incensed by the downfall
of his pal, or plain stupid, he still thought himself the victor in
any battle.

He charged, and Po met him. The thwack of the bat on Murphy's
skull was sharper than when Chapel was struck. The sound rever-
berated in the confines of the underpass. Murphy didn't fall. With
blood streaking his features he came on, his fists pumping. One
of his brutal punches caught Po's midriff and doubled him over
for an instant. Murphy swept up his right hand, knuckles
augmented with brass, to smash down on the back of Po's neck.
But Po was only winding up the bat for another smash to Murphy's
body. It slammed his ribs, and this time the thug staggered away
from the blow. But not out of reach of Po's next swing. The bat
almost tore the jaw from Murphy's face. The big man collapsed
over the armchair, which – weakened and sodden – imploded
beneath his weight. He groaned, blood spattering from his torn
scalp and smashed teeth, and tried to rise. Po's boot buried itself
between Murphy's legs, keeping him down. The bat rose and fell
twice again, these times delivered to each of Murphy's arms. Po
cared less if the man's arms were broken, whatever, he wouldn't
be throwing any punches any time soon.

He spun to face Hawkes, lifting the business end of the bat to
the man's stunned face. He backed up so he was alongside Chapel,
then used a foot to roll the unconscious man over. He quickly
stooped, liberating the gun, and stuffing it in his belt. Hawkes
watched him, face slack with disbelief.

'What?' Po demanded. 'You expected me to play by your rules?'

'You sneaky son of a bitch,' Hawkes whispered. He blinked
first at Murphy, then at Chapel, neither of whom was in a position to continue the fight. Murphy groaned in agony, Chapel was
silent. He snapped his gaze back up to Po. 'You set us up!'

'Of course,' said Po. 'This bat wasn't just lying around.'

'But you chose to fight Murph over in the dunes . . .' Comprehension dawned on Hawkes's features.

'Knowing full well you'd refuse,' Po confirmed. 'I'm not an idiot, Hawkes. I suspected you wouldn't play fair, so wasn't surprised when these goons showed up full of piss and vinegar. In fact, I kind of expected it, so made a contingency. And this . . .' he used the bat as a pointer at the prone men '. . . should convince you I'm not a man to be fucked with.'

Hawkes's gaze zeroed in on the baseball bat. 'So what happens now?'

'I offered you a peaceful resolution; you didn't take it. I should whup you the way I just did your hitters.' Po swung the bat lazily, as if considering doing so. In the end, he allowed the corners of his mouth to turn down. 'We agreed terms. Remember? Well, I'd say I beat your man soundly. Mitchell's debt is clear, you leave him alone, and you don't come near my diner again. Agreed?'

'We going to shake hands on it?' Hawkes asked. His sarcastic grin was back, but he was finding it difficult to hold.

Po declined. He wasn't fooled; Hawkes was livid, but also fearful of refusing. If anyone heard how much of a fool Po had made of him he would never live it down. His options were few though: he could go for broke and hope he could drop Po before he was smashed down alongside his pals, or he could agree to the deal. Whether he stuck to the agreement or not remained to be seen, but it was the least painful choice to make.

'OK. It's a deal,' Hawkes said.

'Then go see to your pals,' said Po, 'I think they're more in need of a hand than I am. And tell them, they ever come at me again, well, I won't be so easy goin' on them next time.'

Hawkes eyed the two disdainfully. Murphy and Chapel had failed in their task. But they'd still want to be paid. Hell, they might even expect him to cover their medical expenses. Po smiled grimly. Hawkes was seriously out of pocket, and that was enough for him for now.

By the time Hawkes looked for Po again, he'd gone. The sound of the Mustang growling to life echoed through the underpass.

TWENTY-FIVE

The two hours they'd agreed on had come and gone, in fact they had almost doubled, and still Po hadn't returned to Tess's house. He was easy going, rarely seemed rushed, but he was never tardy. And he didn't usually ignore her calls: there were times when he'd turned off his cellphone, but it was to protect her, not ignore her. She had a horrible feeling that his no-show and lack of communication meant things had taken a turn for the worse. She'd called Chris Mitchell, who'd spoken to Po a few hours earlier. He had been left to supervise the repair work at the diner, and reported that all had gone well and he was currently cleaning up inside, getting things in order so they could re-open. He was avoiding the issue she'd called about. Tess was tempted to push him on the real nature of the problem, but she could tell from Chris's tone that he was embarrassed to have involved Po at all, and wasn't about to drag her into his troubles.

'I need to know he's OK, Chris,' she said.

'I'm sure everything's fine,' Chris replied. 'He was going over to HappyDayz to speak with the owner there, but I don't know his plans after that. He'll turn up soon . . .'

'Why go back there?'

Chris was reluctant to admit anything more, but knew he had to throw Tess a bone. 'Bernie Addison had nothing to do with the attack on Po's place. He's also a victim of the same people bothering me. Po wanted to make amends with him after what happened earlier.'

'Po mentioned there was another guy, the one bankrolling HappyDayz was behind the vandalism?'

'He was under the wrong impression. Jimmy Hawkes doesn't own HappyDayz, he was leaning on Addison, making him pay protection money.'

'Are you kidding me?' Tess felt her guts clench. 'Is that why Noble and his pals were hassling you? This Hawkes guy's demanding protection money from you too?'

Chris audibly gulped before answering. 'My involvement with Hawkes is more complicated,' he finally admitted.

'Oh! Don't tell me! Po took it on his back to sort that problem too?'

No denial was forthcoming, but Tess hadn't expected one. She knew Po too well: he would take on not only Chris's problems, but also those of Bernie Addison, a stranger before this morning. She thanked Chris and asked him to give her a call if Po turned up back at the diner. He promised he would, and hung up.

'Fool man!' she snapped.

She wasn't positive if she meant Po, or all the men her partner had gotten involved with. It was just like him to come to the rescue of people in need of help. It was his way. His lifelong friendship with Pinky Leclerc had begun after he took the young black boy under his wing in prison. Even his relationship with Tess had started with him pledging to protect her, and though it had blossomed into something more, he still thought it his duty to guard her from harm. There was nothing misogynistic about his attitude towards her, proven by his willingness to protect his friends, and even a man he'd earlier viewed as a possible enemy. Some people still thought of Po in terms of an ex-con, and were suspicious of him because of his past, but Po had shown he had a good heart. There was, however, that *other* side to him, and it was what occasionally sent a tremor of dread through her. She'd never admitted it before, certainly not to him, but she did fear for Po. One of these days his nature would take him somewhere very dark indeed, and she worried that it was a place from which he might not return.

What the hell was he doing taking on a mobster at the head of a protection racket? She had an indirect connection to the district attorney through Emma Clancy and to the police via her brother Alex: Hawkes could, and should, be investigated through proper lawful channels. And yet the issue was moot. Po could no sooner ignore his nature than she could. Various law-enforcement agencies were now involved in the deaths of Chelsea Grace and Kent Bachman, and the assault on Rick Conklin, and now that their cases had all been linked it was only a matter of time before the perpetrators in the crimes were found and brought to justice: but had she backed off from her own investigation? No she had not.

She had returned home, chasing up calls to the other girls from their group of friends when the search for Manny Cabello had gone flat. None of them had heard from Cabello in many years. As her direct conduit to the police investigation, Tess had dropped Detective Jolie Carson of Augusta PD a message, not so much that Manny should be treated as a suspect, but that he should be located at first order. Carson hadn't gotten back to her yet.

She called Po again.

Got the automated message stating he was unable to take her call, and was about to leave a message but thought it unlikely he'd listen. He must have turned his cell to silent mode while doing whatever the hell it was he was up to. She typed out a text instead. CALL ME. There was no tone or inflection to a text message, but he'd read her annoyance in those two short words.

She was surprised when Po immediately replied.

I'M BACK AT MY PLACE. WITH YOU SOON.

No explanation as to why he'd returned to Presumpscot Falls, but it was enough to release a flood of relief through her. At least he was safe. The last she wanted was for him to leave his house, because he was prone to go AWOL again.

STAY PUT, she typed, I'LL COME TO YOU.

Her Prius was outside. Charley hadn't arrived to collect it while she was at Clancy's office, probably because Po had forgotten to ask him. Rather than leave it on a meter that would require further feeding, Tess had chanced its mechanical integrity and driven it the few short blocks home. The grinding and screeching from the undercarriage had grown worse, the shudder transferring through the body of the car to the steering wheel worse than before. Her intention was to have Charley collect it off her driveway instead, but it had come to a point she suspected that she'd need to take a chance on the Prius once more. It could be towed from Po's place instead.

She grabbed her purse and tablet, plus the loose papers and photographs she'd compiled, and headed out.

As she stacked her stuff on the front passenger seat, she heard the tinkle of the bell over Mrs Ridgeway's door, and glanced towards the antiques shop.

'Hi, Anne,' Tess said, as she bustled around her car to the driver's position. She hoped her urgency would dissuade Anne from bothering her too much. She liked the old lady, and would happily spend time chatting on any other occasion, but she was loath to give Po a window of opportunity to escape through.

'Are you going out again?' Mrs Ridgeway asked.

'Duty calls.' Tess continued getting in her car.

'I wanted a quick word with you.' Mrs Ridgeway shrugged her slim shoulders. 'I suppose it can wait. They're long gone anyway.'

Tess paused with the key hovering an inch from the ignition. 'Who are long gone?'

'A pair of liars,' the old woman said. 'They claimed they knew you, but when I think about it, I offered them your name first, not the other way around.'

Tess still hadn't started the engine. 'Sorry . . . were they looking for me?'

Mrs Ridgeway shook her head. Her spectacles jiggled at the end of their lanyard. 'They were ripping me off. They distracted me with lies while stealing my stuff. I thought there was something off about them, but didn't realize what they'd been up to until after they left. It's not the value of the items they stole, more the fact they had the bare-faced audacity to do it under my nose.'

'You should phone the police,' Tess suggested.

'It's really not worth troubling the police over; I'm sure they're long gone by now. They were passing through they said, on their way to . . .' Mrs Ridgeway frowned. 'Now where did they say they were going? Back west?'

'They were probably lying about that too.'

'You're right. They gave me bogus names, for sure. Or at least one of them called the other Shelley. The same one said they were from Wiscasset but I think that was just a place they'd plucked out of their memory. It was probably some other town they ripped off during their travels.'

'How'd my name come up?' Tess asked.

'That was my fault. You see, they mentioned having come to Portland to attend a university class reunion. The big one claimed to have gone to Husson, and I mentioned you were also an alumna. I told them your name, Tess. It was foolish of me, and I see now that they were simply playing me, keeping me distracted while the little one pocketed half the stock off my shelves.'

The key was still poised over the slot.

A steel glove had gripped Tess's heart, and steadily squeezed.

She couldn't tell Mrs Ridgeway that the shoplifters were most likely a pair of violent murderers on a killing spree. But who else could they be? The incident was far too convenient to be a coincidence, especially their admission concerning a 'class reunion'. 'Do you have CCTV in your shop?'

'I've never seen the need to have it installed. Usually my customers are genuine and trustworthy. Plus I have a sharp eye: nobody usually gets anything over on me. Huh! Usually.'

Tess exhaled in defeat.

'I can describe them,' Mrs Ridgeway offered, 'they were rather distinctive. One of them bulging with muscles like one of those wrestlers off the TV, and the other was a waif with a nasty scar to her mouth. I guess she was born with a cleft palate, and the deformation of her top lip was never mended.'

'I think you should call the police.'

'Don't you think I'll be wasting their time? I mean, if the thieves are already long gone?'

'They might still be around, maybe even stealing from other shops in town,' Tess said, offering a plausible excuse. 'The police need alerting about them, so that they can be stopped.'

'You're right. I hadn't thought of that. Thank you, Tess. I'm sorry for holding you up when you're so busy, but I really did need your input.'

'I'm pleased we spoke.' Tess finally inserted the key and the engine kicked to life. She paused. 'Did you see them get in a vehicle?'

'No. They walked that way.' Mrs Ridgeway indicated an intersection further down Cumberland Avenue.

Tess looked. There were various makes and models of car parked further down the street near an elderly care centre, and a couple of delivery vans and a motorhome. With no idea of their mode of transport, Tess had no point of reference. Further up town, near the civic buildings, there were on-street cameras. After Mrs Ridgeway had made her call to the police, Tess promised herself she'd make a follow-up call to Alex and add to its gravitas with a hint that the shoplifters and the murder suspects could be the same people. Accessing the street cameras, the police should be able to identify their vehicle and put out a BOLO alert.

She was suddenly in a flux of indecision.

It was no coincidence that the murderers had visited Mrs Ridgeway's shop. The thefts were merely a means to an end, because if Tess was right, they'd arrived seeking her, and had pumped Anne for information. They knew where she lived, so would be back. Tess thought she should probably barricade herself inside with her grandfather's service revolver, alert the police, and wait for the murderers to return. But she didn't want trouble to come to her at home, certainly not where Mrs Ridgeway could be caught up in the mess. It was better that she follow her original plan and hook up as soon as possible with Po. She'd be out of harm's way up at Presumpscot Falls, and give the killers no reason to invade her home the way they had Rick Conklin's.

'If you see those two again,' she cautioned Mrs Ridgeway, 'don't approach them, call the police immediately, OK?'

'Oh, I'll do that all right,' Mrs Ridgeway assured her, while straightening her spine and throwing back her shoulders. Now that she had a clear line of action, the old woman's spirit had returned. She'd been embarrassed that she'd been made to look gullible by the thieves, and was determined now that they would be brought to justice.

Tess had a brief spark of insight. She waved Mrs Ridgeway closer. She grabbed the file she'd brought off the passenger seat, delved through until she found the photographs taken back when her group had worked as counsellors at the summer camp. She dabbed a fingertip on the grinning image of Manuel Cabello. 'He wasn't the bigger one of the two, was he?'

Mrs Ridgeway fed on her spectacles for a better look.

'Him?' Mrs Ridgeway said. 'No. No I've never seen him.'

But the person the old woman pointed out next almost made Tess's mind explode in disbelief.

'This skinny girl at the back . . .' Mrs Ridgeway said, nodding, as she scored a line under the figure she recognized with her thumbnail, 'it has changed a lot, but . . . I'd never mistake *that* face.'

Tess thanked her, trying to hide the sickness roiling in her stomach. Trembling fingers made putting away the photographs difficult. She didn't explain, only made a quick goodbye.

She'd been on the wrong track all along.

But now that Mrs Ridgeway had potentially identified one of

the killers, it all made sense to Tess, and why their modus oper-
andi had been so different and specific to each victim.

She sped off, keener now than ever to reach Po and to finally
– hopefully – put a stop to the murder spree before it reached
its end game.

Swirling memories distracted her, her mind barely on her
driving, or the escalating shudder emanating from the car's undercarriage. She certainly didn't look back, so missed spotting the
motorhome pulling out from its parking spot, and following.

Distracted or not, common sense influenced her subconscious,
and while driving an unsound vehicle she avoided the major high-
ways where possible, though she'd no option but take the interstate
bridge over Back Cove. As soon as she was on the northern side
of the cove, she took the first exit and drove the surface streets of
East Deering. Thankfully she was keeping below the speed limit
when something integral suddenly sheered loose and her Prius
veered, shuddering and screeching, towards the kerb on the opposite side of the road. Tess fought the steering wheel, but it was
stuck tight, and the car nosed into the sidewalk, coming to a
jolting halt. Fortunately, there was no oncoming traffic. Her tablet
and purse and some of the papers spilled into the footwell. Her
seatbelt held, but Tess had been thrown forward by the impact.
She rocked back, lucky that her face had missed colliding with
the windshield. She sat for a moment, her mind a blank, as she
heaved out a breath. Then frustration kicked in and she called
the Prius a few choice words, hammering the steering wheel with
her palms.

She took stock of her location. Her car had come to rest on
Ocean Avenue, almost at the entrance of a disused landfill site.
Poetic, she thought, considering it was good for nothing but a
garbage pile. As the crow flies, she was about a mile from Po's
place, but could double that if she followed the major streets.
There were ways to shorten the journey on foot, but she was
unfamiliar with the neighbourhood, and had always followed the
main roads in and out from Po's ranch. Even via the longer route,
the walk wouldn't be taxing, but there was an alternative.

She called Po on her cell.

This time she got through on the first ring.

'Hey!' he said.

'Hey, you. Tell me you're still at home, Po.'

He picked up on her tone. 'What's wrong?'

'Remember my car you were going to have Charley take a look at?'

'Damn,' Po said, 'it slipped my mind. I'll call him—'

'Do that please,' she cut in. 'But could you first come and get me? I'm currently stranded on Ocean, near the intersection with Presumpscot Street.'

'Near the old garbage dump?'

'Yep?'

'What's wrong with your car?'

'You're the mechanic, Po. You tell me. All I know is it isn't going anywhere.'

'Fair point, Tess. Stay with the car, I'll be there in a few minutes.'

'Soon as you can, OK? I've something important to tell you . . .'

'Yeah, me too.'

She was about to spill who she thought was behind the killings, and why, but it would take time, and the longer she kept him on the phone the longer it would be until he picked her up. 'Tell me about it when you get here,' she said.

'Setting off now,' he assured her.

They hung up.

The interior of the Prius dimmed.

Her vehicle, pressed at an oblique angle into the kerb, had caused an obstruction to other road users. Its position also foiled her from telling what kind of vehicle had pulled up so close to her back end and casting hers in shadow, as she'd no clear view through her mirrors. She craned around, peering over her right shoulder. All she could see was the grill of a large blocky van or truck. The driver had parked contra to the direction of traffic, had obviously been coming in the same direction as she, and pulled across the road when spotting that she was in trouble. It was best that their vehicles blocked only one lane, so the traffic flow wasn't further hindered.

Fingernails rapped on the window next to her. Startled, Tess spun around and blinked up at the person standing too close to the car door to see them clearly. She'd expected a truck driver, or delivery guy or someone like that, not a slim, young woman wearing a padded jacket with a fur-lined hood.

Tess powered the window down an inch.

'Hey! Are you OK?' asked the young woman.

'I'm OK, thanks,' Tess replied. 'Problem with the steering . . .'

'Looks as if your wheel has come off the hub,' said the woman. She had bent to inspect the front of the car where it was jammed against the kerb. Tess caught a glimpse of the woman's profile. It wasn't a face she knew, a complete stranger. 'The bolts have sheered,' the woman went on, 'there's only the locking nut holding everything together. Wow, you were lucky you weren't going fast when this happened!'

Tess unclipped her belt, and opened the door, as the woman crouched for a closer look at the damaged wheel. She inspected it as if she had knowledge of mechanics: a subject Tess was woefully poor at.

As she stepped out, the woman glanced up at her again, her face still partly hidden by her hood. She smiled reassuringly at Tess, said, 'Good job there was nothing coming the other way too. Things could've ended up much worse.'

'Yeah,' Tess agreed wearily, 'it's my lucky day.'

'You betcha,' said the woman as she stood from her inspection. The light finally hit her face. It was pale, sharp cheekbones and a thin nose. Cloudy grey eyes. Her skin bore the scars of acne, and also where she'd once had piercings in her eyebrows and lip.

Tess's gaze fell on the latter, saw that it was ragged and poorly healed, as if the piercing there had once been forcefully removed, without care for the damage it caused. It gave the young woman a look of . . .

Her mind snapped to the recent conversation with Anne Ridgeway: '*I guess she was born with a cleft palate, and the deformation of her top lip was never mended.*' Anne had come to the wrong conclusion about the reason for the deformity, but she was right about her description: it was a nasty scar to her mouth, made uglier by the way in which the thin lips bowed into a sneer of triumph. The woman understood that Tess had recognized what – if not who – she was, and her notoriety pleased her.

Tess was taller by a couple of inches, and had a few pounds on the woman, and retained the skills she'd acquired as a sheriff's deputy, plus some other dirty tricks picked up from Po. In a straight fight she didn't fear the outcome, but the odds were against her when the waif travelled with a partner in crime. Immediately Tess began to turn to confront the other, but she was a split-second too slow. She barely got a glimpse of the hulking figure standing directly behind her before a palm slammed her shoulder, thrusting her into the open car door. The large figure crammed against her, holding her put. Jammed against the doorframe, pain stabbed through her chest, but it helped galvanize her into a fight for freedom. She jabbed an elbow into her attacker's stomach, but she'd barely room to manoeuvre, and her strike was ineffective.

'Hold her still!' The hot breath of her attacker swirled around Tess's features, stinking of halitosis so strong it was like being washed by molten iron.

The skinny woman lurched forward, her fingernails coming at Tess's face. She dug her chin into her chest to avoid the raking nails tearing at her eyes, but that was never her attacker's intention. The woman grasped handfuls of Tess's hair, held her head down, jamming her jaw against the car door. Tess hollered, kicking and squirming to get free.

A plastic sack was jammed over her head from behind, forcing the grip to relax on her hair. She twisted sideways on, throwing an elbow again, but with as little effect. The sack was tugged lower, bunched in fistfuls around her neck. Tess took a frantic inhalation, and the plastic hood invaded her open mouth. She tugged at the plastic, but the skinny woman grabbed her wrists, yanking them away. Tess couldn't breathe. Panic engulfed her. She was going to suffocate! She screeched, and for a second the bag was expelled from her mouth. But there was no relief from the surging panic in her: reaction caused her to gulp for breath and the plastic sealed her throat once more.

Lights popped and fizzled in her vision. Her lungs hitched and spasmed, and her movements grew spasmodic, heels skidding on the wet asphalt as she was suspended by the rearing back of her larger captor. The lights diminished to a scarlet afterglow, then true blackness swarmed through her mind, weakness assailing her with shocking abruptness and she'd no strength to fight back when she was hauled further backwards, and the slim woman grabbed her up by her ankles and she was lugged semi-conscious towards her death.

TWENTY-SIX

Between Po leaving his ranch and driving to Ocean Avenue, the weather took a turn for the worse. Lightning storms had been a feature of the last week or so, interspersed by grey, brooding skies and heavy showers. Rain had come again, accompanied by a brisk wind, and though he couldn't hear the rumble of thunder above the growl of his Mustang's engine, lightning sheeted across the heavens. He put his foot down: Tess, stranded in her Prius, would be experiencing a miserable time, and each second it took him to arrive would feel like an hour. It was only mid-afternoon, but he had his lights on full and his wipers battled to clear the windshield. He passed traffic heading in the opposite direction, water sheeting from the flash-flooded roads as they forged through widening puddles. A huge, old-fashioned motorhome hurtled past: a deluge of dirty rainwater cast up by its tyres battered his windshield. Po squinted through the spume, barely able to see a dozen yards ahead. Leaves picked up by the wind swirled between the trees on each side of the road adding to the poor visibility. He craned forward.

Ahead, he spotted the intersection of Ocean Avenue and Presumpscot Street. A car idled with its blinkers on at the inter-section, waiting for him to pass. Further on, beyond the entrance to the old landfill site, he thought he could make out the shape of a vehicle sitting at an angle in his lane. No lights. No hazard-warning signal. Tess should know better. He hoped she'd ignored his instructions and gotten out and found a dry place to wait, rather than remain in the crippled car. With no warning lights the Prius was at risk of being involved in a head-on collision. If he hadn't been looking for her, he might not have noticed it until the last moment. He began to slow, and he switched on his own hazard lights. The other car had pulled out the intersection, and now overtook Po's Mustang, having to steer into the opposite lane to pass. Its headlights washed over the Prius, and Po at once saw that it was deserted. The road surface was awash with rainwater and fallen leaves, but Po spotted fresh scrapes in the asphalt where the Prius had veered across the street and come to rest. The car was canted down at the front left, propped on the kerb, and the driver's door hung open.

He got out the Mustang, and jogged, stooping against the icy rain, to the Prius. In his heart he felt there was something decidedly wrong, because even if Tess had abandoned the car for somewhere safe, she would have left on the warning lights, and closed the door. On the phone, she'd sounded harassed but not confused, but what if she had stumbled away from her car before making the scene as safe as possible for other road users? There were houses further along the street, set back from the roadside, and behind him a water-treatment works at the entrance of the old landfill: she could have sought shelter at any of those, but he doubted it.

A quick glance inside told him that Tess had left in a hurry . . . or worse; she'd been forced to abandon her car.

Her case files, tablet, and even her purse lay scattered in an untidy heap in the passenger footwell. There was no reason why she would have left them behind.

His next instinct was to check for blood. There was none. Though the wheel was twisted off its hub, the collision with the kerb hadn't been forceful. The air bags hadn't deployed, and there was no sign of Tess impacting either the steering wheel or windshield. Also, the seatbelt had been unbuckled, and now rested in its proper uncoupled position. He cast around, widening his search. All sensible people had found shelter from the storm. There were no witnesses to what had happened, and no sign of where Tess had gone. He stood, pelted by rain, as he again scanned the near distance. Other than the car that pulled out of the intersection, he'd seen no other road users in the past minute. He was at a loss and feared the worst.

Tess hadn't abandoned her car of her own volition. She knew he was coming to collect her and would be minutes away at most, so wouldn't have flagged down a taxi or another motorist. Even if frustration had taken hold of her and she wanted to get moving, she wouldn't have left her files and stuff behind in the car: second nature would have made her tidy them from where they'd fallen in the footwell, maybe even securing them in the glove compartment if she wanted to avoid them getting wet. She would have switched on her warning lights and locked the car.

Ergo: she'd been forced to leave the car.

Fleeting worry over Jimmy Hawkes impinged on his mind. He had temporarily disabled Murphy and Chapel, but had left Hawkes untouched. When last they spoke Hawkes had been cowed, but Po was under no illusion; he fully expected Hawkes to rally once he got over the shock of witnessing his hitters' beating. Had Hawkes sicked Noble and his pals on Tess, as retribution – or even insurance – against Po?

No. It was too soon and unlikely. Hawkes had discovered his name, but he couldn't have discovered the names of his associates yet, apart from Chris. If Hawkes had launched a counterattack, it would have been against the barman. Tess's disappearance was down to someone else, and he had an idea who – but therein lay the rub: he had no idea *who* the killers of Chelsea Grace and Kent Bachman were.

He delved in the footwell, pulling Tess's stuff into an untidy pile against his chest, and returned to the Mustang. Priority: ring Tess and ensure she hadn't done something stupid like hail a taxi.

The rain drummed on the car, but he heard a corresponding ring tone from a cellphone, nearby. He was out of the Mustang in a flash and crouching alongside the Prius. Wedged under it was Tess's phone, displaying his name. He grabbed it, dashed water off the screen, and stared at it as if it would tell him what had transpired only minutes ago. The fact it had been dropped and had slid under the car spoke volumes. Tess definitely wouldn't have relinquished her lifeline other than during a struggle. She'd resisted her abductors. He cancelled his call and Tess's phone fell silent. He hated the sudden cessation of sound.

He scanned his surroundings again, rain slashing into his face as he peered uphill towards the old landfill site. The old garbage dump had been reclaimed, ploughed over, and landscaped to form a recreation area, used primarily by dog walkers. Trees and shrubs, and undulations in the terrain: any number of hiding places where Tess could have been taken. But no. The abductors hadn't been waiting for her in the random hope that her car would fail at exactly the right spot. Whoever had taken her had arrived in a vehicle, forced her into it, and spirited her away.

Where?

They had likely followed Tess towards his ranch, but that didn't necessarily mean they had continued along Ocean Avenue. They could have turned around, or taken Presumpscot Street back towards Back Cove or I-295: from there who knew their final destination. The abductors would have used a vehicle able to transport a prisoner, and if he knew Tess, one who would resist them all the way. A larger SUV or van would do it, or . . .

He recalled the motorhome that had sped past him only a minute or so before his arrival, and how at the time he thought its driver hasty in the inclement conditions. He ran for his Mustang, hit a screeching Y-turn in the street, and powered back the way he'd come, speeding along Middle Road, across the bridge over the Presumpscot River, praying he'd catch the motorhome before it reached Bucknam Road and got back on the interstate. Once back on the 295, there were options to take the Falmouth Spur west, stay on the highway north, or lose itself on any other county road around Cumberland or North Yarmouth.

It was as if the storm had allied itself with Tess's abductors, trying with all its might to slow down Po's pursuit. The rain battered down in so much volume that the wipers couldn't contend with the wash over his windshield. His tyres churned through puddles, sending up wings of dirty foam. Wind buffeted the car, and Po had to grip the steering wheel to avoid being pushed into deeper water gushing along the kerbs towards the storm drains. Lightning flashed, thunder rumbled, and Po growled a string of foul curses at his own selfishness. He should not have allowed Tess to be taken. Too engrossed in his own need to play the goddamn white knight, he'd failed to protect the one most in need of him.

Driving safely was difficult, and it didn't help that he did so with only one hand on the steering wheel. The other clamped his phone to his ear.

'Alex?'

'Po? What's up?' asked Tess's brother, picking up on Po's urgency in the tone of his question.

'Listen up,' Po almost shouted into the phone, 'Tess has been snatched.'

'What?' Alex babbled out other frantic questions, but none of them coalesced in Po's mind.

'Your sister has been grabbed by the same bastards who hurt her old friends. I'm in pursuit. Now listen to me.'

Alex again peppered him with questions. Who, what, where, when, how? Po ignored them all. In as few terse words as possible he described how Tess's Prius had broken down, and she'd called him to come collect her. He briefly described the scene he'd discovered on his arrival, and how there was no other possibility than that Tess had been forced into a vehicle. He described the old motorhome as best he could – he had only a fleeting image of it in his mind from when it had flashed by on the other side of the road. Alex wanted more detail, but Po had none, only his gut instinct that he was right about Tess's fate.

'Alex,' Po stated, 'I haven't time for more. I'm trying to catch them. Now do your stuff and get your cops looking for that goddamn RV.'

Alex was breathless. Po pictured him charging through the police station, heading for his own cruiser. He'd said all he could for now, and staying on the phone with Alex wasn't helpful. He hung up even as Alex demanded to know more. Fully expecting him to call back, Po found another number in his contacts, attention jumping from the washed-out scene ahead to phone screen and back again, even as he fought the conditions without slowing.

'Pinky?' There was no need of a greeting. He'd spoken to his best friend less than an hour earlier, and twice before that in the preceding twenty-four hours. 'Where are you, man?'

'I grabbed a cab like you asked,' Pinky replied. 'I'm about fifteen minutes away from Tess's place. Nicolas, what's wrong? Things didn't go as planned with that Hawkes dude?'

Po hadn't shared the news with Tess yet. After he'd left her first thing that morning, and while staking out the house before trailing Noble and Lassiter to HappyDayz his first call had been to his friend in Baton Rouge. Po was confident of his own abilities, but he was also a realist. One man was rarely victorious when outnumbered by determined enemies, and he was under no illusion when it came to the necessity of having someone he trusted at his back if the shit hit the fan. Pinky and Emilia, Po's younger sister, had been planning a trip to Maine, but Pinky didn't need convincing when Po had asked him to move his plans forward. Emilia was unable to join him, but Pinky had hopped

on the first available flight. Po had brought him up to speed on
Jimmy Hawkes, and the violent run-in he'd had with Murphy
and Chapel. Explaining how Tess was expecting him at her house
on Cumberland Avenue, Po had suggested that Pinky hail a cab
and go directly there from the airport, where they would meet.
They both thought his surprise arrival would lighten Tess's heart.
But then Po had gotten the call about her breaking down and
their plans had gone to hell since.

'It's not Hawkes,' Po told him. 'It's something else. Pinky, I
need you to check on Tess's home. If she's there, let me know
immediately.'

'Nicolas, you've got me worried, you. What's going on? It's
Tess, right? Something has happened to my pretty Tess?'

'That case she was looking into—' Po had also brought Pinky
up to speed on the attacks on Tess's old classmates – 'she was
right all along. There is someone systematically hunting down
and punishing her old friends.'

'And now they have her?'

'I hope to hell I'm wrong,' Po said.

'If they've hurt a hair on her head,' Pinky warned, and there
was no hint of his usual glibness, 'they'll pay.'

'Yes.'

There was need of nothing further from Po. His tone swore
that hell would come down on the heads of Tess's abductors.

'If she's not home,' said Po, 'come on up to my place. I'll
meet you there. And Pinky, I've told Alex his sister's missing.
He might be at hers when you get there. He's a cop, but he's her
brother first.'

'I get you – on both counts.'

Po rang off. His Mustang swept onto I-295. In a few seconds
he must make a decision. Continue on the highway, or take the
toll road along Falmouth Spur. He doubted that the abductors
would chance the tollbooths and CCTV cameras while trans-
porting a potentially volatile hostage. The Mustang rocketed
forward and in seconds had hit 100 mph. Po pushed it harder,
sweeping by, and even around, slower-moving traffic. The rain
slanted sideways, and spray cast from other hurtling vehicles
hung in foggy clouds, but Po's attention was laser-focused ahead,
watching for the first sign of the motorhome. If it had continued

on the highway it couldn't be far ahead, but if it had taken a different route it could be miles away. Fortune had favoured Po earlier during his run-in with Jimmy Hawkes's goons, but he knew that good luck usually arrived as a short order. Minutes later he knew that providence had deserted him. He pumped the brakes, bringing the Mustang down through a rapid deceleration to a controlled stop. He slammed his palms on the steering wheel.

The traffic had come to an unscheduled halt. Up ahead a flatbed truck had overturned and spilled its load of timber across the highway. Nothing was going to move until after the emergency services were on the scene and cleaned up. There were upward of twenty vehicles between Po and the overturned truck, but not the old motorhome.

Time for another decision, and this one more reckless even than driving at high speed in such awful conditions. There was no way past the jam, so he took the only other option left to him. He yanked the steering to the left, pulling a tight turn on the central meridian, and bulled his way onto the highway south through the cars crawling by so their drivers could gawp at the accident scene. Then he hit the gas again and was speeding back towards Portland. He'd no objective in mind, but at least he was moving, and the sheer act of maintaining forward volition kept frustration at bay. Though not the heart-wrenching concern for his lover.

TWENTY-SEVEN

I t was incredibly difficult to breathe, but what little air she could get was a blessing after her near suffocation. Tess had to rear back an inch or two, sucking as much oxygen through her nostrils as possible, when she wanted to gulp down lungfuls at a time. Her lips were sealed shut with a thick layer of duct tape wound around her lower face. A second layer of tape acted as a blindfold, and muffled her hearing, adding to her disconcertion. She couldn't clearly hear her captors' voices, couldn't tell what they had in mind for her. Did it really matter? They meant her harm, and judging by their most recent actions it would be as agonizing as Kent Bachman's punishment.

Tess was propped on her side. She could feel the softness of a bed but it wasn't out of consideration for her comfort. Periodically her movements caused the bedclothes to move, and a waft of foul air was dragged into her: it stank of stale sweat and something else, rank to the point of putrefaction. She retched on the stink, but her body wouldn't be denied and she soon sucked in more air. Thankfully the overriding necessity to breathe ensured she didn't throw up. If she did so whilst gagged, it would be the end of her. After the method of her recent abduction the thought of fully suffocating to death horrified her.

Under the circumstances she could be forgiven for giving in to despondency, and yet Tess wasn't the type to give up. After almost losing a hand in the line of duty, and through it truly losing her fiancé and her career, she'd fallen into a dark mood, and it had taken some coming back from the brink of despair she'd teetered over, and yet she hadn't given in, she'd fought back, re-established herself, and her life had become rosier for it. She'd had help then, first from her brother Alex and his girlfriend, now her employer, Emma Clancy, and mainly by Po and their friend Pinky. Here and now there was no assistance but for what she could do for herself, and though it was little, she was determined that she would not go down without a fight. Between snatching for what breath could be pulled in through her nostrils, she strove to break her bindings. Not only had the thick silver tape been wound around her face, but both wrists were cinched behind her back, and her ankles were also bound. Given an opportunity to roll and squirm around she might force some play in her bindings, and from there gain enough movement to exert more pressure on them, but each time she moved more than an inch or two the skinny woman took delight in slashing a hand across her face, or thumping her in the stomach. More than once, she had torn clumps of hair from Tess's head, but worse than that she'd nipped her breasts maliciously, twisting them until Tess shrieked through her gag. She had screamed in anger, and had not begged for pity, would not. Seeking pity from the sadistic woman was akin to begging for more punishment.

After some time enduring mind-numbing pain Tess lay still. The woman had leaned close, her words vibrating through the tape covering Tess's ears, goading her to move again. When she didn't, she was hurt. When she did, she was hurt worse. So she remained inert, and soon the woman lost interest and joined the brute in the cab. They discussed their plans for Tess, but her muffled hearing couldn't discern their low drone from the sound of the tyres on the road, or the drumming of rain that continued to cascade on the shell of the motorhome. Tess hoped the tumult would also cover the tiny sounds of her renewed exertions.

The passage of time had grown unfathomable. Each second of torment had been contorted until she felt as if she'd been hogtied in the back of the van for eternity. She had no sense of her location beyond the stinking bed beneath her and the cold wall against her back, no idea of direction or her ultimate destination. Periodically she felt the sway of the van at another corner, the deceleration and speeding up as it negotiated intersections, taking a meandering route that she could only suspect was to throw off any pursuit. But who could be following? Even Po, who would face the devil in her defence, would have been minutes away when she was captured. He would have discovered her abandoned car by now, and perhaps concluded what had become of her. And yet he could have no way of knowing where, or by whom, she'd been taken, so she couldn't depend on him. There was only her and her captors, and they weren't about to free her soon.

It's down to you, Tess. Get free, fight back, or die.

She strained again at the tape around her wrists. More than anything she wanted to wrench her hands free. But she must do so by increments, for fear of alerting her captors.

Was she visible to them? She must be. She had no idea of the layout of the van, but thought that the young woman would keep an eye on her through an open door even if she were in some separate bedroom compartment. She'd been forced onto the bed, shoved into one corner so that she was up against a wall, facing out, and she supposed it was so that she could be watched from the front of the van. Tied up, she'd no hope of making any sudden break for freedom. Even if she were to pull free of one or other of her bindings, then the young woman was probably confident of getting to her and beating her into submission before she could escape. In the knowledge that she was inviting further torment, Tess still strained at her bindings: she'd rather be punished for disobedience than for the pleasure of a sadist. More than she did the muscle-bound brute that had forced the plastic sack over her head, Tess hated the skinny bitch with the scarred mouth. She could understand why the brute would want to hurt her, there was a reason why he might feel that retribution was in order, but the smaller bitch had no personal beef with Tess, only a desire to sate a malignant thirst for inflicting pain. She, Tess had come to understand, was the driving force in the mismatched partnership, because the nasty little bitch had called all the shots since she'd been bundled into the motorhome. She'd directed her hulking accomplice in ensuring that Tess was fully secured, and then sent him packing to the front of the van with the promise she was about to enjoy some *me time* with Tess before 'Cable' got his fun.

Cable.

She'd heard the name, and understood the significance. But it also reminded her how misguided her suspicions had been concerning the suspects she'd formed in the killings of her friends. She had concentrated too long on Mina Stoll and Manny Cabello, when all along she should have known that neither of those two had it in them to physically harm anyone. Time and again she'd studied the group photograph from the summer camp, and all the time the killer had been right there, and yet Tess – as she had back when they'd been at university together – had glossed over the figure as irrelevant. She'd ignored the obvious because it was so unlikely that the thuggish brute now at the wheel of the motorhome could ever be mistaken for the insignificant girl maligned as Thing Two. It had come as a shock to Tess when Anne Ridgeway had earlier scored her thumbnail beneath the image of Gabriella Kablinski and announced it was a face she'd never mistake . . . even if it had changed a lot.

During those brief moments when Tess had glimpsed her attacker, before the bag was forced down over her head, she'd noted the broad, bruised, and acne-scarred face, the spiky, roughly cropped hair, and could barely equate those blunt features with the pale skin and heavy eyeshadow of the young woman who'd hidden her true identity behind the uniformity of make-up. And yet she'd known they were one and the same, because Gabriella Kablinski had always presented a false front. She had hidden behind a disguise, and the face she now wore was no less a facade than the overt masculinity of the body she'd developed. During her youth Kablinski had been extremely uncomfortable in her own skin and had hidden behind the bleak canvas of thousands of other girls and boys who embraced the Goth subculture, but alas it was a disguise that couldn't serve her throughout adulthood. Instead, she'd adopted a new image, and one that had been achieved through God knew what means. Her metamorphosis wasn't about gender reassignment, she'd progressed far beyond the point of any sane transgender person, and become something that was obscenely warped: Cable was as outwardly monstrous as the twisted mind of his companion that guided him.

Throughout her adolescence Gabriella Kablinski had been bullied; as her new persona, the masculine Cable, was she any less a victim of circumstance? Tess could pity the lost girl, but not the pseudo-male that had formed as the product of the abuse the girl suffered. It was a classic case of the victim becoming the abuser, but the former didn't excuse the latter. Through wilful cooperation with her current abuser Cable's actions were unforgiveable, and if Tess had her way, both should be punished with extreme prejudice.

But there lay the problem. How on earth would punishment be served to them when she was hogtied and at their mercy?

Get free, fight back, or die, she repeated.

Easier said than done, but she continued with her exertions, and finally felt the tape around her wrists moving. The small hairs on her forearms were abraded, as was the skin beneath. It was a small discomfort compared to what she could expect. She tilted on her back so that her arms were hidden, and braced her feet in the angle of the wall and a wardrobe, using the leverage to add tension to her body. She listened keenly, worried that the sadist was creeping up on her. The effort required more oxygen. She was feeling woozy, and her face was on fire as blood rushed into her head. She had to slow down, breathe steadily, and not wear herself out. But by moving her hands in a controlled piston-like motion she could feel the tape coming loose, rolling down on itself. She wasn't any nearer to breaking the bindings – in fact she was possibly even strengthening its circle by compacting it into a roll – but she was also forcing more play and movement for her hands. Sensing results she continued, and even managed to hook the pad of her right thumb under the circlet of toughened tape. A few more minutes and her hands would be free. Then she could begin working on her ankles. Hope flooded through her.

It was dashed moments later as the motorhome was brought to a halt. The sudden stop rolled Tess across the bed.

It was still thundering outside, and the rain on the motorhome's roof was constant, but there was no longer any road noise. Even with muffled hearing Tess caught the sadist snapping out an angry curse. Footsteps drummed, and even as Tess began to roll back, to conceal her hands, she was grabbed and pulled almost off the bed. The woman yanked at her bindings, dissatisfied by what she found. A fist caught Tess on the left cheekbone, more painful because of the shock of the assault. Tess yelped, tried to pull away, and was rewarded by a flurry of punches and slaps to her head. Dazed, she shouted in anger, but her words were garbled. She was forced on the bed, belly down, and felt a knee wedge against her side. The woman climbed astride her, knees either side of her hips, and dug an elbow tip painfully between Tess's shoulder blades. With her free hand, the woman tugged down the tape around Tess's eyes and ears. Not so she could see, but so she could hear.

'Trying to escape, are you?' The woman's words were a hot whisper. 'You really think you have any hope of getting away, bitch? Well think again. You're going nowhere I don't make you go. You get me? Do you fucking understand?'

Tess groaned in frustration.

The woman took it as rebellion.

Another hard slap rang off the side of Tess's head.

'I'd like to kill you now,' the woman continued in the same harsh whisper. 'I could beat you to a pulp and there's not a damn thing you could do to stop me. Is that what you want? Do you want me to pulp your skull with this?'

Something wooden knocked sharply against the opposite side of Tess's head. It was a baton of sorts, the wood tempered iron-hard.

'Well? Do you want me to smash your skull?'

Tess mumbled.

This time the woman took her words as a sign of defeat.

'Don't try me again! Do you hear? *Do you fucking hear me?*'

Despite herself, Tess sobbed.

'Rayne,' said the deeper voice of Cable. 'I think you've made your point.'

Suddenly the woman – Rayne – turned her ire on her partner. 'Have I? Have I made my goddamn point? I haven't seen blood yet!'

'She isn't going anywhere, you'll get your chance soon enough.' Cable hadn't left the cab, and his tone was desultory. Had he bought fully into this madness the way his girlfriend had? Tess didn't think so. And the enlightenment ignited a fresh spark of hope. Could she appeal to the girl that she'd once known, get her to understand how misguided and how totally excessive her actions were based on the juvenile slights she'd endured all those years ago? Could she convince Gabriella how unhinged her friend was, and get her to see how she was being groomed into a creature in the psychopath's image? She couldn't if her head was caved in by Rayne's baton.

'I . . . I'm sorry,' Tess slurred through the gag. 'I was stupid. I won't do anything like this again.'

'What? What are you squawking about?' Rayne slapped her head for effect. 'Is that supposed to be an apology? Look at what you did: got me all pissed when I was enjoying myself. Stupid bitch! Have you no consideration for other people's feelings?'

Rayne's demands weren't formed of cohesive thoughts, only a desire to confuse and belittle.

'Sorry. I'm *genuinely sorry!*' Through the gag, Tess's words were garbled, but direct enough.

'C'mon, Rayne. Let her be now.'

'I'll let her be when I'm good and ready,' Rayne said sniffily.

'I need you to unlock the gate,' Cable said wearily.

'What? You think I'm getting out in the damned rain? Think again, Monkey Boy.'

Cable grunted at the insult. But he knew not to argue. 'You drive then,' he said, 'and I'll get the gate.'

Rayne clambered off Tess. But she wasn't done. She used the leverage of her fingers in Tess's hair to force her back on the bed. 'Stay!' she said, as if commanding a mutt. 'Move again and I don't care how Cable wants this game to play out, I'll take personal delight in spreading your brains all over that bed. Y'hear?'

Tess nodded emphatically enough to convince Rayne she was thoroughly cowed.

Rayne marched away, the rattle of her heels indicative of mincing steps. 'Well?' she demanded sarcastically. 'You waiting for me to get you an umbrella?'

The air pressure in the van changed as Cable swung open a door and stepped down from the motorhome. The sound of the storm picked up. But beyond it Tess thought she could hear the roar of wind through treetops, a sound like an angry sea. Metallic clinks followed, then the squeal of unoiled hinges. Rayne had obviously taken the driver's seat. The motorhome lurched forward, and she pushed it up an incline, calling out the window at Cable to run. Her voice had lost its bitter edge, was now almost jovial. The motorhome finally halted, but before Cable could climb aboard, Rayne put down her foot again. She kept up the joke a couple more times, before Cable managed to get aboard, huffing and panting, and shaking off rain water. Tess was sickened by Rayne's immaturity. It was the bilious behaviour of a mean child, the type that took pleasure in pulling the wings off bugs, or holding a flame to a spider in its web. She had the barest hope of appealing to Cable, but any plea to Rayne would fall on deaf ears, and quite probably invite worse punishment than had ever been planned.

Tess made a promise.

There'd be no pleading for mercy.

Get free. Fight back.

She began working at her bindings again.

TWENTY-EIGHT

Tearing around the streets of Portland and its suburbs in the slim chance he'd spot the dilapidated motorhome wasn't the best plan, but Po wasn't the type to sit idle while Tess was still missing. Alex had attended the scene of Tess's abandoned car on Ocean Avenue, and had also concluded that his sister had somehow been snatched but was having a hard time convincing his fellow officers that there was any urgency in finding her. To stir them up, Po had bent the truth, stating that he'd spotted the motorhome closer to the scene than he actually had, and this added some validity to the probability that Tess was inside it: at least the cops in the outlying areas had been asked to watch out for it. To bolster the hunt, Po had taken the toll road back around the northern end of town, then began a high-speed grid search of the streets as he wound his way back down towards the Presumpscot River.

Pinky had gone by Tess's house and was about to hop back in his cab when Anne Ridgeway approached him. The shopkeeper had met Pinky on a previous occasion. The old woman was astute enough to tell he wasn't his ebullient self, and asked if everything was OK. Pinky was reticent in admitting the truth, but only until Anne said: 'It's those two thieves, isn't it? I knew there was something wrong by the way Tess reacted when I told her about them.'

Po's cellphone rang just as he was pulling up outside his ranch. It was a long shot that Tess had somehow escaped her abductors and made it back to his house, but he had to check.

'Pinky,' he said.

'I'm really worried now, me,' said Pinky. 'I just spoke with Tess's neighbour and she tells me there were a couple of wackoes in her shop earlier, who were interested in Tess's whereabouts.'

'What? Who?' Po rushed for his door, key in hand, and pushed inside. He knew without checking that Tess was absent. The house felt morgue-like. He recalled that Tess said she'd something important to tell him when he picked her up: she'd been referring to the couple at the shop, he bet.

'One of them was a gnarly little bitch with a twisted lip,' Pinky said, 'the other built like Schwarzenegger . . . in his heyday.'

Immediately Po matched the description to Rick Conklin's attackers.

'They actually admitted to looking for Tess?' Po made a check of his house anyway, room by room. The silence, the sense of foreboding was enough to tell him he was wasting his time, but he had to do *something*.

'The old girl says she brought up Tess's name first, but then they lied to her about their reasons for being in town. Claimed they were there for a class reunion, them, but she caught the lie. The scumbags stole half the stock off her shelves, and she thought that's all they were, a coupla thieves. But she's a wise one, her. She knew there was more to Tess's urgency than she was letting on.'

'She see a car . . . or a motorhome in particular?'

'She saw an RV, but only after Tess left to meet you. She was about to follow Tess's advice and call the cops, and was still looking out the window. She watched an old Winnebago tear past as if trying to catch up with Tess. She'd spotted it parked down the road earlier, and put two and two together. She passed the description, and get this, the licence number to the dispatcher.'

'Shit! Why doesn't Alex know about that?'

Pinky had no reply. 'She also told me that she pointed out one of the scumbags on a photograph that Tess showed her. Said it was of a bunch of camp counsellors or something, and she marked the photo with her nail for emphasis.'

Po's heart leapt in his chest. 'Get on up here, will ya? Gonna need your help, Pinky.'

'On my way, me.'

Po ran back to his Mustang, grabbed Tess's files and stuff off the passenger seat, and carried them back inside. Before he'd hit the first step up to his porch he was already sorting through the papers. He found the photo quickly enough, but took it into his kitchen and switched on the lights. His gaze was immediately drawn to the guys in the group. He recognized a young Rick Conklin, and a young Kent Bachman, having seen his picture

on the TV news following his immolation. The third one had to
be the dude that Tess had been unable to locate: Manuel Cabello.
Po despised Cabello's face the instant he studied it, but he'd
made the wrong judgement. There was no hint of a mark on the
picture to indicate he'd been in Anne Ridgeway's shop. Po tilted
the photo back and forth, angling it beneath the overhead lights.
His attention slid to a slight figure standing awkwardly in the
back right corner of the group. As he slanted the light over the
face he caught sight of the half-moon impression of a fingernail
dug into the image. A Goth girl. She was grungy then, and if
Pinky was right with his description, a gnarly little bitch with a
twisted lip now. He turned over the photograph. Handily, Tess
had jotted down the names of every person in the picture.
Gabriella Kablinski. Confident he had a name for one of Tess's
abductors, he wondered who the muscle freak was. His attention
went back to Manny Cabello, and he hated him a second time.

He rang Alex.

'Any sightings,' he demanded without preamble.

'Not a damn thing. Goddamnit, Po!'

'Listen up. Your dispatcher took a call earlier. About a shoplifting on Cumberland Avenue. The culprits are the same bastards
that snatched Tess.'

'What? How do you know?'

'Does it matter? The shoplifting was at Anne Ridgeway's
place—'

'Tess's neighbour?'

'—and while they were there they were very interested in Tess.
Ridgeway spotted them following her away from her house in
the motorhome I told you about. She gave the dispatcher the
make, model, and licence number. Is that enough to get your
buddies more interested? Get them out looking for her, Alex.'

'Gimme the number.'

'I don't have it. Ask your damn dispatcher why the fuck they
didn't put out an alert.'

His anger was misguided. The dispatcher couldn't have any
knowledge of what might happen, and had probably prioritized
a call concerning a shoplifting to the bottom of the list. Equating
the suspected thieves with the suspected kidnappers had probably
never occurred, and that was supposing that they'd even heard

Alex pass on the description Po had given of the motorhome
he'd spotted. Calming himself, he said, 'The dispatcher has all
the details you need, Alex.'

'Thank God.' For a moment there Po had forgotten that Alex
was as fraught over his sister's disappearance as he was.

'Alex, there's something else. I have possible names. You need
to put those as a BOLO too. Your friends upstate are already
looking for Cabello, they need to be told about Kablinski too.'

'You only have surnames?'

'I also have their first names. Want me to spell them out for
you?'

'Just give them to me.'

Po told him, hung up. Alex had the facilities to check Cabello's
and Kablinski's criminal records, and get anything on file
relating to them. He hoped there were more recent photographs,
because there was little to go off from the ones he had. Now
wasn't the time to start messing around with one of those
computer programs the cops used to age a suspect or missing
person. If such became necessary, it would be after the event,
and by then Tess would be beyond help. At a loss at what else
to do, Po raced to his bedroom, delved in his sock drawer, and
pulled out a sheathed knife. He slipped the blade down the
inside of his right boot. Tess frowned on him carrying a knife,
but he reasoned that it was a multi-purpose tool, and it had gotten
them out of a number of scrapes in the past: this time he had a
single use for it in mind. If Tess was harmed, woe betide the
bastards that had touched her.

He didn't need much to continue his hunt, only an idea of
where Tess could have been taken. There was a notion that he'd
mulled over between dealing with the situation with Hawkes and
finding Tess missing: if she was correct and the deaths of Chelsea
Grace and Kent Bachman and the attack on Rick Conklin were
all connected, then the attackers were mobile, and with plenty
free time on their hands. Learning that Manuel Cabello had gone
off-grid some time back added to his theory that the killers were
staying constantly on the move. That they travelled around in a
motorhome now made complete sense. He just bet that if he
checked, he'd find that close to the sites of all the attacks he'd
find campsites and layovers where they could park. If he were

a better detective, he might have made the correlation sooner. Tess had posed the question why Chelsea chose a remote spot like Bald Head Cove to commit suicide, but the fact was she'd had no choice in the matter. He fully suspected that the killers had lain low at one of the campgrounds at nearby Popham Beach State Park or Hermit Island while they searched for then abducted Chelsea, and returned with her to a spot they'd scouted out beforehand.

He cursed himself for a fool.

He'd earlier given chase up I-295, before being halted by the overturned truck. The times before when he'd been on that highway were during their return trip from Bangor after visiting Rick Conklin in hospital, and before that when they'd visited the spot where Chelsea died. He'd bet that Tess's abductors had based themselves at various campgrounds between Portland and Bangor while carrying out their plans. He'd bet that they had continued up the interstate to another pre-selected location they were familiar with to deal with their latest catch. But where?

Po wasn't the most computer savvy, but having been around Tess for a while he'd learned enough to start a search engine. He charged through to the small room relegated now as Tess's office away from home and fired up her PC. Soon he'd brought up a map of Maine, tagged with a mass of coloured pins, indicating far too many locations for any one man to search. Po rummaged through Tess's case file again, finding this time another photograph, this one showing a young Tess and another girl posing under a sign at the entrance to the residential summer camp where they'd worked. Tess had theorized that the killings had occurred due to something that had happened there all those years ago, so was it too much of a push to suggest that the killers had returned to where it all began? He typed in the name of the camp, and moments later had the location displayed on a map, though the accompanying note said that the site was now permanently closed. The abandoned Biscay Summer Camp was situated on rugged terrain between the Damariscotta River and a collection of inland lakes, chief of which was Pemaquid Pond. He plotted his course, via Brunswick, Bath, and Wiscasset, to Newcastle and Damariscotta. Almost sixty miles, half of the journey on bad

roads. Obeying the speed limits he could be there within an hour
and a half: Po had no intention of driving slow.

The sound of an engine outside heralded Pinky's arrival.

Po rushed out to meet him, and to urge his friend out of the
taxi and into his Mustang.

Except the vehicle blocking the entrance to his drive wasn't
a taxi but a beaten-up pickup truck, with a bunch of peckerheads
onboard. He recognized faces, some of them from the bruises
he'd put on them that very morning. Aaron Noble and his blond
pal, Lassiter, had rounded up another four punks, and possibly
hearing how he'd earlier levelled the playing field when
confronting Murphy and Chapel they'd come armed with bats
and clubs of their own.

'I haven't got time for this bullshit,' Po wheezed.

He could have retreated inside, barricaded the door, and called
the cops. But he did the unthinkable.

He slammed the door shut behind him and faced them.

His unpredictable move had the desired effect. The group came
to a halt. They shared glances, and nobody seemed keen to be
the first to advance. Noble – their elected leader – sucked in his
gut, aimed the bat he was wielding at Po, and said, 'Jimmy
Hawkes ain't done with you yet, motherfucker.'

'Shame on him,' Po growled. 'If he left things good an' well
alone he might have saved your life.'

His proclamation was delivered dispassionately, but was more
sinister because of it. Red-faced, frothing at the mouth, screaming
challenges – they were signs of a man who'd lost control of his
senses. When a death sentence was delivered with calm surety it
held more weight. Noble's bottom lip drooped, and there was a
perceptible tremble in it. Again glances darted between the group.
They were doing the math. There were six of them against one,
and each of them had come armed. There wasn't a single man on
earth they felt could defeat those odds; but there was still the
chance he could get his licks in and none of them wanted to die.

'I'm a reasonable man,' Po said, 'get back on that truck and
drive away. Come at me, some of you won't be going home to
your wives and children tonight.' He made a slow sweep of every
man in the group. 'Are you willing to die on behalf of Jimmy
Hawkes? Is he really paying you enough?'

'Only one man here's gonna die!' It was Lassiter who spoke. His face was purple from his earlier beating. His eyes were the size of duck eggs. He was crapping his pants.

'You'd better kill me,' Po replied. 'You guys made a mistake this time. You should've worn scarves like you did when stoning my bar. Because I know all your faces, and believe me, if you don't kill me, I will hunt you all down.'

The steam had been taken out of the thugs. A couple of the newcomers shuffled their feet, probably wondering what the hell they'd gotten involved in, and what kind of enemy they were making. The strongest individual often guides a pack – Noble was having second thoughts – but sometimes also by the weakest mind. Lassiter was being driven by outrage at the manhandling he'd suffered that morning. He wouldn't rest until Po was left bleeding in the dust.

'You'll hunt nobody down with two broken legs!' He nudged the guys either side of him. 'Come on . . . what's one unarmed guy gonna do?'

The trio advanced, clutching their bats menacingly.

Po stepped down from his porch, crouching only marginally to slip his hand towards his ankle. He came up with his blade in hand.

Noble and the remaining two guys paused to look at each other, but Lassiter and his duo of pals had committed to the fight: they saw the knife and reacted to the sudden turn of events. They had the numbers; their weapons had a longer reach. They charged in, hollering and swinging.

Po didn't meet their charge. He'd have been beaten down within seconds. He dodged back and hopped up the steps onto his porch. His retreat drew the trio after him, even as Noble and the others still appeared undecided. The steps allowed the trio to follow, but they were bunched together, unable to get a clear swing of their clubs. They all held their weapons in their right hands. Po sidestepped to their left, meaning that they'd be forced onto the porch, and would have to turn to face him before they even got a chance at a clear strike. They were bunched together at the top of the steps, and then Lassiter was suddenly at the front, popping forth like a cork from a bottle. Neither of the others could employ their weapons for fear of hitting him. Po wasn't similarly constrained. He allowed Lassiter to jab at his face before lunging beneath the extended bat with a fencer's grace. The tip of his knife parted flesh. It took Lassiter a few seconds to realize he'd been tagged. His attention dropped to the dark stain spreading down his left thigh, and suddenly he wasn't as keen to continue the fight. But he had no option, the two behind him almost climbed over him to get at Po, and he was thrust into a second stab from the knife, this time to his other thigh. With no idea that their leader had been injured, his pals stumbled on top of him as he sank to his knees crying out in horror. Po was no longer directly before them; he'd vaulted the rail, and then onto the steps. Within the space of two heart-beats he was behind them, and his knife jabbed twice in rapid succession. One man dropped his bat to clutch at the wound on his butt cheek, the second howled, scrambled over Lassiter, and raced along the porch to escape another stab, not yet aware that blood poured from his side.

Po ignored that trio, bounding down from the porch and rushing at Noble, his mouth wide in a challenging roar.

Noble did what any sane person would. He threw away his bat, held out his palms, begged for mercy, and backed off furiously to avoid being similarly skewered. His remaining pals also decided they preferred the truck between them and the crazy knifeman. They ran for it.

Po's furious onslaught had lasted seconds. But the shocking speed at which he'd disabled half of their number had the desired effect. He could easily continue cutting and slashing – follow through on his promise to kill – but he'd defanged the situation, and it was as he'd earlier told himself: he didn't have time for their bullshit.

He grabbed the front of Noble's shirt, forcing him backwards until he slammed up against the pickup. Po's knife was at his throat. A cacophony of voices babbled to each other, all muted by the rush of blood through Po's veins. He could slit Noble from ear to ear, have done with him. But he'd just achieved the miraculous through alacrity and daring, put the fear of God into his enemies, but to kill their leader would ensure a renewed and more vicious attack.

'Last chance, Noble,' he growled, digging in the blade just enough to break the skin. 'Leave or die.'

'Please . . . for the love of . . . don't!'

'Shut up!' Po cast a seething glare at the two men who'd taken cover twenty feet beyond the pickup: their faces were white ovals of terror. 'You two,' he snapped, 'get your friends back on the truck, then get the fuck off my property.'

The two didn't move, fearful that they were being coaxed into a trap.

Po shook his hostage. 'Do it or I'll cut Noble so deep you'll swear he's got a second mouth.'

Already the man who'd been knifed in the side was aiding Lassiter to stand. The guy with the stabbed butt limped down from the porch. Noticeable was the bat he used as a crutch.

'You can drop that,' Po warned, and angled his knife alongside Noble's throat for emphasis.

The guy dropped the bat, showed both empty hands. Sweat plastered his face from the pain in his ass. As his friends came down the steps behind him, he offered a hand to Lassiter, whose legs barely had the strength to support him. Between them they managed to hobble back towards the truck. Po dragged Noble aside, allowing room for the trio to approach. They were bloody and in pain, but Po had cut deeper into their psyches than their hides: their physical wounds would heal in short order, but the fear of challenging Po again would stick. The two uninjured but definitely subdued men helped them on the back of the truck. All eyes were on Po, fearful that he'd renew his assault. He shoved Noble towards the driver's seat, with one final reminder. 'This is your lucky day. Y'know what they say about looking a gift horse in the mouth?'

This time when the truck took off at speed, there was no hollering or taunts from those on the back, they even avoided Po's glare. Noble drove so hastily he almost ran off the road the taxi entering Po's drive. After a moment of stunned reflection the taxi driver pulled into Po's front yard, and Pinky hoisted his bulk out of the back seat. Po stood, hands on hips, really concealing the knife behind his back, while his friend paid the driver, and added a tip – he had commandeered the vehicle for the best part of three hours by now.

As the taxi pulled a rapid turn and followed the truck back towards the road, Pinky stood for a moment, surveying the scene.

Baseball bats lay scattered on the drive. 'You holding a Little League team meet, Nicolas?'

'Didn't work out,' Po quipped, 'they brought the bats but didn't have the balls for a game.'

'More trouble with that punk from Boston?'

'Hopefully that's the end of it. Can get down to what's really important now.'

'Yep, let's go find pretty Tess.'

Pausing only to grab Tess's files from the kitchen, Po closed the door behind him and joined Pinky at the Mustang. His was the third car to speed from his property within minutes.

TWENTY-NINE

Tess was finally free of the blindfold, but it didn't aid her vision that much. She was in a deep, dark place: her ankles and wrists were still wrapped in duct tape, but what little movement her bindings allowed had given her a picture of her prison through touch. The walls were circular, about ten feet in diameter, formed of rocks slick with algae and slime, and she was in muddy water deep enough to slosh around her chest even while she was seated against the wall. The smell was unique, a pot pourri of rank aromas competing to sicken her most. High overhead, there was a suggestion of dim light, at the edges of a board that sealed the entrance. She was chilled to the bone, hair and clothing soaked when she was dumped unceremoniously into the pit. Behind her gag her teeth chattered and shivers ran uncontrolled through her frame. She couldn't sense the ends of her fingers or toes.

The drop had felt endless, but couldn't be that deep. The standing water had absorbed some of the impact: the wind had been knocked from her, but she suspected if she'd plummeted any great depth then her injuries would have been more substantial. As it was she was certain she was bruised and scraped. Her entire body ached but thankfully she could sense no broken bones. The passage of time was a mystery, measured only by her descent into abject misery. One thing she was certain of: if her captors didn't return soon, they needn't bother killing her because hypothermia would have done the job already.

Where had they gone?

She couldn't believe that they'd taken such trouble to snatch her only to dump her in a deep hole then forget about her. Unless that had always been their plan. Maybe the ignoble death at the bottom of a disused well was what they believed best fit Tess's punishment. In an abstract and contradictory way, there was a certain amount of logic in their thinking. Except Tess didn't believe that dumping her to perish slowly from exposure was a satisfying ending when compared to the deaths of her friends. It was more likely the couple had other tasks to finish.

Earlier she had goaded herself to get free, fight, or die. Now she was throwing away an opportunity. While she was out from under Rayne's watchful gaze, she should make more of an effort. All she was doing sitting there was giving in to the inevitable, and that simply was not her way these days. She thought of Jasmine Reed, Elsa Jayne Moore, and even Emma Clancy, who Tess had helped escape their own torturers, and remembered how those young women had impressed her so much through the indomitable nature of their spirits: they hadn't given up. Taking strength from their example, she should not give up either.

'Get free,' she muttered behind her gag. The claustrophobic confines dampened down her words, threatening to subdue the spark of spirit she'd just found. So she repeated the phrase, louder and with anger. 'Get free, goddamnit!'

In the bedroom of the motorhome, under the watchful eyes of Rayne, she couldn't move for fear of being beaten. Now she was under no such constraints. She wasn't as supple as she'd been in youth, but she hadn't seized up fully. Wriggling her wrists down under her butt then shuffling side to side, she easily forced her bound hands beneath her knees. Water sloshed, flicking scummy debris against her face. She snorted like a beast, clearing her nose of the dirty water then sucking in as much air as she could, because now came the difficult part. To get her cinched wrists out from under her feet she must duck under water, lie on her side, and work one foot over her wrists at a time. If she got her wrists caught between her heels she could drown, and when finally her corpse was dragged from the pit it would be contorted like a pretzel. She wouldn't – couldn't – worry about things going wrong, though, otherwise she would never make the attempt.

'Get free, Tess,' she ordered again, then sniffed in more air, before ducking down. Her body flopped on its side, frothy water washing over her, and she bucked her hips forward. Flexing her spine, she jammed both wrists towards her heels. Had there been more play in her legs she could have easily forced one foot through the circle formed of her tied arms, but getting through both at once was nigh-on impossible. She raged against her instinct to give up, to sit up and pull in life-giving oxygen: behind her gag she expelled a wordless scream that sounded almost like the mechanical whirr of an engine. Pressurized blood filled her skull, and her vision: the blackness bloomed with scarlet explosions.

The tape between her wrists got hooked between her feet: the worst-case scenario imaginable. She panicked. And yet, the surge of terror galvanized her, and she kicked and squirmed. All along she'd worked at loosening her wrists, and yet it was the tape around her legs that finally gave, and allowed her numbed legs to flail around. She wasn't entirely free, because her wrists were still hooked around one leg, and the response to her panic had forced her to unfold, so that now she was caught with her left arm to the front, right arm behind her backside, and hands snug beneath her groin. It allowed enough freedom to sit, to rear from the water, and she again inhaled through her nostrils. Trembling at her exertions, she sat numbly for a few seconds. The burning sensation of blood rushing to her feet caused her to jump and squirm. Sharp prickling sensations, pain enough to make her yelp: it kept her moving. She bent forward this time, submerging her face in the water, and lifting her left knee to her chest, she was able to force her wrists under her heel. Her arms popped loose, and she reared back, her skull smacking off the stone. Thankfully the spongy algae cushioned her head, and the impact was more a thing to be thankful of: it meant she was free.

Not yet.

Her wrists were still bound, she was gagged, and she was at the bottom of a well. But at least she could stand. Her legs could barely support her, and she cried behind her gag as circulation continued to ply hot irons to her nerve endings. She forced her backside to the wall to avoid sinking down into the filthy water again. Elbows tucked to her ribs, hands before her like a pugilist under heavy bombardment, she scrabbled unfeeling fingers over the tape encircling her mouth, until she got them wedged in the upper edge and tugged down. The gummy tape gave, but not without a fight. Her skin was raw where she tore it away, but she didn't care. She threw back her head and inhaled the lungfuls of air she'd longed for. She wasn't aware of it, but she shouted with each exhalation. Anyone overhearing would have heard yells of victory: *Yes! Yes! Yes!*

The response of her body was to fold over again, and her wrists were now forced against her abdomen as she gasped and fought to replenish the depleted oxygen. She felt woozy, should have remained bent over, but no. Now she was free she wanted to stand tall. She struggled upright, clenching her fists against her forehead. With one savage yell, she forced her hands directly down, then at the last instant swept them apart. The duct tape was only an effective restraint when there was no wiggle room. It parted with a loud zipper sound.

Now she had total freedom, be it only of the confines of the well, but at least she could move around. She sloshed to and fro, stamping her feet, swinging her arms, flapping her hands, this time welcoming the sting of returning circulation. Her vision was still swamped by swirling clouds of scarlet, some now turning green as their memory faded from her retina. She blinked furiously to clear her vision, and served only to make things appear darker. Or was it? As her vision adjusted, she could now make out the faintest impressions of her own hands as she moved them before her, deeper shadows against the murk. She craned up. At the edges of the board that Cable had dropped over the well she could make out dim light. Standing now, the lip of the well didn't look as high as before, and yet she was under no illusion, it was still beyond her reach. Even at full strength she doubted she could jump high enough to get within a body length of the top.

There had to be an alternative way out. Not a side tunnel or anything so obvious, but perhaps a ladder or rope that could be lowered, otherwise how did Cable and Rayne ever intend fishing her out of the pit to finish her off? Maybe they hadn't thought through the problem themselves. Maybe their intention was to gloat from the top, while hurling down boulders to crush her into the mud. She doubted that was their plan, but who knew? She didn't want to be at the bottom of the well when they finally returned.

Her vision had adjusted enough that she was certain she could make out individual protrusions on the walls. She reached and tested each in turn, wondering if they could be used as hand and foot holds, but they were spongy and slick, some of the old bricks even crumbling to mushy dust beneath her fingertips. There was no way to scale the slimy wall, and its diameter was twice that which would enable her to perform a trick like bracing her feet and shoulders against the opposite sides to inch up it like a hero in an action movie. Climbing out unassisted appeared impossible.

But she kept searching for a way.

She slogged across the well to the opposite side, felt as high as she could reach. Nothing substantial offered a handhold. She began circling to the left, continuing the sweep of her hands, seeking a place to step up with her feet. Her left ankle nudged something. It had sunk into the mud on the floor. As Tess pushed her heel against it, the object gave slightly, moved sluggishly in the cloying muck. It felt like a bar or length of hard wood. Could she use it as a tool to scrape between the rocks, to widen finger holes? It was a long shot, but worth a try.

She crouched, blindly reaching for the object. It felt slick, but wasn't entirely smooth – there were knob-like protrusions at the end. Her fingers encircled the shaft, and she tugged to free it. The mud was slow to release its grip, and then it yanked loose so suddenly that Tess almost fell on her backside. Whatever she held was about fourteen inches long. She held it overhead, moving it back and forth under the dim light at the edges of the pit. Shocked, she dropped the object with a splash.

It was a human femur!

A cloud of putrefaction engulfed her, stirred from beneath the water when she'd disturbed the remains.

Revulsion replaced the shock. When she again reached down for the thighbone she treated it with the respect it was due: yanking the bone out of the filth was akin to desecrating a grave. She cradled the bone in both palms, staring at its vague shape in the gloom. How could she be certain the bone was human? Could it be that of an animal that had slipped into the well and perished? Without letting go of the femur, she crouched and used her other hand to grope in the muck. More bones presented themselves, but she could get no sense of their shapes or dimensions. There was only one thing that would definitely tell her what she'd discovered.

Nausea rose to her throat when her fingers swept over a slick dome. But she had to find out what her companion was. Trembling with trepidation, she dug her fingers into the muck, then gently jostled her find loose. She raised it from the water, using her thumb to wipe off some of the adhering mud. Her thumb traced the edges of orbital sockets. She knew already what she'd discovered, and it confirmed she was correct about the remains. It was a human skull. And she'd a horrible feeling that she also knew whose . . .

'Oh God . . . *Manny?*'

There was the slim possibility that the remains were those of somebody else, but Tess's instincts told her otherwise. Manuel Cabello hadn't gone off-grid; he'd been removed from it. He was the first victim of Cable and Rayne, brought back to the place of his perceived crime to be murdered and dumped in the well.

She was horrified by her old friend's murder, perhaps not as badly if she'd made the discovery out of the blue: when she'd been unable to find Manny during her investigation she'd began to fear the worst. And to be fair, the insane logic used by his killers also made sense to Tess. If she was correct about Gabriella Kablinski's motive in hunting down and punishing her old classmates it was no surprise that Manny should end up here, because it all began at the well . . .

. . . They were only letting off steam. Their summer vacation had been sacrificed, given up for small monetary reward and long hours. Early mornings and late nights. Chaperoning boisterous kids in adventure and leadership exercises. They should be forgiven for letting down their hair, and imbibing the contraband snuck into Biscay Summer Camp by Kent Bachman and Richie Conklin, but they wouldn't be if captured by the camp's directors. If they were caught drinking alcohol they'd be unceremoniously fired, shamed on their return to Husson University, whose faculty had secured employment at the camp for their most trusted students. Tess and a couple of others were nervous about attending the party, but went along with the idea: supposedly agreed by general consensus by all involved, but some were towed along by the stronger personalities in their group. It was a case of 'you're with us or against us', and nobody wanted to be on the outside.

They couldn't party in plain sight, and it was Kent Bachman who'd suggested they use the old farmstead. The farm buildings had been abandoned years ago when the camp directors had purchased the surrounding land: it was far enough away from the children at the camp that it didn't threaten their safety, so money wasn't wasted on its demolition. The counsellors were warned that the farmstead was out of bounds, but their transgression could only be punished if they were discovered. They weren't negligent in their duties: all the kids had returned home, and they were shutting down the site until the fall semester came around, and yet rules were rules. They snuck to their hideout and camped out in the shadow of a sagging barn, where they got a fire going. Somebody brought burgers and ribs, but food took second place to the beer, wine, and spirits being passed around. There were laughs, taunts, pranks, a bit of necking, fumbling and groping too, and Tess had to admit that once she'd relaxed she had actually been enjoying the gathering. Until events took an unexpected turn.

She'd no idea how it happened, but she was gently warding off Richie's overly affectionate hands when somebody swore loudly and there was a sudden rush of bodies towards a dilapidated shack near the barn. Using the opportunity to cool things with Richie, she followed the stampede to see what was going on. Voices were raised inside the shack, one of them hysterically. Tess had rarely heard Gabriella speak above a subdued whisper, so at first didn't recognize the high-pitched shrieks the girl was directing at the others. She pushed inside, jostling for a position where she could see the unfolding drama. Richie pushed in behind her, pinching her backside in greeting. Tess elbowed him gently in the ribs, and he coughed out in drunken amusement. Gabriella stood astride a sagging plank across the mouth of an ancient well. She was stricken, face pale, streaked with runnels of make-up washed by tears. One hand pointed accusingly while she continued shrieking at Manny Cabello and Mina Stoll. The guilty couple were still only partially clothed, though Mina was making an attempt at covering her modesty, while trying to calm down her friend.

Gabriella wouldn't be calmed. She'd been betrayed and she was no longer prepared to remain the silent minority. She wasn't simply upset at finding Mina and Manny in a compromising situation, she was livid. *Briefly Tess wondered if her reaction was fuelled more by the understanding that Mina didn't feel for* her the way she obviously did for her, but that her one and only ally had abruptly abandoned her to fit in with the pack mentality. As absurd as the notion was, she'd been Thing Two, but now she didn't even belong in that disparaging partnership. She was alone, abandoned, bereft even of inclusion in the single club she'd felt part of. Tess felt sorry for the lonely girl.

Others in the group might have too, but the strongest personalities won out. Manny was first to laugh at Gabriella. He grabbed the front of his unzipped jeans suggestively. 'Tell the truth, freak,' he guffawed, 'you're only pissed 'cause you want a piece of me too, but you're just so butt ugly you haven't a hope in hell.' His snarky comment elicited a round of drunken laughter from the others. Gabriella screeched at them to shut up. She bunched both fists in her raven locks. She dropped to her knees on the wobbling plank.

'What a spaz,' Kent Bachman said, unable to hold in his own laughter. 'Who gives a shit about boy-tits anyway? In fact, who the fuck's idea was it to even invite the bitch along? She doesn't belong with us.'

Mina fisted a hand to her mouth, shaking her head as she stared at her friend. 'Gabby, I didn't do this to hurt you,' she moaned. 'I . . . I never—'

Gabriella lifted her face, and stared directly at Mina. Her mouth elongated, and a long howl burst forth that threatened never to curtail.

'She has totally lost it!' Kent Bachman opined. 'What a total freakazoid!'

'Someone should get her down from there before she hurts herself,' Tess suggested.

Chelsea Grace was nearest to the shrieking girl.

'Don't look at me!' Chelsea backed away from the well. 'There's no way I'm going out there. She can fall for all I care.'

Manny's cruel laughter rang out again. 'We should toss her down in the damn well till she cools off a bit.'

Tess turned scolding eyes on him.

'Here,' said Richie Conklin, edging around Tess. 'I'll do it. If I fall in that shit, I swear to God I'll kick the skanky little runt to death.'

'Don't you dare hurt her,' Tess growled.

'It's what she needs, the stupid bitch.' He was talking macho BS. He wouldn't hurt her willingly; his comments were for the benefit of his pals.

'Just help her down,' Tess said.

Before Richie could move, Kent pushed to the fore. 'I'll get her the fuck down before her damn screaming brings the directors here.' He flicked a Zippo lighter to life, waving a guttering yellow flame at Gabriella. 'Get the fuck off there or I'll put a damn light under your scrawny ass!'

'Stay away from me!' Gabriella screamed.

'Off now, bitch,' Kent said, leaning out from the edge of the well to wave his lighter flame within feet of her.

'Kent! For God's sake!' Tess couldn't believe the nastiness the joker of the group was capable of.

'Fuck her then,' Kent bawled back at her. 'Let her fall, I don't care.'

'Gabriella?' Tess called. 'You're going to hurt yourself. Come on down from there.'

She got no response. She wasn't sure that she'd even been heard – the others were still laughing and calling out, and her words were probably lost in the babble. Or ignored.

'What say we throw her the fuck down the well and get back to the party?' Manny Cabello suggested. 'No one wants her here. So we should just dump her down there and forget about her. Let the rats have her.'

'I'm with you,' Kent tittered. 'But I say we set her on fire first; I'm sure those rats prefer barbecue.'

'Go for it,' Richie laughed, caught up in the macho banter. 'Set her alight, Kent. It's the only time you'll ever get a girl hot for you!'

'Fuck you!' Kent and Richie grinned like lunatics.

There was no real intention to follow through their idea. It was a case of high jinks fuelling their cruelty. But Tess had heard enough. She barked something at Richie, and he turned an incredulous gaze on her. He made an apologetic face, but Tess turned away from him, slapping aside his hand as he tried to hold on to her. They were finished, and he goddamn well knew it.

'Who's going to help me get her down?' Tess demanded. She looked directly at her roommate. 'Chelsea?'

Chelsea backpedalled, eyes huge, teeth bared. 'I can't go out there . . . don't make me.'

Tess understood: Chelsea's intense fear of heights overrode any willingness to help. She looked around at the others in the group. All of them ensured they were facing another direction.

Finally she looked at Mina.

Mina only looked back, and then gave a tiny shake of her head.

Not only had Mina betrayed Gabriella, she'd now forsaken her. It was the breaking point for Gabriella. She struggled to rise, perhaps to flee screaming into the woods. But the plank was unsteady, and rotted at one end. It slipped into the gaping maw of the well, and Gabriella squawked in terror. She lunged for the lip of the well, and Tess reached to grasp her extended hand. She missed by inches, her gaze locked with Gabriella's as the girl pitched backwards into the darkness. That final look of hatred aimed at her should have warned Tess what the future held.

THIRTY

'**B**eing around Tess is really rubbing off on you, Nicolas,' said Pinky.

Po's features were set rigid. Teeth clenched, eyes squinting. His knuckles were white on the steering wheel. Driving at excessive speed in the foul conditions took concentration. Pinky wasn't referring to his superlative driving skills.

'She'll make a detective out of you yet,' Pinky went on.

'That's not where my strengths lie.'

'You could fool me, you.' Pinky wasn't built to sit in the bucket seat of a muscle car. He overspilled it somewhat, and that was after tilting back the backrest and sliding the seat to the furthest point on its runners. He'd forgone his seatbelt because it wouldn't fit around his girth. 'You made a connection that even pretty Tess missed, and there's no flies on that girl.'

'I've the benefit of hindsight,' Po said without taking his attention off the road. He swerved around a slower-moving vehicle, then nipped back in to the right. Rainwater stood in deep puddles in the gutters, traps for the unwary motorist. If anything he sped up. 'Tess was unaware of the motorhome the assholes are driving, so didn't know to connect it to where they're probably lying low. If she'd known she'd have figured it out too.'

'Probably. But I'm still impressed, me. Bein' around Tess is better for you than eating brain food: you're not the dumb ox you used to be.' Pinky was trying to lighten the situation with humour. Ordinarily Po appreciated his wit, but he wasn't in a laughing mood.

'You can be impressed with me if we find her alive.'

'We will.'

'I wish I was as confident as you are.'

Pinky looked across at him, and his gaze was steady. 'We will.'

'I should have told Alex where we're going before we set off.'

'Probably best that you didn't. If they've hurt Tess, we don't want the cops around for what we have in mind.'

Po was in agreement but for one thing. 'He's Tess's brother. He's worried about her too and would want to help. He has a right to be there.'

'So give me your cell an' I'll ring him.'

The corners of Po's lips tightened a fraction more. 'We'll ring him when we know for sure we're at the right place.'

One side of Pinky's mouth also turned up. Despite Po's words to the contrary, he wanted to catch up with Tess's abductors before the police – including Alex – could complicate matters. Yet he was torn. Foremost he wanted to find and protect Tess, justice on her abusers was secondary.

'How much further?' Pinky asked.

Wiscasset was behind them, Newcastle ahead. Once they crossed the river and got through Damariscotta the roads would be quieter, but not constructed for speed.

'About thirty minutes.'

Pinky eyed the terrain flashing by. The lightning storm periodically lit up swaying treetops, rocky bluffs and deep gorges through which roared white water – tributaries of the Sheepscot River. The landscape, he guessed, would get more rugged. 'You think you'll even get a signal out here?'

Po shrugged. He'd paid lip service towards involving Alex in the hunt, and that would have to suffice for now. He concentrated on driving, soon sweeping off the Atlantic Highway on the approach road to Newcastle. Without slowing he sped through the tiny town, and took a hard right, flashing over the Damariscotta River Bridge and into the town bearing the same name. He'd set a route in his head, and usually it was as if he had an inbuilt satellite navigation system, but he was unsure of the correct road to take next and was rapidly approaching an intersection offering four different routes. Two of those he discarded, but had to make a snap decision. He took the right turn, his tyres aquaplaning on the sodden asphalt. Luckily no other vehicles were abroad in the storm, and he steered into the skid, taking the Mustang towards the grounds of a Baptist church. Before mounting the opposite sidewalk, he steered out of the skid, and jammed down on the throttle to pull ahead. The Mustang spat wings of spray behind it.

'Somebody up there likes you,' Pinky wheezed. He had one hand braced against the dashboard, the other on the roof.

'Or He didn't want me driving through the window of His church,' Po countered.

'We won't be much good to Tess, us, if we end up in a wreck.'

'I've got everything under control.'

'I'd rather lay my faith in the Good Lord.'

Tentatively Pinky relaxed the hand steadying him against the ceiling. The car was roaring along, its deep tyre treads easily displacing the standing water now. The storm had momentarily abated, but by the look of the heavens – a churning morass of cloud backlit by distant lightning strikes – there was worse to come. Pinky doubted that the car would make such short work of the rougher country tracks they must take towards the summer camp.

Po found the correct road by accident. He knew the general direction where Biscay Summer Camp lay, and that he had to go cross-country towards the bottom end of Pemaquid Pond. Some people who enjoyed their privacy made their homes outside of town. A network of smaller roads that regularly branched or terminated at dead ends serviced the houses, and yet the one that Po took kept on going, winding its way through a landscape dominated by dense woodland and jagged crags. It had grown dark enough that there was little warning of tight bends beyond the reach of the Mustang's lights. But Po barely slowed, driving with the skill of a rally driver. Lightning blazed.

'I just seen a sign!' Pinky exclaimed.

'From God?'

'Naw, you fool. I spotted a signpost for Pemaquid Pond, me. It was back there, on that last cliff we passed. You're going in the right direction.'

'Good to know. Would be a real shame if we had to go all the way back to town to find another way through. I've wasted enough time already, Pinky, time that Tess doesn't have to spare.'

'Ordinarily I enjoy a flair for the dramatic, me, but please, Nicolas, keep those kind of thoughts to yourself.'

The road ended. The Mustang slewed to a halt, almost sideways on to its original position, just as Po intended. He'd angled it perfectly so that he could peer out his side window at the gate without getting out. They'd found the summer camp, although this was a service track once used by the groundskeepers to move their equipment back and forth without troubling the camp's attendees. The five-bar gate was similar to those found on farms to pen in livestock, with steel-framed wire mesh bolted on top to halt any trespassers tempted to hop over it. The wire was rusty, and had been peeled back a foot or so from its frame, allowing enough room for somebody to squeeze through the gap, but the gate was chained sturdily and it didn't look as if anyone had opened it in a few years.

'Son of a bitch,' Po wheezed under his breath.

'They didn't come this way then?'

'I very much doubt it.'

'Then we *need* to find which way they did go in, us.'

Po exhaled noisily. He was thinking hard.

'No time,' he announced. 'And we've no other option.'

'No other option than *what*?'

Po neglected to answer. That was fine, because his actions said everything. He swung the muscle car around so it faced the road they'd so recently exited, threw it in reverse, and then hit the gas. 'Maybe you want to hold onto something, Pinky,' he said.

In the collector's market his car was a classic, and in its pristine condition would command almost one hundred thousand dollars, and yet Po used it as if it were an old beater he'd picked up at a junkyard. He loved his car, but it was just a material thing. It could be replaced or repaired, unlike Tess. He threw it backwards into the gate like a battering ram. The gates buckled, and one side popped off its hinges, but still barred their way. As Pinky braced for a second collision, Po made sure that this time would be the charm. He pulled forward, reversed again at speed. Lightning flashed overhead, so nearby that the roar of thunder was only an instant in its wake, and yet it wasn't loud enough to drown out the crash of the Mustang smashing open the gates. Broken links of chain clattered on the roof and hood, denting the paintwork and cracking the windscreen: who knew how badly the rear end of the car was damaged? Po gave it no thought. He had to drive forward again, the tyres skidding and spinning freely for a few seconds before they found traction on the slick metal bars. He again spun the car around, and without pause drove directly over the busted gate and onto the unused dirt track beyond. Now that they'd forced entry to the domain of the killers, he didn't drive as fast as before because the track was designed for heavier machinery. The Mustang pitched and yawed like a boat on a raging sea as he proceeded. A neglected forest hemmed them in on both sides now, some of the trees having fallen astride the track. Luckily they were rotted, and could be churned beneath the tyres. As an afterthought Po switched off his lights. No need to warn the killers they were approaching.

THIRTY-ONE

The thunder was muted at the bottom of the well. So much so that Tess hadn't given any consideration to the weather since she'd been bundled, half-suffocated, into the rear of the motorhome hours earlier. Recalling the events of the night many years ago had served more than working out Gabriella Kablinski's motives for murder. Tess thought she might also have remembered a way out of her predicament. But she'd best be quick about it, because with the storm there was a deluge, and it didn't take much figuring how the well sustained its water supply. She was certain that the level had risen an inch or two since she'd finally managed to burst free of her bindings. The water table was rising, and the more rain that seeped into the earth, the higher it would get. It now sloshed about her ribcage as she paced again around the walls, this time seeking higher with her probing fingers.

As she searched, she again thought of the look of hatred Gabriella had cast at her as she'd slipped into the well, Tess's grasping hand only inches from hers. It was as if the distraught girl believed that Tess had deliberately allowed her to fall, when that couldn't be farther from the truth. In the intervening years Gabriella had dwelled upon the actions and words of the entire group, and had formed them into twisted versions of themselves: OK, so some of their actions could be deemed horrible, the puerile activities of drunken youths, but they were empty words and threats designed only to provoke cheap laughs. Rick Conklin would never have kicked her when she was down, Kent Bachman would never have lit her on fire, Manny Cabello would never have thrown her down the well, and Tess would never have allowed her to fall if it were in her power to avoid it. Even Chelsea, intensely afraid of heights, hadn't run away when it came to rescuing the girl. And yet Gabriella had taken the individual taunts, twisted them into something more than what they were, and then loosed them back on her tormentors, with fatal results in some cases. If it weren't for the demented nature of Gabriella's vengeance, she should be admired for her ingenuity. No, she wasn't to be admired, but reviled . . . or pitied?

Rayne victimized Gabriella in a more profound manner than any of the name-calling or insubstantial threats aimed at her in youth. Tess believed Rayne was the engine behind Cable's violent spree. Gabriella Kablinski had been devoid of friendship, had only desired to belong, and Rayne had capitalized on the young woman's need. But in forging a partnership with Gabriella it was to feed a sick hunger of her own. The transformation from awkward youth to – God! How did you categorize the *thing* she'd become? Cable had undergone some minor gender modification – to what extent Tess couldn't guess – through surgery, but she . . . no, he, had also been subjected to other agents. Anabolic steroids, Tess assumed, plus weight-lifting and other types of physical sculpturing. Who knew to what depths her mental manipulation had gone? Had Cable been subjected to an intense schedule of punishment and reward, her thoughts conditioned through fear multiplied by the threat of once again being cast aside, abandoned, bereft of love? That was not love, it was *control*. Cable would do anything to please Rayne, and Tess knew that things would not end here. Rayne would demand more, and Cable would deliver: their acts would grow more heinous, and that was saying something. There could be no pity for Cable, none whatsoever. The last time that Tess helped Gabriella from this place it had been swaddled in her dry coat; Cable should be led out in chains.

That thought brought her back full circle. The rising water was now sloshing around her chest. Having disturbed Manny Cabello's decomposing remains the stench had grown almost overwhelming, and disturbing the water again as she waded around wasn't helping. But it was her only hope of escape. All those years earlier, Tess and Rick Conklin had clambered into the well to help Gabriella out, using rungs embedded in the wall during its construction. During her fall Gabriella had struck her head, twisted an ankle, sprained an elbow, and she could not climb out under her power. A rope had been lowered, and even Chelsea had assisted in hauling out the injured girl, albeit she stayed well away from the lip of the well. Tess and Rick didn't need the rope; they'd climbed back out using the rungs. So where the hell were they now?

She must have missed the lowest rung while groping around. Had to have, because during Gabriella's rescue Tess recalled standing in water only up to her hips and had easily stepped up onto the first. It was currently under water!

She moved around the wall again, this time using her feet to probe for the foothold . . . and found it!

She set her left foot on the rung, used it as a step up, and groped directly above. There should have been two more rungs within easy reach of the first, and yet they were gone. Perhaps they'd been knocked loose from the crumbling wall when Manny's body had been dumped unceremoniously over the edge, or, and the thought sent a pang of panic racing through her, they'd been deliberately removed to ensure their prisoner couldn't climb out. She stumbled back down, sending a mini-tsunami to the opposite wall. The sloshing echo reminded her how time was growing short. This time she stepped onto the bottom rung and threw herself up the wall in one fluid motion. Her reaching fingertips scraped something metal, before gravity tugged her down. She stumbled around in the water, hands slapping the murky surface for balance. The next rung was out of easy reach, but not impossible.

'Try harder, goddamnit!'

She waded for the wall, stood on the rung, and hurled her body upward. But too much effort rewarded her by bouncing her away from her objective. She crashed down on her butt, and was swallowed by the deep water. Revulsion assailed her, she knew she was surrounded by the rotting particles of her old friend, but it also filled her with the extra determination needed to get the fuck out of there. She fought upright, then plunged forward, again vaulting off the rung. She snapped the tips of her left fingers over the rung above. The corroded metal abraded her skin, and pain snapped down her arm from a pinched nerve in her index finger. She cringed, eyelids screwed, but clung with every ounce of frustrated rage inside her. Her toes dangled in the water with no purchase. She stretched her right arm. Couldn't reach. Screamed at the effort. She stretched as high as possible, while stabbing her toes at the tiniest of algae-slick seams in the wall.

Her right fingertips groped over the rung. She cried at the effort of worming both hands over so she could grip with her thumbs too. Then she hung there, suspended, but barely a few inches higher than when she'd begun the arduous task of hauling herself out of the well.

She couldn't maintain the grip on the rung for long. Already her shoulder muscles were tortured, and she could feel her arms begin to shudder at the effort. She had to get higher or her hold would give out. She'd regained use of her right hand, if not the finest motor-skills, but she couldn't forget that it had once been practically severed from her wrist. Her injured hand couldn't bear her weight, and neither could her left do it alone. With extreme effort, and the expulsion of a keening moan, she dragged her body higher, feet sliding on the wall, forearms juddering.

It was a hopeless task, because even if she could get one arm hooked around the rung, what then? There was nothing substantial on which she could support her feet while she reached for the next rung up. Hauling herself upward by the strength of her arms alone was an unachievable feat. But she must *try*!

Her right hand gave without warning. She'd no sense of falling until she plunged under water and floundered about, trying to regain her footing. She broke the surface gasping, spitting filthy water, dashing at her eyes and nostrils with abraded fingertips. She cursed, scolding her own weakness, directing her anger on the spasming fingers of her right hand. She was seconds away from pounding the offending limb against the wall . . . but what good would that do?

Use your head, not brawn, she suggested. Depending on how quickly the well flooded, she could tread water and rise to the top, bobbing about like a cork. But hypothermia would kill her long before the water rose high enough.

'Think harder, Tess!' she hissed.

She shook life back into her right hand. A dull, aching sensation extended all the way up the radial nerve to her shoulder blade. She waited for it to subside, breathing deeply, energizing from a depleted stock of determination, while she thought harder.

Her vision had adapted to the darkness. When standing directly under the lowest rungs and peering up against the faintest glimmer of light at the edge of the board, she could make out the shapes of others above. Her worm's eye view made judging the distance between them difficult, but it could only be a foot or so. If she could find a way to grasp that second rung then she could finally get a heel on the lower one. From there the climb would be easier. But those twelve inches could as well be a mile. She'd have to hold the bottom rung with her left, her right wouldn't support her, and reach up for the next with her right . . . and what then? Without a foot support she couldn't secure a grip with her right.

'So give up,' she told herself sarcastically. She shivered, teeth chattering. Then shook her head resolutely. 'The hell I will!'

She wrestled off her sopping jacket. She considered using it as a lasso, then thought it a waste of time and effort. But wait! If she could attach it like a sling under the first rung in reach, it would give her a stirrup.

Before the idea was fully formed, she'd grasped the cuff of one sleeve in her right hand, stepped onto the submerged rung, and thrown her body upward. Her left hand found the rung on the first try, and she let out a scream of challenge as she thrust up with her right fist. She jammed it between the rung and the bricks. Then, as she swung one-handed, she snaked her hips as she shoved and probed the saturated sleeve over the support. It took daring to release the sleeve, but she did so, snapping her hand over it again an instant later, but this time on the other side of the rung. Gravity pulled her down, and she used the movement to yank the coat partly over the rung. She dropped into water now up to her collarbones.

She dragged in air. Tears pouring down her cheeks were hot against her chilled skin: tears of relief. The jacket dangled within reach.

Straining up she brought both cuffs together and tied them in a double knot. She used the submerged rung as a step up, and got her right elbow in the loop, and tested it. The knot tightened, the cloth squeaking in protest, but it held. Next she jumped for the higher rung again, snatched it in her left hand, while bracing her right elbow in the sling. This time, she contorted her body, bringing up a knee. It was a few torturous seconds before she could feed her knee over the sling, but then she was hanging there, not suspended but supported for the first time. She began to laugh, but to her ears there was no humour, just a note of madness. The laughter turned to a hiccup, then a grunt of effort as she straightened out her body, and was finally able to reach for the second rung above her. Her right hand was too unreliable, but she solved that problem by going underarm, pushing wrist and forearm between the rung and wall, and gripping with her inner elbow. Only then did she release her left, and transfer it to the same rung. With two arms secure, she kicked free of the jacket sling, and brought up one foot to the lower rung, already reaching for the next one up with her left hand.

Rock climbers stressed the importance of keeping three points of contact while scaling a cliff, but they didn't have the benefit of a ladder. She went up, now using both feet and only her strongest arm, her right only adding momentary stability as she groped higher.

She'd originally guessed the well was about twelve to fifteen feet deep. She'd misjudged by at least six feet. How she hadn't been seriously injured when dumped, hands and ankles bound, was a miracle. She was thankful that there had been water at the bottom to break her fall, even if her repeated soakings had chilled her to the bone. The effort she'd put in during the last few minutes had warmed her, yet the cold could still finish her if she didn't find dry clothing and warmth soon. The board overhead was tantalizingly close. She only hoped that it wasn't sealing her in, and that her captors had trusted to her bindings and the lack of handholds to keep her imprisoned.

Now she was nearer the top she could hear the storm raging. The incessant rain drummed on the roof and walls of the ancient shack. Thunder rumbled. But there was more. The grumble of an engine that – as soon as she'd distinguished it from the beating rain – was shut off. Doors opened and closed. Voices. The thud of hurrying feet, followed by a clatter and dull rumble as something heavy tumbled to the floor in the shack.

Tess swarmed up the last few rungs, and got an eye to the slim opening between the board and rim of the well. She couldn't identify who was there, could only make out deeper shadows cast on the floor as they moved close to the entrance of the shack, backlit by lightning. She prayed for rescue . . . by Po and Alex, especially. But knew it could be neither of her loved ones. Cable and Rayne had returned.

Disbelief burned through her. She'd almost made it, but fate had dealt her a sickening blow at the final moment. Not that she was going to fold now, because she'd worked too hard to gain her freedom, and wouldn't stop until she'd fully escaped, or was dead.

She exerted gentle pressure to the board, using the back of her head and one shoulder to nudge it an inch or so higher, and was glad to find it wasn't weighted down. She craned to see, just as lightning flashed again. No. Not lightning this time, but a battery-operated lamp flickering to life. She saw a pair of booted feet, and beyond them another figure, this one collapsed on its side, facing away from her, duct tape similarly wrapped as tightly around the face and wrists as hers had been earlier. Who had they brought back with them this time?

The boots belonged to Cable. She was certain even before a thickly muscled arm reached down, grasped the recumbent figure by the belt, and dragged it around a few feet. The figure was contorted, feet and shins twisted beneath them or . . . shit. The lower limbs were missing! It wasn't enough that the bastards had already beaten Rick Conklin senseless that time; they wanted to finish the job. It explained where the demented couple had been the last few hours, off on a mission to grab Conklin while they felt confident that Tess could find no way out of the hell they'd dumped her into.

Her outrage almost overwhelmed good sense. She was a second from thrusting upward, tossing aside the board, and launching herself on Rick's abusers. But caution told her that she'd no hope of defeating the two killers in a fistfight, especially if they were armed. She must even the odds; better still, make them work in her favour. But how?

The chance for clear thought was snatched away. The board was suddenly tilted up and two figures were silhouetted against the lamplight. Tess clung to the uppermost rungs, mouth hanging open as she blinked up in dismay at Cable and Rayne.

'Would you just look at what we've got here,' Rayne crowed. She flicked on a flashlight, the beam searing Tess's eyes. 'It's true! Rats can climb up a drainpipe! Best you throw her down again, Cable.'

Echoing Rayne's insult, Tess felt like a damned rodent. One

caught in the open with a couple of hawks wheeling overhead. But she wasn't as helpless as one. She let out a shriek of challenge and threw herself upward . . .

. . . and met Cable's fist.

The blow struck her directly in the sternum.

Tess tumbled backwards and fell.

She wheeled over once before slapping the cold water, almost flat on her back. Blinded momentarily by the flashlight, now by the pain and the shock of her fall, she sank into blackness. Her fingers clawed at the surface, and her heels kicked it to froth, but she sank butt first into the filth now five feet below. The effort she'd expended trying to climb out had been for nothing. Dispirited she allowed herself to sink into the clammy embrace of the mud almost succumbing to unconsciousness. But the dejection was brief, displaced by the surge of frustration that sent a buzz through her like an electrical charge. She kicked and lashed at the water, righting herself. She broke the surface howling in rage at the two bastards peering down at her from what suddenly felt a million miles away.

Tess would never recollect the actual words she screamed, only that they came out with such vitriol that they made Cable step away. Rayne wasn't as easily moved. She laughed with trademark sadism, and then began hurling small objects down at her, the trinkets and ornaments she had stuffed in her pockets during her thieving spree in Mrs Ridgeway's shop. One ceramic ornament smashed against the wall and sprayed needle-like shards on Tess's upturned face. She hunched over instinctively, and something metallic and heavy bounced off her scalp: a brass figurine about the size of a man's thumb. The pain almost finished the job of knocking her unconscious. She staggered away, but was hemmed in again by the wall. More missiles struck the water around her, each accompanied by Rayne's malicious laughter. Tess dodged away again, wading for where her jacket still dangled.

'Where do you think you can hide?' Rayne called down. 'Run, you rat! I can keep this up all day.'

Tess grasped a handful of her jacket. Clung to it, gasping for breath. The water was up to her chin, but the water table had found its depth. She wasn't in fear of drowning while she remained upright, and she needn't fear succumbing to hypothermia now that Rayne had returned, because it appeared the sadistic bitch intended stoning her to death.

Except Rayne's words were as empty as her pockets.

She turned her ire on Cable.

'I thought you told me there was no way she could climb out of there!'

'There wasn't.' Cable's counter was lame.

'Well *duh*! There obviously was, you idiot. Good job we got back when we did or that little rat would have gotten away scot-free.'

'I broke off the bottom rungs,' Cable argued. 'I'm much taller and couldn't get out without the rope ladder. Besides, she was tied up. I didn't expect her to get free and neither did you, Rayne.'

'Don't presume to tell me what I did or didn't think!'

'I'm only saying . . .'

'Well don't. Go and get me that fucking can.'

'What you gonna do?'

'Make sure the rat isn't tempted to climb out again before we're ready.'

'I . . . I'm not sure it's a good idea.'

'Do I look as if I give a shit? Leave the thinking to me in future, Cable, or I swear to God we're done.'

Tess grasped at the opportunity. 'Gabriella! You don't have to obey her. Don't you see she's insane and making you do things you don't want to.'

'Shut your goddamned mouth!' Rayne hollered.

'Gabriella? Gabby. Please! You have to stop this. It's gone way too far already!'

'I said *shut up*!' Rayne leaned so far over to scream the command that she almost toppled into the well. She grasped the exposed bricks with clawed fingers, her neck taut. 'You don't get to speak to my man. Do you fucking hear me, you bitch? There is no fucking Gabriella. There's only *my* Cable, and there's only *me* who gets to tell *him* what to do.' She turned away briefly to demonstrate. 'Cable, get the fuckin' can. Good. Give it here.'

Tess shut up. Not because of Rayne's words, but at sight of what kind of can Rayne settled on the rim of the well. Oh no, she thought. Rayne unscrewed the cap, all the while staring directly at Tess.

'Yeah,' she called. 'You know exactly what this is, don't you?'

Rayne upended the can, sloshing its contents down on Tess and the surrounding walls. Tess tried to cover her head with her jacket, but it was a futile gesture. The liquid still got all over her, and began to pool on the surface of the water. The undeniable stink of gasoline made her gasp. A memory of Kent Bachman flashed through her mind, as he threatened putting a light under Gabriella's scrawny ass. Another image displaced that one, this time conjured from her nightmares of Kent in flames . . . even more horrible, the figure writhing within the blaze abruptly wore her face.

Rayne threw aside the gas can. But only so she could dig out a cigarette lighter. She struck it aflame.

Tess almost curled up inside. She prepared to dive beneath the water: though she'd no hope of remaining submerged long enough to avoid being immolated. But Rayne didn't drop the lighter. She held it out over the opening.

'If I hear you trying to climb out of there again, I swear to God I will burn you to death.' She briefly turned to Cable. 'What was it that peckerhead Kent said to you about the rats preferring barbecue?'

Enveloped in gas fumes, Tess stood shivering in the well while the demented Rayne turned her screwy attention on a target nearer by. Tess could only listen in abject horror as Rayne goaded Cable into kicking Rick Conklin repeatedly, before the twisted bitch joined in too.

What else could Tess do?

THIRTY-TWO

Pinky squinted at the nearest broken-down cabins. 'How long ago did you say this place closed?'

'Six years maybe.' Po shrugged. He knew that Biscay Summer Camp had been a victim of the economic downturn, but it had struggled against the inevitable for a few years before finally accepting defeat. He hadn't taken too much interest in the details when scoping out where Tess could have been taken, only in getting there fast. But he could tell what Pinky was thinking: even before it had closed it must have been in a state of disrepair, because six years hadn't been responsible for corrupting the site this much. Rather than a vacation or adventure camp where parents would choose to send their children, it looked more like a shantytown in a third-world country. Some of the log cabins were falling apart, roofs sagging, graffiti-daubed doors and windows hanging off their hinges: vandals had put the camp at the mercy of the elements and reduced it to a dump. One cabin had burned down and was a blackened heap: whether that was due to an arsonist or a lightning strike was anyone's guess. The forest had begun encroaching on the site too, reclaiming areas cleared for recreational purposes. Bushes and briar patches had sprung up on lawns and roads, some invading the abandoned structures, and wind-blown branches were scattered everywhere.

'Makes you wonder,' said Pinky as he eyed the evidence of atrophy. 'If the world suffered a real catastrophic event, how soon all traces of our current civilization would be wiped away.'

'That's deep,' Po said, his gaze equally watchful, 'coming from you.'

'Ha! I just play the buffoon, me. Occasionally I do think about things more important than what I fancy for supper.'

Po didn't need convincing. Pinky was a contradiction in terms: his looks, exuberant mannerisms, and exaggerated speech pattern set him apart from the norm, but he was no fool. He was a thinker, a strategist, and his keen interest in the ramshackle appearance of the site went beyond existentialism, he was figuring out the best way to use it to their advantage. So too was Po, but until they had a clue as to Tess's whereabouts there was little to work with. There was no sign of life.

He was watching for the motorhome, guessing that the storm would have pushed the issue, and it would be parked close to where Tess had been delivered. But there was no hint of it within the confines of the summer camp. He was tempted to search every building in the camp, but had the feeling she wasn't there. An equally strong instinct told him she was close by though. He drew the Mustang to a halt and powered down his window. Raindrops pattered his face and shoulder as he leaned for a closer look at the road. 'You see those?'

'I do. Tyre tracks. They could be from an RV,' Pinky said.

There was more than one set of indentations in the wet earth. If the tracks belonged to the motorhome then it had entered the site via a different route than they had, but that had never been in question. The problem was figuring out where it had gone since. The tyre ruts crisscrossed a few times, one overlaid atop the others, and there was little to say what direction the vehicle had been going. Po got out the car and crouched lower. Some of the tracks were older, laid days, perhaps even weeks ago, but some were fresher, one set so new its edges were crumbling under the battering rain. Po stood and spied beyond the camp. Without his headlights he couldn't see far, but he got a sense of an open pasture, then more patches of forest on the other side. The latest set of tracks speared directly for the pasture. He was back in the Mustang in an instant, and got it moving. They left the deserted camp behind as he pushed the Mustang into the field. Briefly he switched on the lights, and spotted the evidence of the comings and goings of the larger vehicle. Some grass was still pressed down by its recent passage, some blades standing back up despite the storm's efforts at crushing them flat.

'Looks as if they already came and went again,' Pinky said. 'I see other tracks; this isn't the first time they've been this way today. It's a bad sign, Nicolas.'

Po had similar misgivings. For all he knew the freshest of the tracks could have been made when the bastards left after doing who knew what to Tess. But they'd no way of telling how recent the tracks were, or if the motorhome – he was confident the tracks were made by the large vehicle that flashed by him near the abduction site – had been coming or going at the time. He could only hope that his intuition played in his favour, and before it was too late. He gave the car more gas and it surged forward, bouncing and swaying on the uneven earth. The backend was already a crumpled mess, and he gave as little concern for the suspension. Ahead, the field sloped to another service road, running across their position. As they approached, Po growled under his breath. The road was hardpack, and he feared there would be less chance of following any tracks on it. He slowed, seeking an idea of which way the motorhome had gone, and real-ized his concern was unfounded. The grass was flattened down in a wide arc to the right, and as he briefly flicked on his lights he spotted fresh breakages in some of the lower branches over-hanging the road to that side, some of the broken twigs also littered the road surface. It was further evidence that a large vehicle had passed that way very recently, though didn't confirm if it had been coming or going. He swung the Mustang to the right.

A quarter-mile further on he brought the car to a halt on a bridge that spanned a ravine, through which tumbled white water. Immediately beyond the bridge, following the contours of the river, the road continued to the left, but Po ignored it. Deeper tyre tracks marked where the motorhome had left the road to drive across another field, this one more overgrown. The winter months had been unkind to the pasture, the grass discoloured and sickly looking, but it was still long enough to show a distinct trail towards another bunch of trees on the far side. He didn't need the trail to convince him of where to go next; beyond the copse of trees he'd spotted the faintest glimmer of light.

'We should get out of here, us,' Pinky said. 'They might hear us if we drive on in.'

'We should.' But Po didn't turn the engine off. 'No. Better idea. I'll get out. You take the car that way and circle in from the road.'

'In case they come that way with the RV and need stopping? That would usually make sense, but it doesn't look to me as if they obey the roads. They've been coming and going across this field, why'd they change things up now?'

'We can't leave anything to chance, Pinky.'

'You want me to go that way, I'll do it, but you ax me, if we leave your ride here, the road's blocked to them anyway. I'd prefer to be with you, Nicolas, when you find those bastards.'

'OK, I guess that's fair. Take a look in the glove box,' Po said. 'Something I picked up earlier you might want to bring.'

Pinky flipped it open, delved inside. He pulled out the handgun Po liberated from Chapel. Pinky made his living dealing in guns, and the gloom didn't stop him from identifying the piece. 'Dan Wesson Razorback.' He dropped the magazine, before slapping it back in, after taking only a cursory glance at the ammunition. 'Point four-five ACP. Yeah, they'll put extra holes in most asses.'

'Use it only as a last resort,' Po advised.

'For sure,' said Pinky with a smile that transformed his usual jovial features to something frightening: the other side of Pinky Leclerc that only his enemies usually witnessed. 'We don't want those fuckers dyin' too easily.'

'They deserve to die, but not until after we find Tess. Depending on *how* we find her, then we'll decide on how to deal with them.' This was also a side to Nicolas Villere that people rarely saw: one that reared its ugly face when his friends were in peril.

He pulled the Mustang around, and parked it sideways across the road. The big motorhome could probably force the car out of its way, but not now. If it were rammed it would only wedge in the entrance to the bridge and block it. Po had to clamber over the hood to join Pinky on the other side. They stood together for a moment, peering across the pasture to the trees beyond. The light Po spotted still glowed faintly between the trees.

The rain suddenly abated, but the wind was as strong as before. Lightning still danced to the south. The storm was passing but another was banked on the northern horizon and would arrive very soon. The break in the deluge was welcome though, because neither of them was ideally dressed for the weather.

'Someone up there's still looking after us,' Pinky noted.

'I'd prefer He looks after Tess,' Po replied, 'and keeps the hell out of my way.'

They set off across the pasture, keeping to the trail where the grass had been beaten down. They were soaked to the knees within seconds.

'Goin' to need some new sneakers after this, me.'

'They aren't the first pair of shoes you've ruined on my behalf,' Po reminded him. 'Next time you visit, we'll think ahead and I'll buy you some gumboots.'

'Does Converse even make gumboots?'

Po grunted in mirth. It was good having his best friend at his side: even at the grimmest of moments Pinky could make him feel better. Yet the time for laughter was over, they were approaching the edge of the woods, and now that they were closer could make out the dim shapes of a cluster of structures beyond the trees. The track they were on swept to the right, around the copse, but Po took the shorter route through it. The undergrowth made moving difficult, but also offered concealment. He and Pinky reached the very edge of the copse, then crouched in the tree line as they studied a farmstead in a worse state of disrepair than the summer camp. There was a house, the roof collapsed at one end. Some ancient barns, one of them leaning precariously to one side, and some sheds. Further away was another structure, a construction of tin sheets and metal girders. Parked between the house and the barn was the motorhome.

Po shared a glance with Pinky, before nodding at the big vehicle. There was a light burning inside it towards the rear, where he guessed there was a bedroom. It wasn't the light they'd noticed from further out. Now that they were close by Po could see other lights – probably battery powered lamps, because the old farm was so run down there'd be no electricity supply. A lamp cast a lambent glow from inside the house, leaking between the laths of shutters on a ground-floor window, and there was a similar glow emanating from the tin shed at the edge of the property. He listened, but the blustering wind roared through the treetops, and plucked and pushed at the ancient buildings, rattling loose tiles and corrugated-tin sheets. The sound was akin to a marching band warming up, a tuneless racket.

'You take the RV,' he told Pinky, 'I'm going to check out the house.'

Pinky nodded at the tin shed. 'You ax me, that's where we should begin.'

'We have to clear the other places first. Tess could be in the shed, but the bastards that took her might not be. We don't want them sneaking up on us from behind.'

Pinky nodded at his wisdom, but couldn't help a lingering glance again at the tin shed. 'OK, let's do it, us,' he finally said.

Po gripped his elbow. 'Hold on. Something I should do first.'

He took out his cellphone, and was surprised to find he had a signal, albeit a poor one. He quickly composed a text and hit send. 'Just covering our asses,' he told Pinky, who nodded in understanding. Pinky began to rise up, but was halted again.

'If you find any of them in the RV, hold 'em there,' Po instructed. 'In fact, wait for me there, OK? I'll join you in a few minutes.'

Without argument, Pinky swept up from concealment and jogged forward, the Dan Wesson down by his right thigh. For such a big man, he was nimble and light on his feet. Po was nimbler, dashing for the house: an observer would be hard put to differentiate him from any of the flitting shadows cast by the storm clouds.

At the house Po paused, one ear cocked towards the motor-home. If things kicked off with Pinky he'd be across to back him up in seconds. His other ear was poised to listen for movement within the house. It creaked and groaned, abused by the wind, but he couldn't get a hint of a living person within. But he'd been truthful with Pinky; he meant it when he said the house and motorhome must be cleared first. They'd be no good to Tess if the killers ambushed them. He edged along to the window, through which light gleamed between the shutters. A quick peek inside told him the room was deserted, and a lot more. It was a kitchen and it looked as if the bad guys had been using it as an extra living space. There was some furniture, old, dusty, scarred, but also newer items, some of them in boxes, some scattered around the work surfaces. Dirty plates had been dumped in the sink, possibly never to be washed. Pizza boxes, Styrofoam fast-food cartons, and greasy burger wrappers littered the table. There were also a number of large plastic tubs. Po distractedly identified them as power shakes containers, the type of strength supplements consumed by bodybuilders and other athletes. Briefly he recalled Rick Conklin describing one of his attackers as *a goddamn steroid freak*, alongside which Po would look a weakling. 'Yeah,' he whispered under his breath. 'Good luck with that, asshole.'

He was unperturbed by the prospect of meeting the muscle freak – in fact he relished the meeting: this was a punk who'd kicked a crippled man when he was down, who'd set light to another man tied in a chair, and quite probably pushed Chelsea Grace to her death from a cliff. It didn't take a tough guy to do any of those things, just a cowardly piece of dirt. He couldn't make the mistake of underestimating the thug, but neither was he going to allow the bastard's inflated appearance to give him pause. Back in Angola, and on a couple of occasions since then, Po had silenced bigger men, when they realized the size of a man's heart was more important than the size of his biceps.

Confident that the house was empty, he turned for the motorhome, and saw that Pinky was making a more thorough search of it than he had the house. His friend was still inside, poking around. By the time he padded over and found the open side door, he met Pinky coming out. Pinky was shaking his head, aghast at what he'd found. 'You won't believe the crap back there,' he said, using his firearm as a pointer towards the bedroom. 'Place stinks to high heaven; I'd say they were breeding pigs in there, them. There's barbells and shit, but that ain't all. Toys.' He made a slow nod to emphasize his meaning. 'Fifty-goddamn-Shades of Sicko! There's even this *thing* for strapping round the pelvis, and it's . . .' He shuddered. 'No. I don't even want to go there, me. You said they beat one of their victims with a baseball bat or something? They were lucky they weren't hit over the head by that humongous thing instead!'

'So the scumball can't get it up? Doesn't surprise me. I already thought he was a dickless coward. Any sign that Tess was in there?'

'Place is too much of a dump to tell. But I did find rolls of duct tape, and a plastic bag that looked as if it had been stretched out of shape. I'm sure there were scratch marks on it too.' He mimed someone clawing for air. 'Hopefully the latter was used first.'

By that Pinky meant he hoped Tess had been secured after the bag was pulled over her head. Tying her up after would have been unnecessary if she'd been suffocated to death. Po boiled as he pictured the horrible attack Tess must have endured during her abduction. He could see how she might have been lured out of her car by one of her abductors while the other snuck up on her and pulled a plastic bag over her head as she stepped out the door. It explained why the car had been abandoned the way it had, with all her important belongings still inside. Suffocating her was their way of subduing her, so they could load her in the motorhome and bring her here, where they could torture her at their leisure. He dreaded how far they'd taken her abuse in the intervening hours: Pinky's discovery of sex toys made him fearful that Tess had been subjected to worse than a beating.

Well, enough was enough.

They headed for the tin shed, flanking it a side apiece, just as the storm returned. This time with more vengeance. Lightning fractured the heavens, and the thunder boomed like cannons. The atmosphere suited Po's mood perfectly. If Pinky's assertion that a deity was watching over them was correct, then He was a god of war.

THIRTY-THREE

Tess lay gasping for an instant on the hard-packed dirt next to the well, but she didn't catch her breath before Cable grasped her by her shirt collar and yanked her to her feet. She was shaken back and forth to make sure the warning was understood.

'Don't dare fight me,' Cable growled, as he – Tess couldn't think of the brute now as a female – pulled loose the rope from around her chest. It had been thrown down to her minutes ago, looped like a noose, with a brisk order to secure it around her, and Cable had dragged her out. The rough hemp rope, a leftover from when the place had still been a working farm, was aged but surprisingly strong, and there was no fear of it breaking and pitching her back into the depths of the well, but Tess had assisted the climb by pushing on each rung her feet met. The rope had nipped tightly, abrading the skin under her armpits and cramping her lungs.

'Sit there and don't move.' Cable forced her down.

Tess sat, her back against the low rim of the well. She stank of gasoline. Rayne stood over her, a facetious smile riding her scarred lips, as she weaved the flame of her cigarette lighter back and forth. 'You know what'll happen if you try to run.' Rayne nodded at Cable, who'd backed away while coiling the rope around one arm. 'And don't try appealing to Gabriella again, bitch. There is no *Gabriella* here.'

Tess purposefully looked away, searching for Rick Conklin. He lay unresponsive about twenty feet from her. His wheelchair had been tipped over next to the entrance door, and she could only guess at the ferocity of his beating that had propelled him so far inside the shed. He wasn't dead: rasping breaths could be heard over the tumult of rain battering the roof.

'Don't expect him to help you either,' Rayne said scornfully. 'Fuckin' cripple's good for nothing.'

'You are an evil bitch,' Tess told her.

Rayne wiggled her eyebrows. 'You don't say?'

Tess glared up at her.

Rayne flicked the lighter again, the yellow flame gouting. She made an exaggerated lunge at Tess. Tess didn't flinch. Rayne wasn't going to burn her yet; she hadn't satisfied her jones for prolonged torture.

'Watch this cow,' she told Cable, 'and make sure she doesn't get any funny ideas about running away.'

Cable had put aside the coiled rope, and now held a gun, an old revolver. Tess wondered if the gun had been used to demand obedience from Conklin when they'd returned for him the second time, or that it was the threat that had compelled Chelsea to step off the cliff. Probably both, but she couldn't know and wouldn't ask now. It was enough that Cable aimed the gun at her, and the look on the bluff features challenged: *Try me.* If she did try to flee, she'd get a bullet in her spine.

Rayne approached Conklin, and dragged the duct tape down off his mouth. 'Still breathing, huh?'

Conklin retained some spirit. He spat a bloody spray of saliva at the woman. Rayne peered down at him as if nonplussed by the crimson strings decorating her sneakers. After this she'd discard the clothes anyway, to rid herself of any incriminating forensic evidence. 'You know something?' she asked in a reasonable tone. 'My friend over there wanted your punishment to fit your crime, but to be honest I'm tired of hitting you. See, it doesn't matter how much we beat on you, you probably aren't the type to beg for mercy.'

'Go screw yourself,' Conklin said, his voice wet with mucus.

'Oh, I would if I could. I bet you would screw me too . . . if you still had a pecker.' Rayne aimed a wicked smile at Cable. 'What say I take a look, eh? See if he's intact or if the bomb got 'im good.'

Cable's face twisted at the suggestion, and Rayne sashayed back towards him. 'What's wrong with my big ol' bear?' she said with a singsong pout. 'Not jealous, are you? Oh, you know I don't want any other man.'

Cable turned his face aside.

How many times had Rayne taunted him in a similar manner, Tess wondered.

'Does she always make a fool of you like that?' she asked.

Cable squinted at her.

'She's using you, but you don't have to do as she says. You've got a gun, Gabriella. Do the right thing.'

'I'll have him put a bullet between your goddamn eyes if you don't shut up.' The singsong tone of Rayne's voice had disappeared, now it was a fingernails-on-chalkboard squeal.

Tess ignored the threat, looking directly into Cable's eyes. 'See what I mean? She's using you again: she'll have *you* shoot me. Do you do everything she demands, even when you know it's *wrong*?'

'Shoot her.'

Rayne's words were a snappy command for a dog to attack.

Cable glanced at her, confused.

'I said *shoot her*.'

'No.'

'No? Do as you're fucking told, Cable.'

'I won't shoot her.'

'Then give me the damn gun and I'll do it.'

Cable held the gun away, a kid protecting a toy from a bully. He looked pleadingly at Rayne. 'I still want her dead,' he explained, 'but shooting her is too easy.'

The announcement caused Rayne to halt, and cock her head wonderingly. 'For a second there I thought you were going to give me trouble. Tut-tut-tut.'

'No. I don't want to spoil our fun.' Cable's wide lips danced uncomfortably, wondering if he'd said enough to appease his girl.

Tess snorted at him. 'So that's what this is: fun? Revenge I can kind of understand, but you're doing this only for your sick kicks? I thought there was hope for you, Gabriella, but I was wrong. You're as insane as that poisoned witch.'

Cable scowled down at her, the gun again pointing directly at Tess's face. 'Are you determined to die?'

'What are my other options? You're going to let me walk away unharmed? Yeah, as if that's going to happen!' Tess shook her head in disbelief. 'That would be the sensible thing to do. The *right* thing. You do realize that you aren't going to get away with this?'

'Nobody knows about us,' Cable responded, 'or where we've brought you.'

'Don't kid yourself. I figured out what you were up to, and

passed everything I had on you both to the cops. You'll be caught in no time.'

Panic flared momentarily in Cable, who looked to Rayne for reassurance.

'Don't listen to the tramp,' Rayne said. 'She's lying. She knows nothing about us. So what if she told the cops about Gabriella Kablinski? She doesn't exist any more.' Rayne bent at the waist to stare directly into Tess's face, checking for guile. 'And you have no idea who I am.'

'My guess is that Rayne is a false name, just as Cable is, but your real identity won't take much figuring out. You were both institutionalized together, right, when you struck up this unhealthy relationship you've got going? The cops will easily get your name from the hospital records.' It was a hypothesis Tess had mulled over, and the solidifying of Rayne's features told her she was on the right track. Cable glanced back and forth between them, shuffling nervously. Tess nodded up at them. 'I thought prison at first, but now I've met you I'm more inclined to believe you met in some mental-health institute.'

'You know nothing about us,' Rayne asserted, but the desperation with which she said it told Tess the opposite was true.

'Yours aren't the actions of sane people,' Tess went on. 'You're both sick in the head.' She made sure that Cable got her next message by staring directly at him. 'Only one of you can still be helped.'

'Rayne, maybe we should—'

Before Cable could finish the thought, Rayne drew back her foot and kicked Tess in the ribs. Tess flinched, but it wasn't the response Rayne desired. She grabbed a handful of Tess's stringy gasoline-soaked hair and yanked her to one side. For an instant Tess feared she'd gone too far with her goading, and that Rayne would light her up. She grabbed for the hand holding the lighter, but Rayne simply snatched it out of the way, even as she laid in another kick to her chest. Rayne's toes found the hollow beneath her sternum, and what little breath she'd gathered was forced from her by the convulsing of her diaphragm.

Releasing her grasp, Rayne stepped back, her arms swinging wide in triumph. Then she rounded on Cable, stabbing one finger back towards Tess. *'That's what we should do to the bitch.* Right there! We should show her what's really going to happen. She's going to die along with all those other bastards, and we are going to get away with it. Don't listen to her lies, Cable. She'll say anything to save her pathetic life. What? She wants you to help her, show her mercy? Did she help you when those other bastards threw you down that well? Did she?'

'Nobody . . . threw you . . . down the well,' Tess reminded Cable, her voice croaky as she tried to find her breath. 'You fell. I tried to catch you.'

'Lies!' Rayne glared at the two of them in turn. 'She's calling you a liar, Cable. Do you hear? She says you fell. That is not what you told me, and I choose to believe *you*.'

'The board you were standing on slipped and you fell,' Tess said, and this time her voice was a bit stronger. 'We were trying to get you down safely, and you slipped. Remember? I grabbed for you but missed. Do you remember the first ones to climb into the well to help pull you out?' Tess aimed her chin at the forlorn figure lying in the dirt across from them. 'Rick and me; we climbed down, while the others sent down a rope for you. Even Chelsea, who was terrified of heights, helped pull you out.'

'That's not the way I remember things,' Cable muttered, and blinked apologetically at Rayne.

'No,' Tess said, 'because the reality doesn't suit your need for revenge. It has to be changed. Your memories of events have been contorted out of shape to fit what Rayne wants you to do. Don't you get it?'

'Does it freaking matter?' Rayne demanded. 'You fell or you were pushed. Who gives a damn? Every last one of them treated you like dirt, Cable, so deserve everything they got. It's their fault you ended up standing on top of the freakin' well in the first place. Mina and Manny started it, you said – rutting like a pair of dogs under your nose – and then all the others joined in to make a bigger fool out of you. Where's that list of yours, Cable? Get it out. See who still needs striking from it—' she jabbed a finger first at Tess and then at Conklin '—to put everything behind you. Once they're gone, there's no need to hang on to Gabriella fucking Kablinski. That pathetic bitch can die along with all those bad memories she holds over you. You'll be Cable; *my Cable*, and that's all we want, right?'

'That's all *Rayne* wants,' Tess emphasized. 'But what happens when she tires of you? It's inevitable that it will happen. You'll end up in a place just like this one, probably burned to ash the way she burned Kent: she won't even wait to scrape your residue off the soles of her shoes before she goes after what she wants next.'

Cable frowned, chewing his lips. But he aimed the gun at Tess. 'You all have to die.'

'Why? Is that what you want? Really?'

'Yes.'

'No,' Tess countered, and she was having none of it. 'It's what Rayne wants.'

'What Rayne wants, Rayne gets,' said Cable.

'Exactly my point!' Tess folded her hands in her lap. The way she sat, they could be friends again, back around the campfire, enjoying a friendly chat. It was a sham. Her fingers, hidden beneath her other hand, wormed in her waistband. 'Just think about it. Did you kill anyone, or was it all down to Rayne? Did you push Chelsea from the cliff? Light the match under Kent?' She nodded backwards at the well. 'Was it you that murdered Manny and threw him down there? Even Rick, over there, I'm betting Rayne has plans to finish him too. The way she finished everyone else.'

'Rayne didn't kill everyone,' Cable said, but the admission didn't sit right with him. 'Mina died because of Chelsea, that bitch pushed Mina into taking her own life.'

Tess shook her head. 'No, no, you've got that wrong. Mina had her own problems, and she had moved on from any juvenile spat she had with Chelsea.' She was desperate to learn how Chelsea had come to schedule the message that reached her after the young woman's death, but she doubted that Cable or Rayne had been aware of it; otherwise they would have ensured that Chelsea deleted it before she'd been forced off the cliff at Bald Head Cove. 'Everyone moved on. And so should you. I don't agree with the way you were bullied at school, but that was then. It means nothing now. We are all different people.'

'Now there's a freakin' understatement!' Rayne crowed. 'Look at what you've become, Cable. You're a goddamn *specimen*! Ain't nobody going to laugh at you now.'

'I'll be laughing from the public gallery when you're both sent down,' Tess told her.

'Only if they bring your ashes to court in an urn.' Rayne turned a devilish leer on Cable. 'You once told me you envied this Queen Bitch's looks: let's see if you still think she's pretty once we've melted the skin from her bones.' She glanced briefly at Conklin, then over at two strategically placed chairs. Before each chair was a metal trough. Her plan was to scorch both prisoners the way they had Kent Bachman. 'Go get that other gasoline can from the RV, we'll need it to light two fires.'

Tess should have been horrified by Rayne's pronouncement, yet with Cable out of the way for a minute or two it might give her the opportunity she'd been hoping for to overpower Rayne.

Cable almost scuppered her plan. 'There's enough gas left in that can.'

'Really?' Rayne demanded. She set herself haughtily before the towering thug, and he visibly diminished under her gaze. 'You forget I poured most of it down the well. She's doused, but the crip over there isn't. Now do as I said and *go get the fucking gasoline.*'

Cable turned quickly without argument and hurried for the exit. As he thrust aside the door, the storm roared inside. Cable averted his face, shoved his gun in his jeans pocket, and plunged into the deluge.

Rayne spun back to Tess. She puckered her mouth, as if there was a foul aroma. Tess hadn't moved, she just sat, peering up at her. 'You think you're such a hot shit,' Rayne said, 'but you're just like all the others. You'll be begging *me* for pity before we're done.'

Tess snorted. 'There we go again, eh, Rayne? It's all about you.'

'Damn right, it is!'

'You don't give a damn about Gabby.'

'There is no Gabby. It's Cable.'

'It? That just proves my point. He's just a tool to you, something to be used.'

'He's good for when it comes to the heavy lifting.' Rayne laughed snidely. 'Would have struggled if I'd had to bring that cripple in here all by myself. But handling you won't be a problem.' She flicked the lighter, got a flame burning, and approached to within a couple of feet. 'Want to try me?'

THIRTY-FOUR

P o watched the hulking figure lope towards the motorhome. The storm had built to such ferocity that the rain bounced off the sodden earth, and from the man's shoulders and head. His spiky hair was pressed flat. Other features were indistinguishable through the deluge, but not the size and shape of the guy: Conklin's assertion that one of his attackers was a steroid freak wasn't wrong. That left the woman still inside the tin shed, and Tess in danger from her. He wished nothing more than to go after the thug, but Tess was his priority. He looked for Pinky.

Hearing the squeal of rollers as the door was pushed open, Pinky had gone to cover. Po spotted him though, crouched behind a pile of ancient farm machinery overgrown by briar and couch grass. Pinky's gaze followed the big guy across the yard. He snapped his attention on Po.

Po pointed, formed a gun from his fingers, and nodded at the loping figure. Pinky got the message. Not that he'd spotted that the man was armed but that Pinky was, and he should go after that one while Po searched for Tess.

Pinky made a brief salute with two fingers of his own, then rose up, and began stalking the big guy, his Dan Wesson poised for action. Pinky was equal to his prey in size, if not in form. The sculpted physique of the thug should give him the advantage, but Pinky's strength was born from genuine struggle and hardship, and the tougher for it. He had a medical condition, but not one that hampered him. Po almost pitied the thug if he took Pinky's bulk for softness. Confident that Pinky would handle the guy, he concentrated on his own task. He too had taken cover when the door opened, crouching and blending alongside a fallen wall. He came out of his crouch and stalked forward. He didn't have a gun, but his knife had come to his hand as he rose. He wasn't a monster: he didn't intend sticking the woman with a blade, but that all depended. To save Tess he'd cut the murderous bitch's head off.

The thug had left the door standing open to the elements. The angle Po approached from didn't give him a clear view inside the shed, but he could make out an unexpected object tipped on the floor just beyond the opening: a wheelchair. It didn't look as old and abandoned as everything else at the farm. Had her abductors used the wheelchair to transport Tess from the motorhome to the shed? Whatever, it didn't matter. He moved close to where the door had been rolled aside, standing beyond the wash of faint light from within. Creeping sideways, he peeked around the open door. A quick sweep of the interior told him everything. Rick Conklin, beaten and in a state of semi-unconsciousness, lay on his side about ten feet to his right. Tess – thank God she was still alive – sat with her back against a low wall that he thought might be the top of an ancient well, and a young woman stood over her, waving a cigarette lighter dangerously close to Tess's face.

'Want to try me?' he heard the woman snarl.

Tess tightened up, about to launch at the woman in a do or die effort. But then her gaze slid past her tormentor and met his. She was too switched on to make an obvious sign she'd spotted him, but he caught the brief narrowing of her eyes as she peered back at him. He lifted a finger to his lips, and stepped inside. He was silent, and even if he'd clumped his way inside, the racket made by the storm would have deadened his step, and yet something made the woman glance his way. Immediately Po moved, springing forward, but was brought short when the woman aimed the guttering flame at Tess and hollered: 'Don't you smell the gasoline?'

Po skidded to a halt. He searched Tess's face for proof, and her grimace said the woman was telling the truth. Tess was saturated and he didn't doubt that it was in highly inflammable gasoline. Now that he'd taken stock of the situation, he realized the severity of Tess's plight: the stench of gas was almost overpowering within the shed. How the fumes hadn't ignited already was a miracle. 'OK, take it easy,' he said.

'I don't know who you are,' the woman said, 'but unless you want her to go up like a Roman candle, back up.'

It was unwise admitting his relationship to Tess. One look at the woman, with her crazy eyes and ugly screwed up mouth, told him she'd delight in burning Tess before the eyes of her lover.

Instead, he said: 'Maybe you should douse that flame before we all go up. You included.'

'Maybe you should drop the knife,' the woman countered, 'or we all will go up in flames. That isn't water you're standing in, buddy.'

Despite himself, Po glanced at the ground. It was damp underfoot, but that could have been from the windblown rain. Could he take the chance? He held the knife out to his side, allowed it to fall.

The woman nodded satisfactorily, then jerked her head at him. 'Now come sit down over here where I can keep an eye on you till my friend gets back.'

'Nope.'

'You aren't in a position to argue,' the woman reminded him with a wave of the lighter.

'I can just walk outta here,' Po reminded her.

'Before you burn?'

'Why not throw that lighter over here and we'll see.'

She seemed to consider the idea, but knew as well as he that the threat she held over Tess would end. Plus, the moisture underfoot was only water; more of it had blown inside in the past few seconds. Her attention slipped past him as she searched for her partner in crime.

Flashes lit up the darkness outside. This time it wasn't lightning, and the thunder that followed was the higher *crack-crack-crack* of competing gunfire . . .

Seconds earlier Pinky met the muscle-head coming back around the motorhome, where the big guy had been rooting around in a storage compartment. He was lugging a jerry can that sloshed as he came to a halt as Pinky stepped in front of him.

'Who are you?' the big man wondered aloud. His eyes showed their whites when his gaze alighted on the Dan Wesson held alongside Pinky's hip.

'If you've hurt Tess Grey, I'm the man who's goin' to make you sorry.'

The thug seemed stunned to find Pinky blocking his path, more for his appearance – you'd think he'd never seen a black guy before – than the threat of the gun. His reaction proved that he didn't give the presence of a gun much respect. He swung

the jerry can at Pinky. The sudden move was startling, and Pinky
ducked. The big man followed the swing of the can with his
shoulder and crashed into Pinky, knocking him aside. Stumbling
against the side of the motorhome, it was a second before Pinky
could gain his balance and bring around the Dan Wesson. The
man was running for the tin shed, had only made a few paces,
but Pinky had to stop him before he got to the shed and spoiled
Po's rescue attempt. He brought up the Dan Wesson, but the guy
hurled the jerry can backwards, and again Pinky had to dodge
to avoid being struck. The metal can caromed off the motorhome
and fell between Pinky's feet. He danced to find his footing,
buried his heels in the soaked earth, and fired.

Po had warned him to use the gun only as a last resort.

He did so now as a warning only, to alert Po of the guy's return.

The muscle freak had another idea. He pulled a revolver from
his jeans, and fired twice as he raced for the shed. The bullets came
nowhere close to Pinky, but he ducked nonetheless. Then, as the
thug powered towards the shed, Pinky struck out after him . . .

Rayne heard the gunfire, the shock of it causing her to take
an involuntary step backwards, and her thumb off the lighter. It
snuffed out.

Tess, seeing her opportunity at last, yanked out the object she'd
concealed in her waistband before she'd been dragged out of the
well. It was five inches long, tinged dark ivory by the filthy water,
with some tough ribbons of sinew still attached. It was a bone,
broken at one end from when Manny Cabello had been thrown
unceremoniously to his final resting place, and spear sharp. With
a shout, Tess drove it deep into Rayne's right thigh. 'That's for
Manny, you bitch!'

Rayne screeched, and staggered away, forgetting about igniting
her prisoner as she slapped at the rounded end of the bone jutting
from her leg in an effort to knock it free. Po made a lunge after
her, but was brought around as Cable rushed inside the shed.
There was a brief moment of confusion, before Cable hollered
for Rayne, then began to bring up his gun to seek a viable target.
But by then Po flew at him and grappled with his gun hand. The
revolver fired, the bullet ricocheting off an I-beam overhead.

Chaos reigned, both within and beyond the tin shed. Booming
thunder echoed the sharp retort of the revolver as two more rounds

were spent into the ceiling. Po didn't have time to check the gun
– it could be a five- or six-shot – so didn't waste his time. He
drove under the burly chest of Cable with his right shoulder,
forcing him backwards. Cable dug in his heels, but they skidded
in the wet earth. He tried to bring around the barrel of the revolver,
to shoot Po in the chest. Po abruptly brought up his skull, directly
under Cable's chin. He couldn't tell if the gun had fired again or
if the crack was from the impact of bone on bone.

Pinky charged inside the shed, his head snapping back and
forth as he checked for friends and foes. His gaze alighted on
Tess. She'd pushed up from a seated position, and was going
after a skinny woman. Tess appeared pained, as if every muscle
in her body ached, but she was gaining on the other woman, who
limped badly as she tried to pull something free from her leg.
Both women's voices competed furiously. He saw Po wrestling
with the muscle-freak. The revolver in the big man's hand
discharged, muzzle flash visible in the gloom at the side of the
shed. Pinky aimed his own gun, but didn't have a clear target:
Po was in too close a grapple with his opponent. Undecided who
needed his help most, Pinky only watched the unfolding drama
until the right moment presented itself.

Rayne yanked the bone out of her leg. It trailed droplets of
blood as she slung it aside. She hadn't relinquished the lighter
in her other hand. As she rolled her thumb over the striker wheel,
Tess caromed into her, and both women went down on the
floor. They squalled like wild cats caught in a death grip as they
fought. Tess clawed at Rayne's hand, trying to rip away the
lighter. Rayne clawed at Tess's eyes. They rolled, now fists in
hair, now pounding each other's faces. They crashed into one of
the metal troughs earlier set up, and it spilled over on its
side. The spreading puddle reached for Conklin.

'Pinky!' The voice was Tess's. 'Help him!'

Pinky hadn't at first noticed the man lying semi-conscious to
his right. He wasn't the prejudiced type, had experienced it enough
in his lifetime, but even he blinked in dismay at where the guy's
legs had been removed – it simply wasn't something he'd expected
to see, and it gave him a second's pause. But then he spotted what
it was that Tess and Rayne fought for control over, caught a waft
of the acrid stench of gasoline, and he rushed to drag the disabled

man out of harm's way. Conklin's head lolled in dazed confusion
as Pinky loomed over him, and his response was to throw a weak
punch. The fist bounced ineffectively off Pinky's side, but offered
a good handhold. Pinky grasped the wrist, his other hand still
encumbered by his gun, and dragged the guy away from the
spreading puddle. Missing his legs, Conklin should have been easy
to manoeuvre, but he was a dead weight, his upper body dense
with muscle. Pinky had to push away his gun, get two hands on
the guy, and lift him to safety. He pulled Conklin up so they met
chests, and the confused guy tried to headbutt him. 'Take it easy,
you,' Pinky scolded, 'I'm one of the good guys, me.'

Conklin expelled bloody spittle in Pinky's face.

'Talk about ingratitude,' Pinky wheezed, as he swung Conklin
around and set him up against the wall next to the exit.
Conklin pushed against him, still in a state of confusion. Pinky
swung around.

His task had taken less than twenty seconds, and yet the tableau
had changed dramatically.

Po and Cable's fight had taken them to the rear of the shed,
beyond the open mouth of a well. The revolver had been lost
somewhere along the way. Now it appeared that the muscle-freak
wasn't as keen to engage, because Po stalked him, and the big
guy backpedalled, throwing useless punches and kicks that fell
short. They cursed each other, but their voices made little sense,
not exactly drowned by the storm, but melding with it along with
the continued spat between Tess and Rayne.

The women had spilled apart.

But Tess scrambled after the skinny woman, who was on all
fours, hands slapping at the sodden earth.

Enough was enough. Pinky raced to help Tess.

Just as Rayne rose to her feet, a full body length beyond Tess,
and her mouth twisted into a sneer of victory.

Tess faltered, but couldn't halt her forward momentum.

Rayne sparked the lighter, and a yellow flame stood four
inches from her fist.

Tess was half a body length away now, and Rayne swung the
flaming lighter towards her.

There was an audible *phoop!* as the gas fumes ignited,
and flame billowed.

With a strident shout of alarm, Pinky dove, scooping Tess around her waist with his bent elbow, and they both landed in a rolling heap in among a stack of piled clutter, farming equipment left over from decades ago. Unidentifiable tools and buckets and parts of an old bench all collapsed on them as they came to rest. Pinky's mind was full of panic as he slapped and patted at Tess. But her faint groan was enough to tell that she wasn't aflame. He rolled off her, shedding a cascading pile of junk, and looked for the firebug.

Rayne stood in place, arm extended. The flame on the lighter now stood four feet tall, and growing. It also wreathed up her arm, and the entire right side of her clothing had caught. Her sneer of victory was replaced by a look of abject terror, of disbelief too. The blaze coughed, billowed, and suddenly she was engulfed in searing flames. A secondary flicker of flame danced briefly across the floor, and then fire raged around Rayne. She stood at the centre of the conflagration, a wail of agony rising from its midst.

Flames spread unerringly after the trail of droplets shed from Tess as Pinky had bowled her aside.

Pinky grabbed her unceremoniously, and sprinted for safety, hurdling smaller puddles of flame, seeking safety but with no idea where to go. A ribbon of flame writhed along the floor in their wake, a thing alive and with a hunger to consume.

It was not the only thing to chase them.

Rayne, senseless with agony, gouting dirty yellow flames stumbled to meet them. Nobody would ever know if her intention was to wrap them in the flames that sheathed her body, or if her stumbling progress was made in some hope of assistance, because there was no way she could have been thinking clearly. Surely, in her final moments, she wasn't so bent on murder that she'd die while trying to take down her enemies? In the end, it didn't matter.

Pinky and Tess came to a halt, the well to their backs, with no way to safely escape the conflagration while Rayne barred their way.

Pinky drew his gun.

It had come to the last resort, and the choice between shooting the blazing woman or joining her in agonizing death was a no-brainer.

But Tess had another idea.

She set herself directly in front of Rayne, and screamed at her to *come on*!

Rayne stumbled the last few feet, her blazing arms reaching to grasp Tess.

But Tess wasn't for dying engulfed by flames.

She ducked away from the fiery hands, and as Rayne stumbled past, she swept a kick into her back. Overbalanced, Rayne had nowhere to go but down. She fell trailing flames and smoke into the well.

'Get away!' Tess shouted, grabbing at Pinky.

He was tugged along with her as Rayne splashed headlong into the water below. Water on which floated a layer of gasoline. It ignited with a roar, and flame boiled between the walls, then reached for the ceiling.

Pinky fell flat on his face, stunned by the sudden explosion, the Dan Wesson sliding away across the floor. But then he was crawling, assisted by – and assisting in turn – Tess as they sought safety. It was seconds before he realized that Tess was on fire. Blue flame danced on her jeans, crawling towards her sodden shirt. Pinky bellowed a wordless roar as he flattened his bulk over her, rolling her across the floor as again his hands slapped and patted at her. This time her groans were punctuated by hisses of pain. Yet she squirmed out from under him, and rose to her knees, smoke rising from her singed jeans.

Thankfully, she didn't appear seriously burned. Her face was pale with shock as she stared at him. Then she gave a little yelp, comprehension flaring in her eyes and she began slapping frantic-ally at him. Flames had been licking up his front. Pinky's larger palms joined the slapping. Then they were both on their knees, dazed, but checking out each other for errant sparks that would flare up again. Pinky checked his hands. They were reddened, but not charred, and the heat he could feel in his face was as much from effort as any scorching he'd received. Tess had also escaped serious harm, though her hair was a mess equally hanging in wet ringlets, or singed to dirty curls at their ends. Pinky couldn't help a laugh of disbelief, and Tess was only a moment away from joining him.

A scream broke them out of their relieved stupor.

THIRTY-FIVE

The danger didn't end with Rayne's death.

Cable was still alive, and though he'd met more than his match in Po, was still intent on putting up a fight. Po was happy to oblige, but for one niggling point. He was unsure when he'd grown aware that there was something different about the man he battled with – likely it was when Cable had him in a headlock and he'd grabbed and twisted the brute's genitals to force him to let go. He'd heard that steroid abuse could have some unsavoury side effects, where a man's testicles could shrink to the size of peanuts, but surely there'd be something there to squeeze? As they fought on, Po peppering well-timed punches into Cable's solid abdominal muscles and ribs, palm thrusts to his face and neck, Cable had responded with clubbing blows that grew wilder by the moment, to a point they became flailing slaps and scratches: the deep throated curses had grown higher in pitch too.

Again they smashed together in a grapple, and this time Po was the one applying a headlock, and as Cable squirmed out, Po grabbed the tails of his jacket and yanked them up over his head. He controlled him a moment with the jacket pulled over his head, while he battered a knee into Cable's ribs. Cable wrenched backwards and his jacket and T-shirt were dragged off him. He windmilled his arms, freeing himself from the entangling material. Face rigid, teeth clenched, the muscles in his jaw bulging, Cable lurched back from Po, who for a moment halted the chase. Po stared, while allowing the clothing to drop to the floor.

Before him, Cable stood, bared to the waist, and Po's suspicion was confirmed. On entering the shed and spotting the woman who threatened Tess, he'd wondered why she looked nothing like the Goth girl in Tess's photograph. The guy he'd battled wasn't Manny Cabello either . . . he wasn't even a guy!

Cable wore vivid scars on his chest, both below the pectoral muscles and around his nipples. They were indicators that Cable's breasts had been removed, and some cosmetic work had been done to reform him, but not by the most skilled of surgeons. It wasn't that he fought a woman that gave Po momentary pause, but the fact he had suspected it and had been deliberately holding his punches. Now the confirmation made him hold back again: he was no fool, there were plenty women capable of giving him the fight of his life, but it was apparent that his opponent wasn't one of them. Cable was all about brawn and fury, but both had burned out rapidly, strength fleeing as rapidly as the heart for a real fight had gone out of her. Weakened, and fearing she'd bitten off jerky tougher than she could chew, Cable was folding beneath the understanding that she wasn't the *specimen of perfection* Rayne had made her believe in. She was a scared little girl once more.

But then the flames rose and Rayne pitched into the well and the subsequent fireball plumed among the rafters.

Something snapped in Cable.

'Rayne!' she screamed. 'Nooooo!'

She lunged, as if to hurl herself headlong down the well after her girlfriend.

Po barred her.

'Get the hell out of my way,' Cable screeched, 'or I swear to God I'll tear you apart.'

'That's enough, Gabriella,' Po growled. 'It's over with.'

'I said *get out of my waaaay*!'

Cable hurtled forward, hands grasping for Po's throat. If she got a hold on him, he'd topple into the blazing well too.

'I said *enough*, goddamnit!' he snapped.

He met Cable's lunge with a straight blast of his right fist. The punch was thrown with intent, and would save his life, but also spare hers. It connected squarely on the point of her chin and Cable's legs collapsed under her. He caught her as she tumbled forward, knocked cold. He rolled her onto her butt, settled her a moment while he looked for Tess and Pinky. Curtains of flame separated them, but he could make out their shapes beyond, where they were helping Rick Conklin outside. He caught Tess looking back for him, and shot her a nod, and a grim smile. Cable was big, though not inordinately heavy, and yet while he could toss her over his shoulder, carry her out like a firefighter coming to the rescue, there was no clear path through the flames. Poisonous smoke roiled overhead, creeping lower by the second.

Po kicked corrugated metal panels from the side of the shed. Returned for Cable, and got a grip under her armpits. He dragged her outside, looked for his friends and spotted Tess running towards him. She was bedraggled, soaked through, hair a frizzy mess, but he'd never been so happy to see her.

'I knew you'd find me,' she said.

'Knew?'

'OK. I hoped.'

They clinched briefly, Po kissing her forehead and cheeks, before she planted her mouth over his. Their kiss was brief though, because the fire continued to rage within the shed. The tin and steel structure wasn't in danger of going up completely, but the heat emanating from it was growing uncomfortable, and the smoke choking.

'Help me with her?' Po asked.

Tess looked down at the figure at his feet.

In sleep Cable had lost much of the faux-masculinity in her face, her muscles lax, so that her features were softened. Tess could see something of the girl she'd once known, and to be honest had pitied, so bent without any rancour to help drag Gabriella to safety.

After helping to haul Conklin outside, Pinky had dashed back for his wheelchair. He'd gotten Conklin seated, and used it to wheel him to safety near to the motorhome. As Tess and Po deposited Cable on the earth before him, Conklin stirred, blinking in wonder at those surrounding him. His face was a swollen mess of cuts and bruises. His gaze flicked down to the recumbent form on the ground. His bottom lip trembled, but no words came out. Maybe he'd never expected to get out of the shed alive, because his instinct was to weep. Pinky placed a comforting hand on his shoulder and squeezed. Tess held onto Po. The rain continued to beat down.

Cable's naked upper body glistened under the rain.

'We should do something about her,' Tess suggested.

Po pulled out of his jacket and laid it over the unconscious woman. He didn't mind knocking her out, but wasn't a heel about protecting her dignity.

'I meant to secure her,' Tess said.

Cable was blowing spit bubbles as she slept.

'She's going nowhere.'

They were still arranged around their prisoner when the first sirens rose above the tumult of wind and rain.

'The cavalry have arrived,' Pinky announced with a swift clap of his hands. 'Yay!'

Tess peered up at Po.

'I sent Alex a text after I confirmed you'd been brought here,' he explained. 'He has probably sent out the local cops for a look-see.'

'They won't get past the bridge you blocked,' Pinky said, reminding him that the Mustang was wedged across it.

He frowned. 'Hope they don't decide to ram it outta the way. Oh, well, I guess it's going to have to go into the body shop any way. Your Prius too,' he added to Tess.

He walked to the motorhome, drew open the driver's door and laid his hand on the horn. Summoning the cops to them.

THIRTY-SIX

D ays later Po met with Jimmy Hawkes for a powwow. He wanted to knock Hawkes cold the way he'd resolved the issue with Cable. But if Tess could find a modicum of forgiveness for Gabriella Kablinski then he thought he should probably attempt to initiate a peace plan with his enemy. The alternative was a continued feud, and it wasn't long ago that he'd ended one that had beleaguered him for more than two decades. If terms weren't agreed, more people would get hurt, and anyone with a brain could see that it was not good for either of them.

'This is the last time I lay my cards on the table,' Po warned, as they sat opposite each other in a booth in Po's recently reopened diner.

'I hear you,' Hawkes said. 'I'm listening.'

'Then listen good, because I'm not going to repeat myself. This ends here, now, peaceably. Or you can send more of your boys after me, but we both know how that will end.'

'Coming from anyone else, I'd say you were overconfident, but I've seen the proof of your words. You went through my boys like a dose of salts.' There was actually a note of grudging respect in his voice. 'More than once.'

'And that was me taking things easy with them. That last bunch you sent to my home, I cut 'em to hurt, could have done much worse.'

Hawkes nodded at the truth of his statement.

'If there's a next time I won't waste my time with them, I'll come directly to you,' Po went on.

'There won't be a next time,' Hawkes said. 'You have my word on it.'

'Your word means shit to me.'

Tess slid into the booth alongside Po. Her fair hair had been cropped short to remove the singed ends. Her brand-new neat style, coupled with the navy blue trouser suit and crisp blouse she wore, gave her an official look. She pushed a folder across the table.

'Open it,' Po said.

Hawkes exhaled slowly, but did as he was told. He turned back the flap, and teased out the first of a dozen sheets of paper. He exhaled once more as he read the uppermost sheet: a witness statement signed by Bernard Addison, owner of the HappyDayz diner.

'That's a copy of a file I've compiled,' Tess explained. 'It contains sworn statements from those you've already extorted cash from. I have times, dates, and video footage of you and your associates threatening various business people and taking pay-offs. The evidence contained in it would be of great interest to the district attorney. Oh, did I mention that the DA and I are like that?' Tess held up two crossed fingers.

'This,' said Po, holding up his right fist, 'is your order to cease and desist. Take another look in the file, Hawkes.'

Hawkes delved behind the sheets of paper, pulled out a small vinyl wallet. He shook his head in disbelief even before he opened it.

'One-way bus ticket back to Boston,' Po confirmed.

'You want me to leave town?'

'There's nothing to keep you here,' Po reminded him. 'Except maybe a prison cell. If, no, *when* the DA makes those charges stick, you'll be going away for a long time. Your choice, buddy. If I were you I'd take the bus.'

'You can't run me out of town like this.'

Po only smiled.

'This is bullshit!' Hawkes announced. He glanced around for support he already knew wasn't available.

His pals Noble and Lassiter were at the bar, squirming uncomfortably under the watchful gazes of Pinky Leclerc and Chris Mitchell. Both still carried the evidence from the last time they'd met Po, in the form of bruises, and in Lassiter's case stitches in the wounds on his thighs. He stood because he couldn't get comfortable on his bar stool. Noble's swollen eyes were now purple grapes. They'd already received a prediction about their futures if they dared move against Po or his friends again. They hailed from Portland, so had the option to stay, but with the caveat they also added statements to Tess's files detailing their part in Hawkes's protection racket. Neither man had refused.

Hawkes knew he was sunk. Extortion only worked when victims were fearful of the consequences. But judging by the stack of witness statements nobody feared him any longer, not when they had Villere championing them.

'I can't go back to Boston,' he whined. 'Murphy and Chapel were my only contacts there, and we didn't exactly part on good terms. If I show my face in my old neighbourhood, they'll take what you did to them out on me.'

'My heart bleeds for you,' said Po. 'Actually, it doesn't. Use the ticket to Boston, or feel free to buy your own elsewhere. Only, you get gone, or all deals are off.'

'Do as he says,' Tess added, 'or I send that file to the DA.'

'You'll be cutting your own throat,' Hawkes said to Po in desperation. 'If I'm arrested, you will be too. There's a matter of . . .' he made a quick tally in his head '. . . six of my guys you injured, a couple of them seriously.'

'I acted in self-defence.'

'Not that first time at HappyDayz.'

Po jerked his head at Noble and Lassiter. 'Think they want to make a complaint? Or maybe you think the cops will take Murphy and Chapel's word over mine, 'specially when it comes to light they were hitters brought in by you to hurt me? And the gang you sent to my ranch, they weren't there with good intentions either.' He reached across and drew the file out from under Hawkes's fingers. 'Tell you what, I could always burn this thing, then come visit you at *your* home.'

'Son of a bitch.' Hawkes's insult was self-directed. 'Did I step on your toes or something? Is that it? Did you have this town under your heel first?'

'Nope. My protection doesn't come at a price. You just chose the wrong town, Hawkes. And now you've overstayed your welcome.' Po aimed a finger at the door. 'The bus station's a few blocks that way. Run, Hawkes, run.'

After Hawkes shuffled off, head down, and Noble and Lassiter were also shown the door, Pinky joined his friends in the booth.

'You think he'll finally see sense?' Pinky asked.

Po shrugged. 'Who knows?'

Pinky gave a surreptitious squint to either side. 'You want me to make him disappear, Nicolas? There's room in that well now the bodies have been recovered.'

Tess snorted at him. Then she held his gaze steadily, wondering if indeed he was being serious. Sometimes she forgot he was a criminal. Pinky broke the moment with a wide grin and a wink. 'I'm kidding, me,' he said. But was he?

'The farm's due for demolition,' Tess said quickly. 'And that well is going to be bulldozed over.'

She wasn't lying in order to dissuade him from doing something stupid. The abandoned farm at Biscay Summer Camp had been subject to deep forensic examination as part of the crime-scene investigation. The remains of Manuel Cabello – since positively identified by dental records – and Rayne's corpse had been exhumed from the well, and an order was in place to bury the site. The last anyone wanted was for the old farmstead to become a destination of those fascinated by the ghoulish aspects of the crimes that took place there. Tess still shuddered when she thought about her time in that well: the order couldn't be carried out fast enough for her.

Detective Carson of Augusta PD was helming a cross-jurisdictional task force charged with investigating the full breadth of the crimes Cable and Rayne were responsible for. Cable – Gabriella Kablinski – was being held pending a full psychiatric evaluation at a secure mental-health facility upstate, and had undergone a series of interviews with the detective. As a nod, and as a token of gratitude in bringing the reign of terror to an end, Tess had been kept in the loop and was now on first-name terms with Jolie. She'd learned Rayne's real name and it proved innocuous: Mary-Anne Clarke. The young woman had a troubled past, one that began with sexual abuse at a very early age, where first she was the target of her father, and his brother, before a succession of paying customers had their evil way with her under the very noses of her parents. At age thirteen, Mary-Anne had set light to her parents' marital bed while they both slept in a drunken slumber. That was the first time she was institutionalized. When finally released, she had fallen into prostitution to make ends meet, and had been subject to violent assault on more occasions than were on record. One particularly brutal attack had left her with a cloven lip after her abuser tore out a metal piercing after he didn't appreciate the way it felt when she was giving him oral stimulation. In response, the newly rebranded Rayne had gone after the john with a kitchen knife, and had come close to ending his life before the cops arrived. Before their very eyes she had begun carving deep gouges in her arms in what they understood to be an attempt at ending her own life. She avoided criminal charges, but was again locked up, this time for her own safety in a second mental-health institute. That was where she met the equally troubled Gabriella, and took her under her wing, both as lover and co-conspirator. Rayne was not a lesbian, but she had developed a – some would say understand-able – hatred of men, and was at first perturbed by Gabriella's sexual advances, but had also seen where she could have the best of both worlds. She'd agreed to, then assisted, and lastly controlled the physical changes in Gabriella, moulding her idea of the perfect specimen of man from the clay of Gabriella's desperation to be loved. She controlled the performance drugs, the steroids and hormonal injections, and it was she who had travelled with Gabriella to a back-street plastic surgeon in Los Angeles who'd performed her double mastectomy. She'd also renamed her man: Rayne was illiterate, barely capable of stringing together the letters when reading Kablinski: 'Kay . . . buh . . . lhu . . . aw, fuck it, let's just call you Cable and have done!'

The plan to punish those responsible for causing Gabriella's suffering came later, and began with the hunting and taking of Manuel Cabello, who had stolen her first love. Rayne had previ-ously committed parenticide, and a violent assault on the john who'd scarred her face, but it was only after the murderous attack on Manny that she found her true self. Her sadistic streak was a mile wide and unquenchable. From that point on she'd been the directing force behind snatching the others, encouraging Cable to write up a death list of all those who'd wronged his former self. Their first attempt at grabbing Chelsea Grace had failed, but had forced her to flee Massachusetts where she'd held her teaching post and run home. That they later caught up with Chelsea and then forced her off a cliff at Bald Head Cove was a given, but Gabriella had been sketchy with those details during interview.

Tess was yet to fathom why Chelsea hadn't gone directly to the police and had instead scheduled a Facebook post to alert her about her death. Perhaps she had issues of her own, that she preferred didn't come to light; maybe she was afraid to involve the cops who might treat her as a paranoid flake and had instead reached out in the first way that had occurred to her – who knew? Sadly she might never know, and the reason was probably unknown by Gabriella too. If she or Rayne had suspected that Chelsea had left the scheduled message they would have forced her to delete it prior to her fall from the cliff. If only Chelsea had been specific about the danger, then Tess might have been able to save Kent Bachman's life, and Rick Conklin from not one but two severe beatings, and herself from a violent abduction and fight for life. The killers must have disturbed Chelsea in the act of typing, grabbed her without realizing what she was up to . . . there was no other answer Tess could think of. Ordinarily she loved a mystery, but not one that couldn't be solved. But she'd have to accept it.

She'd make do with the fact that the murder spree was over, and justice done. Rick Conklin was on the mend, and her worst injuries happened to be a sprained wrist and a few minor burns on her legs. Now that Hawkes was out of the picture all could return to normal.

That thought caused her to chuckle, and draw the attention of Po and Pinky. She waved away their puzzled frowns.

'I just had a funny thought,' she said and laughed harder.

Normal?

Since she'd met those two, there was no such thing.